Book 3

Darkness

By J.D. Crist

Dedication

To my family, both by blood and by not. It is each of you who continues to give me the strength and confidence to keep telling Emily and Marley's story. Each of you has contributed to this in some way, and that is more than a dedication. It makes up the very pages of this book. Without every one of you, this story would not exist.

Trigger Warnings

This book explores several themes and topics that may be uncomfortable for some readers. These include:

Death

Zombies

Killing

Blood

Child Abuse

Sexual abuse

Strong Language

Loss of Pregnancy

If you are unable to continue, I understand. But if you are, thank you for coming back to the world of The Dead Flash.

.

Chapter 1

Emily stood on the wall of Sanctuary with Marley, the wind whipping around her. Emily strained her eyes to look at the figures walking up the logging road. The man had said his name was Charles, and Emily couldn't help but believe that it could be her father. Emily felt Shawn wrap his arm around her as she continued to look at the figures. Emily already knew it wasn't her family walking towards them, but she kept watching, hoping she was wrong.

"It's not them, is it?" Shawn asked smoothly.

"No," Emily replied, trying to hold back her emotions.

"I'm sorry," Shawn said as he held her tighter.

"I need to open the gate," Emily replied emotionless as she turned to head for the control room.

Shawn released his grip on Emily and allowed her to walk away. Emily entered the gate code and collapsed into the wooden chair. She watched as the group entered through the gate and then entered the code to close it. Emily rubbed her face, trying to get herself in the mindset to welcome the new arrivals. Marley nudged Emily's arm with his nose, forcing her to look at him. Emily could tell that he was worried about her and wanted to make her feel better.

"I'm okay, baby boy," Emily reassured him as she petted his head. "Let's go meet the new people."

Emily forced herself to stand and walk out of the control room. Marley followed her out and back into the wind. Emily glanced around and found that Shawn was gone. Emily led Marley to the stairs, assuming that Shawn had already gone to meet the new arrivals. Emily made her way through the open inner gate and looked at the people who stood there.

It was apparent they had been traveling for a while and were underfed. Emily could hear Shawn talking with an older man, whom Emily guessed was Charlie. Charlie was holding his arm, and Emily could see the blood dripping between his fingers. Emily walked over to join them as quickly as she could.

"This is our leader," Shawn said as Emily joined them.

"Emily," Emily smiled at the man.

"Charles," Charles tried to smile back. Emily could tell that
he was putting on a brave face but was in a lot of pain.

"Charles hasn't told his family yet, but he was bitten on the way here," Shawn whispered to her.

"I know what you have to do," Charles spoke up. "I would just like a chance to see that my family is safe."

"You will," Emily tried to comfort him. "We don't have to do anything unless the infection takes your life."

"I appreciate your kindness," Charles says softly. "We've seen it happen, though, and it's not necessary." Emily looked at Shawn, and Shawn nodded at her. Emily walked closer to Charles and pulled the sleeve of her shirt to expose her scar.

"And I've seen it not happen," Emily replied, allowing Charles to look closely at her scar. "There is a small percentage who are immune to the bite, like me."

"I want to believe you," Charles said, taking a step back.
"But it sounds like a long shot."

"It is," Emily nodded. "But it's a shot, and we want to try to help if you'll let us."

Charles nodded and adjusted his grip on his arm.

"We will get you set up in our quarantine area, and Doc will examine the rest of your family, just to be safe."

Charles nodded again and followed Shawn into the quarantine area. Emily could see that Doc was watching from the clinic door. Doc quickly made his way over to Emily.

"What's going on?" Doc quickly asked, looking back at Charles and Shawn as they walked through the quarantine door.

"He got bit," Emily explained. "Shawn is taking him to a cabin."

"How long ago?" Doc asked, and Emily could hear the urgency in his voice.

"I'm not sure," Emily replied.

Doc said nothing and ran towards the quarantine door. Emily quickly followed him with Marley right behind her. Emily and Marley followed Doc into the cabin, where Charles was sitting on a bed.

"How long ago were you bitten?" Doc asked, not bothering with pleasantries.

"I'm not sure," Charles said with hesitation. "It was back by the last sign, where the road turned to dirt."

"Emily told you there is a small chance that you are immune," Doc quickly spoke. "However, I have an experimental vaccine that will give slightly higher odds of survival. It only works one in a hundred times and is more effective if given directly after infection. However, it is a higher chance than the one in ten thousand odds that you are immune."

"Are you serious?" Charles said, looking at Doc.

"I have a dose," Doc said, removing a syringe from his pocket. "I'll have to inject it directly into the bite."

Emily watched as Charles held out his arm to Doc. Doc didn't hesitate, removed the tip of the syringe, and injected the liquid the syringe contained directly into the bite. Emily watched as Charles gritted his teeth and couldn't imagine the pain he was feeling.

"You rest," Doc said as he quickly wrapped Charles's arm in a bandage. Doc then turned and walked back out of the cabin. Emily smiled at Charles and followed Doc out with Shawn and Marley. They follow Doc to the door of the quarantine area.

"Doc!" Emily called as Doc showed no signs of stopping. Doc slowed and waited by the door. "What was that?" Emily asked as she neared him.

"Exactly what I told him," Doc replied shortly, irritating Emily.

"Why didn't I know that you had any type of vaccine?" Emily asked with authority in her voice. "How long have you had this?"

"I've been working on it for a while. But this latest attempt, I've had for about a month," Doc slowly admitted.

"Why didn't you tell me?" Emily repeated more firmly.

"I didn't want to give false hope or advertise it yet," Doc said shortly.

"And you think I would be a gossip and wouldn't know how to handle this information?" Emily said, not trying to hide her frustration.

"I just..." Doc began and then trailed off.

"You can't keep this stuff from me," Emily quickly spoke. "I could have let this man sit here, lowering his chances of survival, because you wanted a secret!"

"It still has a low chance of working," Doc said, adjusting his glasses.

"But he still has a chance," Emily said, stepping closer to Doc. "We agreed you would keep me informed on your experiments and findings."

"We did," Doc said with defeat thick with defeat. "It won't happen again."

"It better not," Emily said as she pushed past him.

Charles's family stood huddled together, obviously scared and confused. Emily walked towards them, trying to find the words to explain what was going on with Charles.

"Where is my husband?" an older woman demanded to know.

"Charles is resting in our quarantine area," Emily said, as comforting as she could. "Charles informed us that he was bitten on your way here."

"Oh my god," the woman said as she began to cry and visibly shake.

"Our doctor has done everything he can to help Charles fight the infection," Emily continued. "Unfortunately, at this time, all we can do is wait and see."

"Are you saying he might live?" the woman asked. The hope in her voice cut Emily's heart like a knife.

"It's a small chance," Emily explained. "But we want to give him that chance."

The woman continued to clutch the front of her shirt over her heart as she nodded at Emily.

"Our doctor will need to examine each of you," Emily continued. "Just to ensure that none of you are in danger of infection."

"After, can I see my husband?" the woman asked more calmly than Emily expected.

"Of course," Emily nodded.

The woman stepped forward towards Emily, volunteering to go first.

"My name is Emily," Emily said to her as she walked closer.

"Susan," the woman replied.

Susan followed Doc into the clinic and reemerged a few minutes later. Emily watched as a man, slightly younger than her, stepped forward to go next.

"Do you wish to wait for the rest of your family?" Emily asked Susan as she walked towards her.

"I would like a moment alone with him if I can," Susan said, looking back at the others.

"Of course," Emily replied as she turned to lead Susan to where Charles was resting.

Emily stood outside the cabin door and allowed Susan to enter alone. Emily could hear the pain in Susan and Charles's voices as they began to talk. Emily felt like she was spying on a private moment. Emily turned and headed back to the quarantine area and watched as Doc worked through the exams.

Doc walked towards Emily as he finished the last exam. Emily could tell by the look on his face that he was still ashamed of what had happened earlier. Emily knew that he felt terrible, but still felt that she needed to remain stern with him.

"They all are malnourished and a little banged up," Doc reported. "However, none of them are in danger of infection."

"Can we see him now?" A sandy-haired woman stepped forward.

"Mia," Doc whispered to Emily.

"Susan asked for a few moments alone with him," Emily explained. "I can go see if she's okay with all of you joining her."

Mia was visibly upset with Emily's response as she rolled her eyes and crossed her arms. Emily pretended not to notice and calmly walked back to the quarantine area. Emily knocked on the door of the cabin as she entered. Susan was sitting next to Charles, holding his hand. Emily could tell by the amount of sweat on Charles's face and pillow that the infection had set in.

"Mia is asking to join you," Emily explained softly.

"It's not working, is it?" Charles asked in a weak voice.

"I can't be sure," Emily replied. "Doc will be able to answer that question better than I."

"I am here," Doc said as he walked through the door. Doc made his way over to Charles and quickly examined him. After a few minutes, Doc stood, and Emily could tell by the look on his face that she was correct. "I'm sorry," Doc said to both Charles and Susan.

"How long?" Susan asked, looking at Doc for the first time.

"An hour," Doc said slowly. "Maybe less."

"Emily," Charles said, prompting Emily to step forward.

"Promise me you won't let me turn into one of those things."

"I..." Emily began.

"My family can't be the ones," Charles interrupted. "I know it's a lot to ask, but I must." Charles coughed, and Emily could see the pain it caused him. "Please, ensure I stay at rest and take care of my family."

Emily had never had to put down anyone before they turned, and part of her believed she would never have to. Emily looked at Susan, and the tears streaming down her face broke Emily's heart in two. "I promise," Emily finally nodded. "I will get the rest of your family."

Emily walked out of the cabin and found no comfort in the wind as she usually would. Emily said nothing as she walked back to where Mia and the rest of the family were waiting.

"I'll lead you back to them," Emily said to the group, hearing the pain in her voice.

"Is he going to be okay?" Mia asked.

"We did everything we could," Emily explained, "But the infection is spreading."

"Take us to him," Mia said firmly.

Emily nodded and led the family back to the cabin. It was a tight fit, but the family all managed to gather inside around Charles. Emily left the family to share Charles's final moments while going to the armory. Emily picked up a small knife as she heard someone enter behind her.

"I can do it if you want," Shawn said behind her.

"He asked me," Emily said as she turned, tucking the small knife into her pocket. "We need to give him a funeral. Can you speak to Jose and see if a coffin can be made?"

"I'll take care of it," Shawn said in a comforting voice. "Do you want the grave where you buried Robert?" "Yes," Emily nodded as she replied.

Shawn stepped aside, and Emily walked past him with Marley and back to the quarantine area. Emily waited outside the cabin, trying not to overhear the family's private conversation. However, she had to at least listen in part to know when she was needed.

"They are letting you die!" Mia was yelling at Charles. "You want us to stay and live with the people who let you die!?"

"They gave me more of a chance than I would have had out there," Charles replied in a forced voice. "Emily is a good person, and these are good people."

"Good people!?" a man exclaimed next. "They took our weapons and are not going to allow us to make sure you stay at rest. What's their plan? Just let your corpse walk out the gate?!" "I've asked Emily to ensure that I do not come back," Charles spoke once again, the pain more obvious. "She wasn't comfortable with it, but is going to do it because I asked. I don't want any of you doing it."

"This isn't right," Mia spoke once again. The anger in her voice had turned to pain.

Emily could hear that she was crying, realizing that Charles was nearing the end of his journey.

"It is the world we live in," Charles forced himself to speak.
"You must stay here; you have to live. Promise me." "I promise," a chorus of voices rang out.
"I love you," Charles barely spoke.

Emily knew that he was taking his final breaths. Emily waited a few moments and allowed the family to each say their final goodbyes, knowing that Charles was gone. Emily walked into the cabin, still hiding the knife in her pocket.

"He's gone," Susan said, trying to speak between sobs.

"It may be best if you all step out," Emily said smoothly.

"He made it clear he didn't want you to have to handle this part." Emily could see that Mia was preparing to argue when Susan stood up. Susan motioned for her family to leave the cabin. Emily stood alone, looking down at Charles lying on the cot. Emily walked towards the head of the cot. Emily knelt by Charles's head and looked down at his face. Emily slowly lifted Charles's head off the cot and removed the knife from her pocket.

"I'm sorry," Emily whispered to Charles as she slid the knife into the base of his skull.

Emily returned Charles's head softly to his pillow and felt warm tears begin to roll down her face. Emily sat for a few moments, cleaning the knife and pulling herself back together before she stood up. Emily made her way back out of the cabin to where the family now stood. Emily could see Shawn and Father Nathan standing near the door.

"Is it done?" Susan asked softly.

Emily nodded and could tell by the look on Susan's face that Emily's pain from what she had done was showing. Emily wiped her hands on her pants nervously before looking back at the family.

"We would like to give you all a proper funeral for Charles," Emily said to the family. "I only knew him for a short time, but in that time, I could tell that he was a great man." Emily looked to Shawn, who nodded. Emily knew that the arrangements were well underway. "Our people are working on preparing everything, and Father Nathan is available if you would like him to perform the service or if any of you need to seek his guidance."

Susan turned and looked over to where Father Nathan was standing. "Thank you," Susan replied as she looked back at Emily.

"Thank you for everything."

Emily tried to find the words to respond, but none seemed fitting. Instead, Emily nodded and made her way to where Shawn was standing with Marley. Shawn opened his arms, and Emily walked straight into his embrace. Shawn said nothing and simply held Emily for several minutes. Emily could hear the family speaking with Father Nathan, discussing Charles's life and the prayers they would like said at the service. Emily didn't move until Cole spoke from behind her.

"Everything is prepared," Cole said softly. "If the family is ready, we can move him to the coffin."

Emily felt Shawn's grip loosen and forced herself to stand up independently.

"Thank you," Emily said to Cole. "Give me just a moment."

Cole nodded as Emily walked over to where the family was gathered around Father Nathan.

"I'm sorry to interrupt," Emily spoke, and everyone turned to face her. "Everything has been prepared. With your permission, we would like to move Charles into his coffin."

Emily watched as most of the family cringed at the word coffin. Emily wished there was a better, softer word she could have used.

"We will do it," one of the men said as he stood.

"I'll have them bring it into the cabin," Emily said as she backed away and made her way back to Cole. "They wish to set him in it themselves," Emily explained. "If it could be carried into the cabin, that would be a great help."

"Of course," Cole replied as he walked out the door.

Emily stepped aside with Shawn and Marley as Cole, Derick, Jose, and Alec carried the coffin through the door and into the cabin.

Once they all walked back out, the family walked in with Father Nathan. Emily waited with everyone until Father Nathan walked back out.

"They want a private service," Father Nathan explained.

"That's understandable," Emily nodded.

"They do want you to be there," Father Nathan added. "Susan insisted that Charles would want you to be included."

"If that's what they want," Emily replied with hesitation, "I will be there."

"They are saying their final goodbyes, and we will be ready in just a few moments."

"I'll meet you after," Shawn said to her as he squeezed her hand and walked back through the door with the others.

Emily waited with Father Nathan for several minutes. Emily stood quietly as the family walked out of the cabin, carrying Charles's coffin. Emily opened the door to the quarantine area and held it while Father Nathan led the family out. Emily closed the door and joined Father Nathan in leading the family to the burial site. Marley ran up to join Emily, unknowing that he wasn't invited. Emily hoped that the family wouldn't be offended by his presence.

Once they reached the site, Emily walked around the grave with Father Nathan and stood in silence while the family lowered the coffin into the grave. Once the family stepped back, Marley left Emily's side and went to the children. Marley sat with them, allowing the children to hug him and cry into his fur. Emily listened as Father Nathan spoke of Charles, telling him things the family shared with him.

As Father Nathan finished the final prayer, each family member took a handful of dirt and sprinkled it onto the coffin. Emily followed their lead as Susan nodded at her. Once they had all finished, the men each grabbed a shovel and began to fill in the grave. Marley remained by the children, and Emily stood silently with Father Nathen.

"Thank you," Susan spoke as the men finished.

"I wish we could have done more," Emily responded.

"You did more than we could have dreamed possible," Susan said. "You gave him a chance and gave us a place to lay him to rest."

"So, what's next?" Mia asked, her tone less angry than it was earlier.

"Next, we take you inside, let you get cleaned up, and I make you a warm meal," Emily replied warmly.

Chapter 2

Summer in Sanctuary was the busiest time of year for everyone. They all worked hard to ensure that things were ready for the winter months. Even though they had plenty of supplies because of the work they had already done and the backstock that Robert had gathered, everyone continued to work as if they could run out of stores at any moment. Emily admired their dedication and was amazed at the group of people who had gathered inside the walls. Emily still remembered when she had vowed to let no one in. Emily now could not imagine her life without all of them.

July's thick, hot air flowed around Emily as she walked towards the clinic with Hope and Marley. Hope has been seeing Doc once a week to monitor her accelerated growth rate closely. Emily had told Hope that it was normal for kids her age to go to the doctor so much to make sure that they were growing okay. Emily didn't want Hope to think that something was wrong with her.

Emily opened the door to the clinic and allowed Hope and Marley to run in ahead of her. Hope waved hello to Isabelle and headed straight to the exam room. Marley followed her and sat down next to the exam table. Emily followed them and helped Hope up onto the exam table just as Doc walked in.

"Good morning," Doc greeted them as he closed the door. "Good morning," Hope smiled back.

Emily stepped back and allowed Doc to work through his standard exam. Hope was getting used to the routine, and the process went quickly.

"Still healthy," Doc said as he finished writing on Hope's chart.

"I know," Hope smiled.

"Why don't you go get your treat from Isabelle while I talk to your mom?" Doc smiled as he helped Hope down from the table.

"Then I can go to school?" Hope asked excitedly.

"Then you can go to school," Emily nodded.

Hope turned and ran out of the room with Marley. Emily closed the door behind them and then turned back to Doc.

"She is healthy?" Emily asked.

"Very," Doc nodded. "She is perfect for a five-year-old girl." "She's one," Emily said, trying to contain her shock.

"I know," Doc said smoothly. "The good news is it seems to be slowing down, her physical development at least." "So, no more big jumps?" Emily asked.

"It's like she grew up to an age where she would be able to defend herself quickly. I would say it's evolution because of how the world is, but...."

"But what?" Emily asked.

"We don't know another child born after the flash," Doc continued. "We have no way of knowing if it will affect all newborns the same or if it's just Hope."

"But it is slowing down?" Emily asked.

"Yes," Doc smiled. "Her growth chart has leveled out, and I see no reason to think it will accelerate again. We will continue to monitor her once a month, but I don't expect a change."

"That's great," Emily sighed. She couldn't help but feel that at the rate Hope was growing, she was going to be full-grown before she was three. However, Emily couldn't get something Doc said out of her mind.

"You said physically it should level out?" Emily asked Doc.

"Yes," Doc replied. "Hope is very smart, beyond a normal five-year-old. I know she enjoys school. You may want to ask June to test her to see if she may be happier in a higher grade level." "She can't even read yet," Emily remarked, shocked by Doc's suggestion.

"I think she can," Doc continued. "I've watched her looking over my notes as I write them. I think she may be hiding what she can do from you."

"Why would she do that?" Emily asked, confused.

"She listens to everything that is said, long before she could talk. You used to say all the time how she was growing up too fast, and you wanted to slow it down."

"You think she is hiding it to make me happy?" Emily asked more of herself than Doc.

"It's not your fault," Doc said, trying to comfort her. "All parents say the same thing at one point or another. You had no way of knowing she could understand you."

"But she did," Emily couldn't believe what she had done.

Hope was hiding who she was to keep Emily happy.

"You just need to talk to her," Doc continued.

"I will," Emily said as she headed for the door.

"Thanks, Doc."

Emily walked back into the lobby where Hope and Marley were waiting.

"I'll be late!" Hope exclaimed as soon as she saw Emily.

"You will be fine," Emily insisted. "We are leaving now."

Emily opened the door and followed Hope and Marley outside. Hope took Emily's hand as she closed the door to the clinic and began to drag her in the direction of the school. Emily followed, and they reached the school just as Bobby was running inside. Emily walked through the fence and to the door with Hope.

"Are you coming in?" Hope asked as Emily opened the door.

"I just need to talk to Ms. June for a moment," Emily replied.

Hope nodded and led Emily and Marley through the halls. Hope waved goodbye to Emily as they reached her classroom.

"Have a good day," Emily said as she waved back.

"She's adjusting nicely," June spoke behind Emily.

"She loves coming here," Emily replied as she turned around. "She hates the weekend because it means no school."

"I can see that," June laughed as she turned to lead Emily down the hall.

"I wanted to talk to you about Hope," Emily said as she followed June.

"Is something wrong?" June asked.

"No," Emily quickly replied. "I just wanted to get an update and discuss if she may need more of a challenge."

"Hope performs at the level of a normal preschooler," June began. "However, it seems like she is capable of more but is holding back. We have tried to get her to open up, but she hasn't yet."

"Doc believes she's holding back because of me," Emily explained.

"I'm sure that's not true," June comforted her.

"She may have understood when I wished she'd stop growing up so fast," Emily explained. "I'm going to try to talk to her about it and see if it's true."

"I will make sure we continue to push her and let you know if there's any change," June smiled. "If this is true, this girl is going to be smarter than all of us."

"She's already smarter than me," Emily laughed. "I'd better get to work before she gets my job."

"Not without finishing her education," June smiled. "So, you may have a few weeks."

"Comforting," Emily laughed as she turned to leave the school. Marley followed Emily out the school doors and into the hot July air. Emily made her way to the town hall and soon was behind her desk, looking through reports. Marley took his usual spot on the floor and fell asleep.

Emily had each division turn in a report regarding their supplies, work, and production. She had been dedicating more time to reading through them to keep any surprises from happening. This was one part of her responsibilities that she felt confident doing. Her years with the landscaping company had prepared her for this job.

Emily couldn't help but notice how low they were running on lumber. It had been a year since she and Shawn had last gone out for any. Jose had gotten a lot done and made it stretch, but it was becoming evident that they would need more soon.

Emily made a note for herself and finished looking over the reports. The farm was producing more than Jacob had predicted. While their current storage system was still holding everything, at this rate, they would need more soon. Emily thought back to the lumber and knew that building a new structure was not an option without more building supplies.

Emily finished the reports just as her stomach began to growl. Emily hadn't realized how loud it was until Marley stood and walked over to her. Emily stood, knowing she needed to eat if her stomach was loud enough to wake him. Emily walked out of the town hall with Marley and made the short walk to the bakery.

Inside, Julia was hard at work kneading some type of dough.

"Hey," Emily greeted Julia as she walked in.

"Forget your lunch again?" Julia smiled at her as she continued to work.

"No, I just wanted to stop by and see how things are going," Emily replied with a sheepish smile.

"On the counter," Julia said, shaking her head.

"Well, if you have something, I don't want it to go to waste," Emily said as she walked over and grabbed the paper bag on the counter. Emily looked inside and saw that there was too much food for just her. "Am I getting fat?" Emily asked, looking down at her waist.

"Shawn forgets too," Julia said, rolling her eyes. "I figured one of you would be by and could take lunch to the other."

"Good excuse," Emily said as she took the bag and headed back towards the door with Marley. "Thank you," Emily said as she walked out the door.

"You're welcome," Julia called back.

Emily walked towards the wall with Marley and saw that Shawn was coming down the stairs. Emily smiled as she made her way towards him.

"Hungry?" Emily asked, holding up the bag.

"Julia?" Shawn laughed.

"Yeah," Emily admitted. "Apparently, neither of us can ever remember lunch."

"I'm not complaining," Shawn smiled. "Let's go to my place so we can relax."

"Lead the way," Emily smiled.

Emily and Marley followed Shawn up to his apartment. Shawn led her over to the couch, and Emily spread their lunch out on the coffee table. Emily and Shawn ate while Marley worked through the apartment, sniffing everything. Emily talked to Shawn about everything going on with Hope and the upcoming issues she found in the reports. Shawn smiled and offered his opinion and advice on each subject.

"I don't think I've ever been in here before," Emily said as Marley finally returned.

"You came to the door and thanksgiving," Shawn said. "But other than that, we are normally at your house."

"I like what you've done with the place," Emily said, looking around. There were a few pictures that Hope had drawn hung on the refrigerator, but nothing else she could see that looked like he had done.

"I don't spend much time here," Shawn admitted. "Just a place to sleep and eat."

"And hang Hope's pictures," Emily smiled.

"Of course," Shawn laughed. "It wouldn't be complete without those."

"I should get you something," Emily said, looking around.

"I've got all I need," Shawn said, turning her face back to him.

Emily couldn't help but smile as Shawn pulled her closer.

Emily wrapped her arms around his neck and fell into a deep kiss. Everything around them seemed to melt away. Emily felt the world come back as Shawn slowly drifted away from her.

"I wish we could stay here forever," Shawn said softly.

"Can't we?" Emily asked as she looked at him.

"I have to get back to the wall, and Hope will be getting out of school soon," Shawn reminded her.

"We should go," Emily replied, still not moving.

"We really should," Shawn replied as he pulled her closer.

Shawn and Emily kissed once more, but were careful not to get lost in it. They both backed slowly away from each other. Shawn stood from the couch and helped Emily to her feet. Emily held on to his hand as they left the apartment and headed back down to the street with Marley.

"Try not to worry too much," Shawn said once they were back outside.

"No promises," Emily smiled as she kissed him once more.

Shawn let go of her hand and headed back to the wall. Emily walked through the streets, checking in with everyone as she went. It wasn't long before it was time for her and Marley to head to the school to pick up Hope. They arrived just as the children began to pour out of the school doors. Emily waited as Hope was the last to leave, like always.

"How was your day?" Emily asked as Hope ran up and hugged her.

"Good," Hope smiled. "We are learning colors."

It was a simple enough phrase, but Emily couldn't help the pain that happened in her heart. Knowing that Hope was so intelligent and hearing talk about learning colors like it was exciting hurt her heart.

"What's wrong, mommy?" Hope asked, looking at Emily's face.

"Nothing," Emily quickly smiled. "I was just thinking about dinner."

"Can we have chicken?" Hope asked with excitement.

"Sounds good to me," Emily replied as she took Hope's hand and began the walk home. Hope continued to talk about the colors she had learned about that day, and Emily smiled as she opened the front door.

Emily made her way to the kitchen, quickly prepared the chicken, and put it in the oven. Hope quickly refilled Marley's food and then headed to the living room. Emily followed her once the chicken was baking. Hope was sitting on the couch, looking at a book. Emily walked closer to see that she held one of the children's books from the bottom shelf. Emily walked over to the shelf and grabbed their copy of The Wonderful Wizard of Oz.

"Would you like to read this?" Emily asked, turning back to Hope.

"Yes," Hope said as she quickly ran over to return the book she was holding to the shelf.

Hope sat down on the couch and waited while Hope and Marley climbed up to join her. Emily opened the book to where she and Hope left off.

"Why don't you read this time?" Emily said as she handed the book to Hope.

"I can't," Hope said as she pushed the book away. "That looks too big for me, mommy."

"You promise?" Emily asked as she offered the book to Hope once more.

"I'm not growing up too fast," Hope insisted. "I promise."

"Why would you say that?" Emily asked, already knowing the answer. Hope didn't answer and was instead staring at her hands.

"You don't need to worry about being able to do things. It just makes you even more amazing."

"I'm growing too fast," Hope said, sounding ashamed. "I'm trying to slow down like you asked, but it's not working."

"I didn't mean that," Emily said as she lifted Hope's face to look at her. "It's something all parents say because they are afraid." "Afraid of what?" Hope asked, sounding confused.

"Afraid of their babies growing up and will not need them anymore," Emily replied.

"I will always need you, mommy," Hope said as she hugged Emily.

"Then I have nothing to worry about," Emily said as she hugged Hope back. "Now, why don't you read this time?"

Hope took the book as Emily offered it this time. Emily wrapped her arm around Hope and waited patiently while Hope adjusted the book in her hands. Emily couldn't help but smile as Hope began to read. Hope read the words crystal clear and with no hesitation. Emily listened patiently and did not interrupt until the timer in the kitchen sounded.

"Sounds like dinner's ready," Emily said to Hope.

"One more page," Hope pleaded. "Then the chapters are over."

"One more," Emily agreed as she settled back in.

Hope read through the last page quickly. Hope closed the book and smiled up at Emily as she handed it back the book.

"I'm proud of you," Emily said as she finished it.

"Really?" Hope grinned.

"Really," Emily said as she stood and returned the book to the shelf. "You get washed up while I set the table."

"Yes, mommy," Hope said as she jumped down from the couch.

Emily looked back at Marley as she headed for the kitchen. Marley simply stretched out on the couch and showed no signs of moving. Emily made her way to the oven and pulled out the chicken. The smell instantly filled the house while the sound of the chicken, potatoes, and carrots sizzling filled Emily's ears. Emily carefully set the pan on the counters and pulled out the plates and forks.

"Can I have milk to drink?" Hope asked as she walked in and climbed up into her chair.

"Sure thing," Emily replied as she grabbed a plastic cup and filled it with cold milk from the fridge.

Emily quickly made each of their plates and then sat down beside Hope to enjoy their meal. It was always easier to eat in the kitchen when just the two of them. Sitting in the dining room always made it seem like they were alone or somehow abandoned.

"All done," Hope said as she finished clearing her plate.

"Are you full?" Emily asked as she took a bite of a carrot.

"All full," Hope smiled.

"You can go play for a while. I'll clean up," Emily replied. "Why don't you see if you can wake up that lazy dog and get him to play?"

"Yes, mommy," Hope said as she jumped down from her chair. Hope ran into the living room and began to wake up Marley.

"Marley!" Hope yelled. "Do you want to play?"

Soon, Emily could hear Marley running upstairs and knew that Hope was leading the charge. Emily finished the last bit of food on her plate and set to cleaning up. It didn't take Emily long to put away the few leftovers and wash the dishes. Once she finished, Emily headed upstairs to check on Hope and Marley. Emily walked to Hope's door and could tell that Hope was ready for bed. She had her favorite doll out and was trying to play, but kept yawning and rubbing her eyes.

"Time for bed," Emily said as she walked through the door. "Let's get dressed and those teeth brushed."

"Yes, mommy," Hope yawned as she stood and put her toy away. Emily walked with Hope to the bathroom to ensure that Hope didn't fall asleep while brushing her teeth.

Once Hope was dressed and ready, Emily helped her into bed.

"Good night," Emily said as she kissed Hope on the forehead.

"Good night," Hope yawned as she pulled the covers even higher.

Emily went to stand up and noticed something was under Hope's bed. Emily reached under and pulled out the storybook she had made for Hope for her birthday. It contained all the family pictures Emily had, turning them into a fairy tale for Hope. Emily smiled at Hope as she slid the book back under the bed before standing and leaving the room.

Chapter 3

Emily set to work the next day to find solutions for their lumber and food storage issues. Emily was sitting at her desk in the town hall, feeling like she was working on an unsolvable puzzle. Marley seemed to see that she was not at ease and was staring at her instead of sleeping like normal.

"I'm missing something," Emily said to herself.

Emily suddenly felt like the walls of her office were shrinking in on her. Emily tried to ignore it and focus, but couldn't shake the feeling.

"I need some air," Emily said as she stood up and walked out of the office.

Marley quickly followed her out onto the street. Emily walked with no real intention of where she was going. Soon, Emily found herself wandering the wall with Marley. Emily kept thinking that there was more lumber in town, but she knew there had to be a better solution closer to Sanctuary. Emily stopped and leaned against the wall.

Emily looked out at the tree line and suddenly remembered the conversation she had with Shawn months ago. The trees on this side of the wall were blocking the view of anyone on the wall. They couldn't see any encroaching threats, living or dead. Emily couldn't help but think that the trees would provide more than enough lumber for what Sanctuary needed.

Emily was so deep in thought that she didn't notice Cole walking towards her.

"You look like a woman deep in thought," Cole said as he stopped beside her.

"We need to cut back that tree line," Emily said, pointing outside the wall. "It will help with our visibility and give us the lumber we need to continue to grow."

"Not an easy job," Cole said, looking to where she was pointing. "It will be difficult to defend anyone out there working from the dead."

"I hadn't thought of that," Emily admitted. "I was focused on whether we had everything we needed to harvest the trees."

"Even if we don't have the exact tools, I'm sure we have enough here to make it work," Cole assured her. "However, keeping the workers safe is a real concern. We can't see the dead until they are on the wall. Not much help to the people out there cutting down the trees."

"We need some way to draw them away from the area while the work is being done," Emily continued. "That's the part I can't figure out."

"I don't think you will get a lot of volunteers for bait," Cole smiled. "But if you ask, count me in."

"I'm not," Emily laughed. "There has to be a better way."

"They're drawn to sound, right?" Cole asked. "Maybe something could be set up to draw them out."

"That could work," Emily said with a smile. Emily remembered using the police siren to draw the zombies. They seemed to come from everywhere and were drawn to the sound.
"You're a genius!"

"Don't go spreading that around," Cole smiled back at her.
"Then people will start expecting more from me."

"It will be our secret," Emily replied. "Though I will now depend on you for everything."

"Well, shit," Cole laughed.

"What's done is done," Emily laughed. "I should probably go see if Sarah can come up with something to make the noise.

"Don't let me stop you," Cole said as he walked back to patrol his stretch of the wall. "Just use me and leave!" Cole yelled back to her.

"You know you love me!" Emily yelled back.

"I know it!" Cole yelled once more.

Emily laughed as she turned with Marley, walked back around to the control room, and made her way down the stairs. It didn't take Emily long to find Sarah in the COM building. Margaret was sitting in front of the radio, working on some stitching, and Emily could see Sarah working on something on her workbench.

"And contact today?" Emily asked as she and Marley walked in.

"Silence," Margaret replied. "But we will be ready."

"What are you working on?" Emily asked, motioning to the cloth Margaret was stitching.

"I thought I could help by fixing clothing while I sit here,"
Margaret said. "I felt like I wasn't pulling my own weight."

"That is really good," Emily said, looking closer at the cloth.

"We can't afford to waste anything," Margaret said.

"Just my
small way of helping out."

"You are amazing," Emily said.

"Is something wrong?" Sarah asked, turning away from her project, realizing for the first time that Emily was there.

"No, I just had an idea I wanted to run by you," Emily assured her as she walked closer and sat down in a wooden chair. "We need to clear the tree line on the south side, but the dead make it impossible."

"And you think I can help?" Sarah asked as if thinking Emily was talking to the wrong person.

"They are drawn to sound," Emily explained. "Could you set up something that could draw them out to another spot? It would have to be pretty loud."

"A speaker deterrent," Sarah nodded. "I've been toying with the idea for a while. I was thinking of making a PA system for us inside, but it would be the same concept."

"So, it's possible?" Emily asked as Sarah's face showed she was going into the planning portion of her brain. When Sarah got like this, she forgot that people even existed. If Emily did not pull her back quickly, Sarah would be lost for hours.

"Oh, yes," Sarah said, coming back to the conversation. "There are plenty of speakers here, and I can make the modifications to make them work. I can probably have something ready in the next few days."

"Modifications?" Emily asked.

"I can't run wiring outside the wall," Sarah explained. "There's too much of a risk that it will get damaged. However, I can rig up some Bluetooth speakers that will charge with solar batteries."

"And you have everything you need to do this?" Emily asked. Emily couldn't help but fear that Sarah would need them to do a run for more supplies. It was a run to town that she was trying desperately to avoid right now.

"I do," Sarah nodded, looking around the room.

"Do you need anything from me?" Emily asked, hoping that the answer was no. Emily was less than useless when it came to electronics.

"You will just need to pick the place you want to set it up,"
Sarah continued. "No more than a mile outside the wall, though." "Why only a mile?" Emily asked.

"Any more than that, and the range will become an issue,"
Sarah explained. "I can probably extend it more, but that will take more time and require things that I don't have here."

"No more than a mile," Emily replied quickly. "I will pick a spot and make sure we are ready."

Emily turned to leave when she heard Sarah suddenly stand up from her chair.

"Actually, when this is done, I would like to set up the PA system inside," Sarah continued. "We have the walkies for leaders inside, but no way of letting the rest of the people know if there is an emergency. If we continue to grow, just yelling at each other could get problematic."

"I agree," Emily nodded.

"If I don't do this, I would feel like it was my fault if something went wrong," Sarah confessed. "I just can't...."

"I understand," Emily replied. "Once we handle the tree line, I will help you any way I can to get the PA system set up."

"I've got work to do then," Sarah said with excitement as she turned back to her work table.

Emily knew that Sara was done with the conversation and would not remerge until she finished her work. Emily waved goodbye to Margaret as she walked back outside with Marley. Emily had not realized that Sarah took so much personal responsibility for the safety of everyone inside the wall. Emily promised herself that she would not break her promise and would help Sarah set up the PA system. Emily made her way to the Security building and found Sam, Shawn, and Alec sitting around a table.

"They're increasing in number," Shawn was saying. "And there's more that we can't even see on the south side."

"Maybe I can help with that," Emily said as she walked over and sat down to join them.

"Sarah is going to make a speaker system for outside the wall to draw the dead out of hiding and towards it. That will allow us to clear the tree line, opening up visibility, and provide more lumber to increase our food storage capabilities."

Emily felt proud as all of the men at the table looked at her in shock. "It solves all of our most pressing issues with one move,"
Emily continued. "Unless there is something that I'm not seeing."

"Told you we should have asked her," Alec laughed while looking at Shawn and Sam, who both still sat silent.

"The only issue I see," Shawn finally spoke, "Is that we may draw more dead to Sanctuary. While our ammo supply is more than enough, we will burn through it quickly if we don't find a way to keep them away or another way of putting them down."

"Maybe we set up more than one speaker system," Sam spoke. "That way, we can divide them between four different spots, keeping them away from the wall."

"But the groups will continue to grow if we don't put them down," Shawn replied. "The more they grow, the harder they will be to handle, and they will still end up surrounding Sanctuary."

Emily realized that while her plan did solve most of their issues, it did leave one big loose end. "What about a mass clean-up once a month?" Emily suggested. "We could take out the dead at each of the systems, burn the corpses the next day, and wait another month to do it again. It would keep them from building up."

"Once a month or once a day equals the same amount of ammo used," Shawn pointed out. Emily could tell that part of him hated to point out the flaw in her plan. However, she loved that he was comfortable enough to do it anyway.

"Unless we don't shoot them," Emily offered. "There has to be a better way to kill a massive group of stationary zombies."

"We're listening," Shawn grinned at her. Emily knew that look; he was challenging her. Usually, Emily liked the challenge, but she was out of ideas this time. Emily was not just going to admit that, though, and had to think of some way out of this fast.

"Do I have to think of everything?" Emily laughed as she sat back and folded her arms.

"You all are part of security. What would you suggest?"

"We could do spike pits," Sam offered. "Though it would require a team to clean frequently and may not always get the brain."

"That's a lot of maybe," Alec answered with a look of doubt on his face.

"A deep enough pit, though, would keep them contained," Shawn said, obviously deep in thought.

"But we still need a way to kill the ones we catch," Alec said. "Burning would be preferable. Then we wouldn't need to clean up."

"But we have to be careful not to burn down the entire forest," Emily spoke next.

"Otherwise, we will put Sanctuary at risk."

"Yeah, there's that," Alec nodded as he sat back in his chair, looking defeated.

"A controlled burn is something we could figure out," Shawn spoke. "I will look through what we have and come up with something."

"I will let Sarah know we need a total of four speaker systems," Emily said as she sat back up. "We will just need a group of volunteers to set them up."

"I assume the four of us are going," Shawn said, looking around the table as everyone nodded.

"Cole will volunteer," Emily added.

"I will ask around to see if we can get a few more," Shawn said. "I assume you want to do this by the end of the week."

"Of course," Emily laughed. "You know I'm not good at being patient."

"And you wonder where Hope gets it?" Shawn teased.

"I think she's learning it from you," Emily teased back as she stood up.

Sam and Alec both laughed as Emily and Shawn glared at each other. Emily and Shawn both broke the glare at the same time and laughed.

"Well, I'll leave you guys to figure that out," Emily laughed. "I've got work to do."

"Are you saying this isn't work?" Alec asked, trying to sound offended.

"I didn't say it," Emily smiled while holding her hands up and backing out the door. Emily continued to laugh as she and Marley made their way back to the COM room.

"I'm back!" Emily announced as she walked through the door with Marley.

Margaret smiled at Emily and nodded to where Sarah was still working. Emily walked towards Sarah and waited patiently until Sarah set down her tools.

"How's it going?" Emily asked, making Sarah jump.

"Just working on the solar charging plates," Sarah replied, placing her hand over her heart.

"I wanted to let you know that we will need to be able to set up four systems outside," Emily said, and then waited for Sarah to be upset.

"I thought that might happen," Sarah replied. "I have the materials and can still have it ready in a few days." Sarah picked up her tools and set back to work.

"I'll let you get back to it then," Emily said as she turned and headed out of the building.

Emily worked through the rest of the day, checking in on everyone as she went. Soon, it was time for her to pick up Hope. Emily made her way to the school with Marley and waited for Hope to come out. Hope burst through the doors and came running towards Emily.

"I did it!" Hope exclaimed as she hugged Emily. "I showed everyone what I can do, just like you said."

"I'm proud of you!" Emily smiled with excitement.

"She sure did," June said as she walked over to join them.

"She is quite a smart young lady."

"I know it," Emily said as she stood back up.

"Turns out she could probably teach the preschool class," June smiled. "We are going to let her start on the kindergarten curriculum tomorrow."

"Good job," Emily said to Hope with a smile.

"She may need to be in the first grade, but we are going to take it one step at a time," June smiled. "We'll see you tomorrow," June said as she waved goodbye to Hope.

"See you tomorrow," Hope waved back.

"I think we need a parade or something," Emily said as she began to lead Hope and Marley home.

"Can we go ride Buttercup instead?" Hope asked, looking up at Emily.

"Let's do it," Emily smiled as she turned and began the walk to the farm.

Hope let out a happy squeal and skipped to the farm. Emily couldn't help but smile at how excited Hope was. Emily spotted Jacob walking out of the barn. Emily walked Hope towards him, still laughing at her excitement.

"Hello, ladies," Jacob smiled at them.

"Hello, Jacob," Hope smiled, trying to contain her excitement.

"We're celebrating how well Hope is doing in school," Emily explained. "We were hoping that Buttercup could use a run."

"Of course," Jacob said as he ushered them towards the barn.
"It will just take me a second to get Buttercup ready."

Hope played with Marley while Emily helped Jacob to saddle Buttercup. "Maybe it's time for her first riding lesson," Jacob said as they were finishing.

"You mean, let her ride by herself?" Emily asked.

"She's big enough, and I think she can handle it," Jacob smiled. "No running or anything like that, of course."

"I think she will love that," Emily said, looking back at Hope. "Let's ask her. Hope, come here for a second."

"Is Buttercup ready?" Hope asked as she walked over.

"Yup," Jacob grinned, "but your mom wants to ask you something."

"Yes, mommy," Hope said as she looked at Emily.

"Would you like to have a riding lesson today instead of riding with me?" Emily asked Hope.

"You mean I can ride by myself?" Hope asked with excitement building in her voice.

"That's what I'm saying," Emily smiled back at her.

"Riding lesson," Hope said as she jumped up and down, clapping her hands.

"Alright," Jacob laughed. "You have to promise to listen to what I'm saying."

"I promise," Hope said, trying to force herself to calm down.

Jacob lifted Hope and set her on Buttercup's saddle. Emily followed them as Jacob led Buttercup out of the barn. Emily leaned against the barn and watched as Jacob explained to Hope how to ride. While Hope was excited, Emily could tell that she was focused on every word that Jacob said. Emily knew that there wasn't a better riding teacher or horse for Hope to learn how to ride.

"I'm surprised you're so calm about this."

Emily turned to see Shawn walking out of the barn. "I have to let her grow up, right?" Emily smiled, looking back at Hope.

"Yeah," Shawn nodded. "But it is okay to be a little upset about it."

"Not with her," Emily smiled. "She sees everything."

"You're right about that," Shawn laughed. "I think we have figured out our problem."

"What's the plan?" Emily asked as she waved at Hope.

"We have a store of kerosene that we can use for a while, and Kathy says there is a way to use scrap wood to make more," Shawn explained.

Kathy had arrived last year and had become their local scientist. "She thinks it will burn long and hot enough to take care of the zombies?" Emily asked.

"As long as we clear the trees around the pits, it's also controlled enough that the fire will not spread," Shawn continued. "Jose is working with Cole to build a delivery and ignition system for the kerosene so we can do everything from inside the wall."

"Sounds like you have solved the puzzle," Emily smiled.

"I'm afraid that we won't be able to meet your timeline, though," Shawn said firmly. "It's a lot more complicated than we had initially, though, and if we don't do it right, it will blow up in our face, literally!"

"Are you trying to tell me I have to be patient?" Emily asked, looking offended.

"I am," Shawn laughed. "Just a little bit."

Chapter 4

It was nearly two weeks before everything was ready to set up outside the wall. Shawn had set up a strategy to help them set up the radio systems, dig the pits, and keep everyone safe in the process. Emily could not help but be impressed. He had gathered a group of volunteers who would help get everything done. The plan was to finish one of the systems each day and start the clearing project next week.

The speakers would need to be playing through the weekend to ensure that the dead were all drawn out that were close, and a burn would be done on Sunday to make room for more. They had decided not to use the speaker systems during the day to avoid drawing more of the dead to them. However, if they found themselves overrun, they would turn on select speakers to pull the dead away from the workers.

Emily hadn't wanted the speakers to cause any panic inside Sanctuary and had arranged a party for Saturday night. She hoped that the party's fun would help drown out the sounds of the zombies outside and show everyone that there was nothing to worry about right now. As she expected, no one was willing to turn down the event. Everyone who was not working outside the wall was already hard at work making the necessary preparations.

Emily made her way towards the gate with Marley after gathering her weapons to meet up with the rest of the crew. Shawn was already there and was giving instructions to everyone. Emily joined everyone and waited while Shawn finished explaining the plan to them. Emily was part of the perimeter crew that would ensure the safety of those working.

If everything went according to schedule, they should all be home in time for dinner. However, Emily knew that the rocky Missouri soil might prove difficult. Emily had watched the crews at the landscaping company run into it all the time. Sometimes they could dig forever, but other times they would hit bedrock less than a foot into the soil.

Jose had done everything he could to prepare the digging crew, but it would not be easy. They would have to dig mostly by hand to avoid any unnecessary noise. They had brought a couple of jackhammers if there was no other choice.

Shawn had finished giving his instructions, and everyone was beginning to climb into the trucks. Emily made her way to the control panel and opened the gate. Emily walked back through and walked out amongst the trucks. Shawn was the last to drive out as Emily shut the gate. Several people were loaded in the bed of the truck with Marley. Emily climbed into the truck's cab with Shawn as he began to drive.

The caravan had stopped, allowing Shawn to drive to the front and take the lead. The plan was to go as close to their chosen spot as possible. While they would still have to walk some ways, they wanted to waste as little time as possible walking back and forth. Shawn led the caravan onto the paved road and drove for a few more minutes. It wasn't long before Shawn pulled over to the side of the road, bringing them all to a stop.

"We walk from here," Shawn said to Emily.

Emily nodded and opened the passenger door. Emily climbed out just as everyone, including Marley, climbed out of the bed of the truck. It only took a moment for everyone to unload and gather up their supplies. Once they were all ready,

Shawn, Emily, and Marley led the group to their chosen location. Shawn stopped as they arrived, and everyone began to spread out. Those on guard duty circled the area, weapons in hand. Sarah was with them to ensure that the speakers were installed correctly, and Jose set to work clearing the trees that needed to be removed. For now, they would be gathering the trees but wouldn't return for them until all of the stations were set up. Once the trees were cleared, Jose's crew would begin digging the massive pit to capture the dead.

Emily stood, watching her section of the forest, with Marley by her side. Shawn stood a few feet away from her, doing the same. Everything remained calm, but it wasn't long before the sound of trees falling drew the attention of the dead. Shawn had instructed them to use melee weapons unless they had no other choice. Emily pulled her knife and took a few steps towards a woman with milky white eyes, reaching for Emily with her mouth open. Emily quickly stabbed the zombie in the head and stepped back to her position.

This process continued for a few hours, and soon they were encircled by a ring of corpses. The number of the dead began to decrease as the trees were finished and the digging began. The plan was for the pits to be eight feet deep, thirty feet long, and thirty feet wide. Emily knew that the goal was lofty, but she also knew that everyone was determined to make sure it was done. The hours continued to go by, and Emily could see that the progress was beginning in the pit. It was long past noon, and the crew was only about halfway done.

"We need more hands," Jose said to Shawn. Emily could see that Jose was soaked with sweat, and exhaustion showed on his face. Shawn nodded and walked over to Emily.

"There's almost no dead now," Shawn said to her. "Maybe we should ask some people to switch to digging."

"The speaker system is in place," Emily said. "Sarah can take my place, and I will join." Shawn nodded, knowing that there was no way of talking her out of it. "I will try to get some more people to volunteer and then join you."

Emily nodded as she returned her knife to her waist and turned to climb down into the unfinished pit. Marley remained up top, keeping a watchful eye on the area. Emily grabbed a shovel and began digging. Emily worked with several others to fill a wheelbarrow. Every time it was full, it was taken away and replaced with another. Emily lost track of time and ignored her aching muscles as she continued to work.

"You need to drink," Shawn said as he placed his hand on her shoulder.

Emily stuck the shovel into the dirt and turned to take the water bottle from Shawn.

"I think we bit off more than we could chew," Emily said as she took a drink.

"We won't make dinner, but we will make it," Shawn replied. Emily looked around at their progress and realized how far they had gotten. Ramps were set up so that the wheelbarrows could be pushed up. "We are mounding the dirt between the pit and the wall," Shawn continued. "An extra deterrent to keep the dead away from us."

Emily took another drink of water and nodded. "How's everyone holding up?"

"No one is complaining," Shawn said. "Jose said as long as you are working, they will work."

"No pressure," Emily said, wishing she had the energy to laugh or even roll her eyes.

"Maybe you should go back to guard duty," Shawn offered. "We should be done within an hour or so."

"I can help," Emily insisted as she handed the bottle back to Shawn and grabbed her shovel. "I'll just sleep well tonight."

"If you insist," Shawn said as Emily went back to digging.

Emily continued working aside everyone and felt a sense of relief as it was announced that they were finished just as dusk began to settle in. Shawn helped Emily walk up the ramp as her muscles started to betray her. Emily held on tight to her shovel, still trying to help, as they all made their way back to the trucks. Shawn took Emily's shovel as he opened the door to the truck. Emily was too exhausted to argue and sat down. Emily watched as everyone loaded up, and Marley jumped into the bed of the truck.

Emily remained still as Shawn joined her in the truck and led everyone back to Sanctuary. Emily had to fight her limbs to move to climb out and enter the code. Shawn waited for Emily to make her way back to the truck and climbed inside, too exhausted to walk back into the gate. Once inside, Shawn walked with Emily and Marley to the control panel to close the gate. Shawn attempted to lead Emily home, but she walked back to the trucks instead. Emily could see the exhaustion on everyone's face as they climbed out of the trucks.

"Thank you," Emily said to all of them. Everyone turned to face Emily, stopping what they were doing. "I know it was hard, but I appreciate you all staying out there as long as you did."

"We will be here in the morning," Cole said, smiling at her.

"We won't let you down, ma'am."

Emily felt tears in her eyes as Shawn wrapped his arm around her waist. Emily allowed Shawn to lead her back through the gate and into Sanctuary. Emily had made arrangements for Hope to stay with Julia while working on the pits. Emily knew that she would be exhausted when they returned and couldn't say exactly when she would return. The night was settling in around them, and Emily knew that Hope was already settling into bed. Shawn continued to walk with Emily and Marley into their house.

"You need to take a hot shower," Shawn said as they entered the living room.

"I just want to go to bed," Emily said as she headed for the staircase.

"A hot shower will make sure you can move in the morning," Shawn insisted. "Unless you are planning on taking the day off?"

"Fine," Emily sighed.

"I'll make you something to eat and be up in a minute," Shawn said as Emily began to make her way upstairs.

Emily simply nodded as she was too tired to argue with him. Emily made her way to the bathroom and began to peel off her dirt and sweat-stained clothes. Emily felt the pain in her limbs as she undressed, but forced herself to continue. Emily turned on the shower as hot as she could stand and stepped under the steaming water.

Emily watched as the water around her feet turned brown, and she could feel some relief from her sore muscles. Emily stood for a long time, allowing the water to run freely over her. Finally, Emily felt capable of washing herself. Emily, once again, took her time and tried to relax. Emily eventually turned off the water and stepped out. Emily dried herself and put on a clean t-shirt and panties before heading out into the bedroom.

Shawn was already sitting on the bed, obviously showered. He had set a plate on the nightstand with a sandwich and a large glass of water. Emily made her way over to the bed and sat down.

"I know you don't feel hungry," Shawn spoke. "But you need to eat."

Emily picked up the plate from the nightstand and began to eat the sandwich. Shawn smiled and put his feet up on the bed.

"You'd better have already eaten," Emily said as she forced herself to take another bite.

"I did," Shawn assured her. "I promise."

Emily finished her sandwich and returned the plate to the nightstand. Emily grabbed the glass of water and began to take small sips.

"We barely finished today, and everything went in our favor," Emily said to Shawn.

"We didn't hit bedrock, and tomorrow our crew will be tired to start," Shawn agreed.

"I don't know what to do," Emily said as she set the glass back on the nightstand.

"You keep going," Shawn said as he took her hand. "Did you see their faces tonight?"

"They were exhausted," Emily replied as she wrapped her fingers around his.

"It was more than that," Shawn insisted. "They are dedicated to what they are doing because they believe in you."

"I don't want that kind of power," Emily admitted. "They are willing to work themselves to the grave because I say this needs to be done."

"Are you wrong?" Shawn asked, turning her face towards his. "Does this need to be done to protect Sanctuary?" "It does, but.." Emily tried to argue.

"No, but," Shawn interrupted. "We are all working to survive here. Not just for now but for many years to come. You have inspired us to do that, made us believe it was possible. Don't waiver on us now."

"You have a way with words," Emily smiled at him. "Did you know that?"

"I like to think so," Shawn said as he slid down into the bed. "We need to get some rest. I'm sure you want to see Hope before we head back out."

Emily slid down and lay her head on his chest. Moments later, Marley jumped up and spread out behind her. It didn't take long for Emily to fall asleep that night.

Emily continued the process for the next few days, only seeing Hope on her way to school in the morning. Emily continued to help with the digging as soon as the dead became fewer. Emily had never been so exhausted in her life, but she kept working alongside her family to complete the task. They had only hit solid rock a few times but had quickly worked through it. They continued to return home each day around dusk. The crew always promised to see her in the morning before they all headed home.

It was the final day, and they had been struggling to get through the bedrock for hours. Every time they thought they had made progress, they hit more. The pit was nearly done, but dusk was nearing, and the bedrock was refusing to take it easy on them.

"Maybe we should stop," Emily said to Jose, who had just handed off his jackhammer to Shawn.

"We'll get it," Jose insisted. We're only a foot off."

"Is a foot enough to worry about?" Emily said, looking at the pit. "It's more than deep enough to contain the dead."

"It's your call," Jose replied. "We'll follow your lead.

Emily made her way over to Shawn's work and signaled for him to stop.

"Problem?" Shawn asked, short of breath.

"What are the consequences of leaving it a foot short?" Emily asked, looking around.

"It may require cleaning sooner than the others," Shawn replied. "Are you thinking about calling it?"

"The jackhammers are calling in more and more," Emily said. "Staying out here after dark is asking for someone to get bitten."

"I agree," Shawn breathed, still waiting for her to make a decision.

"Good work, everyone!" Emily called out. "Let's go home."

Emily watched as they all nodded and began to gather up their supplies. It was quite a walk back to the trucks. It would be hard for them to make it before dark. Emily pulled her knife as soon as she was out of the pit. The dead continued to come at them, and she was determined, despite her exhaustion, to protect her people. Marley ran over to join her, his fur covered in blood, showing that he had been busy helping the guards. Emily worked with the crew to begin fighting their way out. Emily felt her last bit of energy draining away with each zombie she killed. Emily felt like she was on autopilot as she continued to work forward. They were nearing the road where the vehicles were waiting when things went wrong. Emily heard the dead coming but didn't realize how many there were. Emily continued to fight as she lost track of everyone amongst a sea of the dead. Emily worked her way through the sea, killing as she went.

"Get to the truck!" Emily yelled to each person she saw.

Emily had just killed another Zombie when she heard a noise behind her. Emily turned, just a zombie grabbed her by the front of the shirt. Marley didn't hesitate and lunged at the zombie. Emily rushed towards him and plunged her knife into his skull.

"Good boy," Emily breathed as she climbed back up to her feet. Emily noticed that Cole was pinned on the ground with a zombie woman on top of him, a short distance away from her. Emily ran towards him and stabbed the zombie in the head. Emily pulled the corpse off of Cole and helped him to his feet.

"Are you alright?" Emily asked him quickly.

"No," Cole said as he looked down at his arm.

Emily followed his gaze and saw it. Even with the limited light that remained, the bite on his arm was visible.

"We have to get you to the truck," Emily replied. "The crew has the vaccine needles."

Cole nodded and ran with Emily and Marley back to the trucks. Emily ran to Shawn, who was helping load the supplies.

"I need a needle!" Emily yelled at him as she ran.

Shawn pulled a needle from the supplies and held it out to her. "Who?" Shawn asked as he ran back with her towards the truck.

"Cole," Emily answered.

Cole had climbed into the bed of the truck and was holding his hand over the bite.

"I have to inject it into the bite," Emily said as she pulled his hand away. Cole didn't fight her and watched as Emily thrust the needle into his arm and injected the liquid it contained.

"We have to go," Shawn said as he reached to pull her away from Cole.

"Let me at least wrap it with something!" Emily insisted as she tried to push him away.

"The others will help him!" Shawn yelled. "We have to go!"

Emily looked up and could see the dead pouring out of the trees and coming towards them.

"Fuck!" Emily said as she shut the tailgate and ran towards the passenger door. Emily pulled the door handle and allowed the door to swing open. Emily climbed inside and reached back for the door to slam it shut. The pain was just as intense as she remembered. A zombie man clamped down on her outstretched arm before she could shut the door. Emily held back her scream and used her free hand to stab the zombie in the head. Emily quickly shut the door as soon as it fell to the pavement. Emily allowed herself to react as soon as she was safe inside the cab of the truck.

"Son of a bitch!" Emily yelled as she held her arm by the wrist.

"No," Shawn said with panic as he pulled her arm closer.

"I'll be fine," Emily insisted as she pulled her arm back. "We have to get Cole back." Emily pulled the walkie from her waist and pressed the button. "Doc, we need you to meet us at the gate."

"On my way," Doc simply replied. Emily dropped the walkie on the seat next to her and reapplied pressure to her bite.

Shawn drove as fast as the old truck could go to get them home. The burning pain had spread up Emily's arm by the time she jumped out to open the gate.

"Go!" Emily insisted as she turned to see Shawn waiting for her.

The look on Shawn's face told her he wasn't happy, but he drove inside. Emily followed the rest of the trucks and made her way to the control panel to shut it.

"What happened?" Doc said as he rushed over and tried to look at her bite.

"Cole first," Emily insisted. "I gave him the vaccine within minutes of the bite."

Emily led Doc over to where Cole was passed out in the truck.

"Let's get him into quarantine," Doc said after looking at the bite.

"Is he going to be okay?" Emily asked as Shawn and Sam lifted Cole out of the truck's bed.

"There's no fever," Doc said as he followed where Sam and Shawn were carrying Cole. "I'll stitch up the wound, and then we have to wait."

"Isn't there something we can…" Emily began to ask.

"You gave him a chance," Doc replied. "That's all we can do."

Emily stopped and leaned against the wooden wall. After a few minutes, Shawn walked back through the door.

"We should get you home," Shawn said as he wrapped his arm around her.

"I need to stay in quarantine," Emily insisted as she made her way towards the door. "Just in case."

Shawn walked with Emily and took her to the second cabin. Emily walked to one of the cots and sat down. Shawn sat down beside her and wrapped his arm around her.

"I'm going to be fine," Emily insisted as she lay her head on his shoulder.

"You better be," Shawn replied softly. "I can't lose you."

"You won't," Emily replied, trying to comfort him despite the pain that was now spreading up her arm and through her torso.

"I'm not going anywhere."

Chapter 5

Emily and Shawn didn't have to wait long for Doc to come into the cabin. Doc set to work without a word. Emily held out her wrist and sat still as Doc cleaned the bite, stitched it shut, and wrapped it in a bandage. The pain continued to spread, but Emily was hiding it as best she could. She was surprised that she hadn't passed out. The last time she was bitten, she passed out almost immediately.

"How's Cole doing?" Emily asked as he finished, and she pulled her arm back close to her body.

"He's still passed out, but no fever yet," Doc said as he put his tools back in his bag. "I've never seen anyone go unconscious from a bite before."

"I did," Emily replied. "The first time I was bitten. I passed out almost immediately."

"Interesting," Doc said, adjusting his glasses. "This may be a sign that the vaccine is working."

"When will we know for sure?" Shawn asked.

"If there's still no fever in the next hour or so, I feel confident that he will beat the infection," Doc explained.

"Will he become immune like me?" Emily asked.

"No," Doc replied, shaking his head. "It will lower his chances of the vaccine working a second time."

"Let's not let there be a second time," Shawn said. "How's she looking, Doc?"

"I think she'll be fine," Doc replied. "She's in quite a bit of pain, though."

Emily looked down and couldn't even try to deny what Doc knew. She wasn't good at hiding her pain from Doc.

"I just need to rest," Emily said as she could feel Shawn looking at her.

"Can you give her something to help?" Shawn asked, looking back at Doc.

"I could try," Doc replied. "But her body would burn it off in minutes."

"I don't need it," Emily insisted. "I just need to rest."

Shawn stood up from the cot and allowed Emily to lie down. Emily stretched out and tried her best to relax.

"Let me know if there is an update on Cole," Emily said as her eyes became too heavy to hold open any longer.

"I will," Doc replied.

"Shawn, you will take care of Hope, right?" Emily asked, fighting the urge to fall asleep.

"I got it," Shawn said as he took her hand.

Emily didn't have the strength to talk anymore. She could hear Shawn and Doc continue talking, but it was like she was hearing them from the opposite end of a tunnel. Their voices were too faint and distorted to make out. The voices drifted away, and Emily fell into a dreamless sleep. Emily felt herself slowly wake up, still lying on the cot. Emily glanced at the cabin door and could see the light shining under the door. Emily readjusted on the cot and realized that Shawn held her hand. Emily looked on the ground beside her to see Shawn and Marley lying there. Emily tried to readjust on her cot without waking either of them. However, as soon as she moved, both Marley and Shawn opened their eyes.

"How are you?" Shawn asked as he sat up.

"Right as rain," Emily said, replied. "A little hungry." "I'll get you something," Shawn said as he began to stand.

"How's Cole?" Emily asked.

"No fever, but he was still asleep last I heard," Shawn said.

"I'll stop and check on him while I'm out."

"Why don't we go together?" Emily said as she started to stand.

"You rest," Shawn said as he gently pushed her back down on the cot. Emily knew he was scared. He hadn't seen her go through this before. She felt fine but knew he wasn't going to accept that.

"Okay," Emily smiled. "But after breakfast, I need to get up and moving."

"We'll see," Shawn smiled as he brushed his hand against her cheek. Shawn turned and walked out of the cabin. Marley stood and walked over to lay his head on Emily's lap.

"Did I scare you, too?" Emily asked as she petted his head.

Emily took Marley's lack of movement as confirmation. "I'm sorry.

I am fine, I promise."

Marley looked up at her with his big brown eyes. Emily could see the pain and worry in them. Emily continued to pet his head, trying to comfort him. They remained this way until the door of the cabin opened once more.

"I thought we could have breakfast together," Cole said as he walked into the cabin.

"Cole!" Emily exclaimed, and she stood and hugged him.

"You're alright!"

"Yeah," Cole said as he hugged her back. "I woke up a little bit ago. Shawn said you were bitten, too."

Emily held up her bandaged wrist to show him that she was also sporting her own battle scar.

"Sit down," Emily insisted, motioning to the cot.

"Everyone keeps telling me to rest," Cole said as they sat down. "But I feel fine."

"I know," Emily laughed. "But it's best to humor them a little."

Shawn walked in carrying two plates of food. While Shawn was a decent cook, Emily felt confident that Julia provided their breakfast. Emily took her plate as Shawn held it out, and Cole did the same.

"I thought you were told to rest?" Shawn said as Cole took his plate.

"You never said it had to be in that cabin." Cole pointed out.

"Smartass," Shawn said as he sat on the floor beside Emily.

"Did you see Hope?" Emily asked as she took a bite.

"Yes," Shawn nodded. "She and Tiffany will come by once Doc says you are both fine."

Emily hadn't had much interaction with Tiffany, Cole's sixteen-year-old daughter. However, she knew that Tiffany was everything to Cole. Cole smiled as he began to eat his breakfast.

"I see you both have an appetite," Doc said as we walked into the cabin.

"Part of fighting the infection," Emily replied with a smile.

"Which you have both done," Doc replied as he checked each of their temperatures. Doc unwrapped the bandage on Cole's arm, revealing his bite. Emily watched as Doc cleaned the bite and put on a fresh bandage. When he finished, Emily held out her wrist and allowed Doc to repeat the process on her bite.

"You both are going to be fine," Doc said as he stood up.

"I'm clearing you both to go back into Sanctuary."

"Are you sure?" Shawn asked from his position on the floor.

"I would recommend taking it easy for a few days," Doc said. "Which shouldn't be hard with the festivities tonight."

"So, just to be clear," Emily began. "We can still go to the party?"

"I don't see any reason why not," Doc said.

"Just no zombie fighting until you get the stitches out."

"Can I go?" Emily asked, looking down at Shawn, sticking out her bottom lip. "Please?"

"Alright," Shawn said, rolling his eyes. "I'd better get you both out there to your daughters before they start to go crazy."

Shawn stood from his spot and held his hand out to Emily. Emily took his hand and stood up on her feet. Cole quickly stood and began making his way out of the cabin with Doc. Emily, Shawn, and Marley followed them. Emily couldn't help but enjoy the sunlight on her skin as she walked. Emily didn't focus on anything else until they were back inside Sanctuary.

"Mommy!" Hope yelled as she ran towards Emily.

"Dad!" Tiffany joined as she ran towards Cole.

Emily bent down and pulled Hope into a big hug.

"Hey monkey," Emily breathed into Hope's long hair.

"I was so scared," Tiffany was saying to Cole. Emily glanced over and could see that the girl had a death grip on her father. "I thought I lost you like mom."

"I wouldn't let that happen," Cole insisted as he hugged Tiffany.

"Let's get home," Emily smiled at Hope.

Hope took Emily by the hand, but Emily couldn't help but notice the look of concern that was now on Hope's face. Hope had simply looked like she missed Emily before, but now she looked scared. Emily walked, holding Hope's hand, to the house.

"I'm going to make sure everything is ready for tonight," Shawn said as they reached the porch. "You get cleaned up and try to relax."

"She will," Hope insisted as she dragged Emily up the stairs.

"I don't think I have a choice," Emily laughed as Hope dragged her inside the house.

Emily allowed Hope to drag her through the house and up the stairs. Marley followed them as if thinking they were playing a new game.

"I can clean up on my own," Emily insisted as Hope began to pull her into the bathroom.

"Okay," Hope said with hesitation.

Emily shook her head and turned to grab herself some fresh clothes. Hope headed back out of the room with Marley as Emily shut the bathroom door. Emily assumed that she was going to her room to play. Emily removed her clothes from before and tossed them into the basket.

Emily took a shower, careful not to get her bandage wet. Emily dressed and brushed her hair before heading back out into the bedroom. Emily couldn't help but pause at the scene that unfolded in her bedroom. Hope had brought up a couple of DVDs and set them on the dresser, a glass of water was on the nightstand, and the blankets on the bed had been folded back. Hope was sitting on the bed holding a book while Marley lay on the foot of the bed.

"What's going on?" Emily asked as she walked towards the bed.

"Shawn said you needed to rest," Hope said innocently.

"He did," Emily said as she sat down on the bed. "But I got permission for us to go to the party tonight."

"Are you sick?" Hope asked with a look of concern on her face.

"No," Emily assured her as she pulled Hope close. "Why would you think that?"

"Why do we live behind a wall?" Hope asked.

Emily took a deep breath. She knew that Hope would ask questions about the world outside one day, but didn't expect it so soon. Emily had to remind herself that Hope was no average oneyear-old. While she was not ready for all of the gory details, Emily needed to give her some information about the world.

"There are creatures outside the wall that try to hurt people," Emily explained.

"What kind of creatures?" Hope asked.

"They were once people," Emily continued. "Just like you and me. But one day, there was a bright flash in the sky."

"Just like in my story," Emily said, holding out the book.

"Just like in your story," Hope nodded. "The flash sent a lot of people to heaven, and monsters took their place."

"That's not nice," Hope said with a stern look.

"No, it wasn't," Emily agreed. "The monsters want to send more people to heaven and bring their friends here." "How will they do that?" Hope asked.

"If they bite a person, the person gets sick and goes to heaven," Emily explained.

Hope's eyes went straight to Emily's bandage.

"Tiffany said you and her daddy were bit," Hope said as tears began to pool in her eyes.

"We were, but the monsters didn't win," Emily assured her. Emily could see that Hope was confused. Emily took Hope's storybook and opened it to where Emily lost her family. "On this day, one of the monsters bit me. I wanted to save my family and told them to run. Marley pulled me inside my old house and protected me. I waited to get sick, but never did." "Why not?" Hope asked.

Emily flipped ahead to the part where the story is about Robert.

"Robert discovered that there were a few people in the world who the monsters could not get sick, and I was one of them." "Is Cole one of them?" Hope asked.

"No," Emily said while shaking her head. "Doc was able to make a medicine that can help people get better. It doesn't always work, but we were lucky that it did for Cole." "Am I one of them?" Hope asked.

"No," Emily said with a knot in her stomach. "But I will make sure no monsters come near you."

"Are the monsters what everyone calls zombies?" Hope asked, closing the storybook.

"Yes," Emily said.

"And sometimes you have to fight the zombies and send them to heaven?"

"Sometimes," Emily nodded.

"If they are so tough, how do you fight them?"

"Well," Emily said with hesitation, trying to find a way to explain it that wasn't so gory. "The monsters have one weakness, big brains. If you hurt their big brains, then they go to heaven."

"Did the monsters send my daddy to heaven?"

"I don't know," Emily admitted. "They hadn't last time I saw him."

"Why would my daddy leave you?" Hope asked next. Emily had thought the questions would be over. "Shawn didn't leave you even though the monsters tried to make you sick."

"I wasn't your daddy's happily ever after," Emily explained just as she did in the book. "He had found his happily ever after and had to go save her."

"And no one knew that I was in your tummy," Hope said, looking at Emily for confirmation.

"Nope," Emily smiled. "But you were the best surprise I could have ever asked for."

"Will we ever find our family?" Hope asked, looking down at the closed book once more.

"I hope so," Emily smiled. "But even if we don't, we have built an amazing family here."

Hope nodded and turned to set the book on the nightstand. "Can we watch movies until it's time for the party?"

"I could use a movie day," Emily said as she leaned back against the pillows.

Hope handed Emily the remote. Emily pressed the button and brought the television to life.

Emily and Hope spent the rest of the day in bed, working their way through the movies that Hope had chosen. They only took a break to get lunch, which they promptly brought back up to the bedroom along with a bowl of popcorn. Occasionally, Emily could hear everyone out on the street setting up for the party. Emily was determined to remain exactly where she was and trust everyone else to take care of it.

"Hello?!" Shawn's voice echoed up the stairs.

"Up here!" Emily yelled back. "I think it's party time," Emily smiled at Hope.

Hope clapped her hands with excitement as Shawn made his way into the room.

"Have you two been in here all day?" Shawn asked as he looked at them lying on the bed.

"No," Hope insisted. "We had to eat."

"Well, as long as you ate," Shawn laughed. "Everyone's gathering if you guys would like to come out."

"I think we're ready," Emily said, looking at Hope, who nodded.

"Then let's go," Shawn said, motioning towards the door.

"Come on, Marley," Hope said as she jumped off the bed and ran out the door, Marley right behind her. Emily stood up and walked towards the door to follow them.

"Are you feeling alright?" Shawn asked as she neared him.

"I feel fine," Emily insisted. "I'm ready for a night of fun."

"Then let's get going!" Shawn said as he swept her off her feet and ran down the stairs with her in his arms.

"Me too!" Hope yelled as they reached the bottom.

"You too," Shawn grinned as he kneeled, and Emily pulled Hope on top of her. "Someone get the door," Shawn said as they reached the front door.

Emily and Hope reached out and pulled the door open. Marley ran out the door ahead of Shawn, and Shawn carried Emily and Hope into the party.

"Bobby!" Hope yelled, waving at where Bobby and Terra were standing. "Can I go play, Mommy?"

"You sure can," Emily smiled back.

Shawn knelt once more and allowed Hope to run off to join the kids.

"Are you going to let me walk?" Emily asked as Shawn stood back up.

"Try to spoil a woman, and she complains," Shawn said, rolling his eyes as he set Emily down.

"I know," Emily laughed. "I'm just so difficult."

"You know you scared the hell out of me," Shawn said as he took her hand.

"You can't focus on that," Emily said as she wrapped her arms around him. "Nothing is guaranteed in this world. We just have to enjoy all the moments we have."

"I can do that," Shawn grinned as he lifted Emily off her feet. Emily pulled his face closer and fell into a kiss.

"Ewww," Hope and the other kids yelled.

Emily and Shawn both laughed but continued kissing.

"If you two are about done," Sarah interrupted them.

"Not really," Shawn said as he gently set Emily back on her feet.

"I think we can take a break for you," Emily teased.

"We are ready to turn on the speakers," Sarah said, laughing.

"Let's do it," Emily said excitedly. Shawn and Emily followed Sarah back to the COM room hand in hand.

"Each system has its marker," Sarah explained, pointing to a set of toggle switches by the radio. "The ones inside are all set up on this one."

"We will get those up right away," Emily said.

"We got the ones on the main street up tonight," Sarah smiled. "Thought it would give us better music quality for the party."

"Always thinking," Emily laughed.

"The placement of the speakers and their volume settings will make it so they can't be heard outside the walls," Sarah explained. "The outside ones are loud enough that they should be heard in a two-mile radius around the systems."

"What are we going to play?" Emily asked.

"Tonight, we'll use the same music we are playing inside," Sarah smiled.

Sarah flipped on all of the speakers and hit play on a stereo setup. Even inside the COM building, Emily could hear rock music playing in the street.

"Everything's working!" Sarah said with excitement.

"Then let's party!" Shawn yelled as he led them both back outside.

Chapter 6

Emily couldn't help but look at everyone as they walked back into the party crowd. Everyone was smiling and enjoying the music selection Sarah had set up. Some people were dancing, and those who weren't were either singing along or at least swaying to the music.

"Do you want to dance?" Shawn asked as he continued to walk with Emily.

"I want to get some food," Emily said, looking at the food tables.

"Good idea," Shawn said, following her gaze. "The kids are going nuts."

Emily could see Hope holding the plate, and Tiffany was helping her with the food. Emily wished there was less sugar, but decided to let Hope have fun tonight. Shawn and Emily made their way over to the food and started loading their plates. Emily's standard cookies were missing this time, but no one complained. They all understood that Emily was a little preoccupied this time.

Once they had both loaded their plates full of food, they headed to a couple of open seats by Hope. Hope smiled at them as she took a big bite out of a cupcake.

"She is going to crash hard," Shawn whispered.

"I know," Emily smiled. "That's the plan."

Emily ate her food and enjoyed all of the small talk around her. These get-togethers were becoming the highlight of being inside the wall. It gave everyone a chance to relax and have fun for a night. They all worked so hard. It was important to Emily to provide them with these moments. Everyone knew what was going on outside the wall, but the party kept everyone from worrying.

Hope finished her plate and ran with the other kids to dance to the music. Emily turned in her chair and watched them with a smile. Hope and the other kids looked like normal kids before the flash. Emily enjoyed watching the kids have fun as a variety of music played through the speakers. Hope started to yawn and rub her eyes as the sun began to set.

"She's going," Emily said as she stood up.

"I'm going to check on the wall while you tuck her in," Shawn said as he turned to head towards the wall.

Emily made her way to where Hope was still trying to dance.

"I think it's time for bed, kiddo," Emily said as she reached Hope.

"Can I go to the slumber party?" Hope asked, looking at the other kids.

"Slumber party?" Emily asked, looking at the other kids.

"Margaret is having all the kids stay at her place so the parents can keep having fun," Terra answered. "We couldn't find you to ask if Hope could come."

"We are all going there now," Bobby said. "Can Hope come, please?"

"I don't see why not," Emily smiled. "I just need to make sure it's okay with Margaret."

Hope smiled back at all of the other kids. Emily took Hope by the hand and led all the kids towards where Margaret was sitting.

"I hear there's a slumber party?" Emily smiled at Margaret.

"I thought it would give the parents a chance to relax," Margaret grinned. "Hopes invited, of course. We are going to let them sleep in the living room and watch movies."

"She wants to go," Emily laughed as Hope began to jump up and down. "I just wanted to make sure it was okay with you."

"Us old people are partied out about the same time they are," Margaret laughed. "I would love for her to join us."

Marley began to jump around and bark as if insisting he go as well.

"Marley is welcome as well," Margaret laughed.

"Alright," Emily smiled. "You be good and listen to Margaret, and I'll see you in the morning," Emily said to Hope and Marley.

"I will, Mommy," Hope said as she quickly hugged Emily and ran off with the other kids and Marley towards Margaret's house.

"Have fun," Emily smiled at Margaret as she followed the kids to the house.

Emily found herself entirely alone with no responsibilities. It wasn't long after the kids had left that Cole appeared with jars of a clear liquid that Emily knew to be moonshine. Emily noticed Derick staring at the bottles, obviously struggling with his problem. Emily made her way over to where Derrick was standing.

"Everything alright?" Emily asked as she reached him.

"I keep thinking one drink wouldn't hurt," Derrick admitted to her. "But I know it will only take one to ruin everything."

"You don't need to drink to have fun," Emily said as she bumped her shoulder into his.

"I don't know about that," Derick said, straightening up. "But it's what I got to do."

"I'll prove it to you," Emily said as she grabbed Derrick by the hand.

Before Derick could say no, Emily had pulled him out onto the make-shift dance floor and began to dance. Derick looked uncomfortable at first, but he was laughing and twirling Emily within minutes. Emily continued to dance with Derick for a few songs, having just as much fun as he was.

"I need some water," Emily laughed as the song ended.

"I'll get it," Derick smiled as he walked over to where the water pitchers were sitting.

Emily made her way over to an empty chair and took a seat.

"Did I see that right?" Shawn said as he sat down beside her.

"Just proving to him that he doesn't need to get drunk to have fun," Emily laughed. "He's trying."

"It's just hard to believe that last year you broke his nose, and tonight you two were dancing like old friends," Shawn grinned slyly. "It is friends, right?"

"Shut up," Emily said as she punched him in the arm.

"Here you go," Derick said as he handed Emily a glass of water. "If you don't mind, Cara has said she would like to dance." "Go for it," Emily smiled as she took a sip of water.

Derrick didn't hesitate and practically ran over to where Cara was waiting. It was only a moment before Derick and Cara were dancing, both laughing and having fun. Emily caught another couple dancing that took her by surprise.

"Is that Jacob and Mindy?" Emily asked, pointing to them.

Mindy had arrived with the group rescued from Jeff's camp. She had been quiet and scared, not surprising because of what she had been through with Jeff. Now she was laughing, and the look on their faces told Emily there was something between them.

"Yup," Shawn answered. "They have been spending a lot of time together lately."

"Love is in the air," Emily mused as she looked at Shawn.

"Well, I'm not going just to sit here while everyone else has all the fun," Shawn said as he stood up and held out his hand. "Can you dance sober?" Emily asked as she took his hand and stood up.

"I'm not sure," Shawn teased. "I guess we are going to find out. We have to enjoy these moments."

Emily followed Shawn out onto the dance floor. The song changed to a slow ballad just as they reached their spot.

"Oh, they're giving you a warm-up," Emily teased as she reached her arms up towards Shawn's shoulders.

Shawn wrapped his arms around her waist and pulled her close. Shawn was ignoring what Emily had said and proving he could slow dance. Emily lay her head on Shawn's chest and allowed him to lead her around the floor. Emily felt like everyone else had disappeared, and it was just the two of them. The song seemed to go by too fast, and the tempo increased once more.

Shawn didn't hesitate for even a moment. He reached up and grabbed Emily's hand before she could realize what was happening. Shawn quickly spun Emily around, causing her to laugh and trip over their feet.

"Can you dance sober?" Shawn laughed as he pulled her close once more.

Emily and Shawn danced for several songs before Shawn led her off the dance floor.

"I got the next shift," Shawn explained. "I'll only be gone an hour."

"I'll go with you," Emily said as she took his hand. "Unless you don't want the company."

"I'll always say yes to you," Shawn replied as he wrapped his fingers around hers.

Emily walked with Shawn to the armory and waited by the door to grab his gun. Shawn walked back out and immediately took her hand once more.

"Is Marley with Hope?" Shawn asked, realizing that Marley had not joined them.

"Margaret took all the kids for a slumber party tonight," Emily explained. "Naturally, he invited himself and went."

"That dog is so weird," Shawn laughed.

"Don't get me wrong. He's a good dog. But he's just different from every dog I've ever met."

"That's what makes him Marley," Emily laughed.

"I'm not complaining," Shawn grinned. "It's rare that I get to spend an evening alone with you."

"I forgot what it's like not to have anyone to worry about for a night," Emily admitted as they climbed the stairs. "Normally, I always have something or someone to take care of."

"Just enjoy it," Shawn said to her. "Don't go for something to worry about."

"I think I can do that," Emily said as she lay her head against his arm just as they reached the top of the stairs.

Shawn and Emily walked around the wall together to the south side, where they would be clearing the trees. Shawn took a report from each person who passed about what had happened during their shift. Emily remained silent and allowed Shawn to ask his questions. They finally reached the spot that Shawn would be patrolling and were alone once more.

"This is good," Shawn said to her, looking out over the wall. "The dead are being drawn away from the wall."

"And into our pits of fiery death," Emily added.

Shawn nodded and pulled her close as he continued to keep his eyes focused on the other side of the wall.

"I think we should keep playing music out there," Emily said.

"Well, the dead will at least get to listen to some good music before we roast them."

"Exactly," Emily said. "And the pits are a half-mile from each station. People could hear it, and it would help them find us."

"I thought you weren't going to worry?" Shawn said as he glanced down at her.

"I'm not," Emily insisted. "Just a thought I wanted to get out of my head."

"It is a good idea," Shawn admitted. "I'm sure the logging crew would appreciate the music while they work as well."

"See, no worry," Emily smiled. "Just good ideas."

Emily leaned her head against his shoulder once more and looked out into the distance. They couldn't see much as the trees still blocked their view, but both of them remained vigilant.

"This is the longest wall shift ever," Shawn finally spoke.

"It's half the time of a normal shift," Emily laughed.

"But it feels twice as long," Shawn said, looking at her once more. "I would much rather be dancing with you in my arms than standing here."

"We all have to make sacrifices," Emily said. "At least we are together."

"I just know that the dancing will be pretty much over after this," Shawn said. "You deserve to be out there having the time of your life."

"I'm right where I want to be," Emily said as she leaned up on her toes and kissed Shawn.

Shawn pulled her close as he turned his attention back to the tree line. Emily stood with Shawn for the remainder of his shift and couldn't help but jump when Jacob appeared to relieve him.

"Didn't mean to scare you," Jacob laughed. "Please don't jump off the wall."

"Make some noise or something next time," Emily teased.

"I'll work on that," Jacob laughed.

"Oh, no," Shawn said as he looked away from Emily.

"What?" Jacob asked, looking between them.

"She's about to be noisy," Shawn explained to warn Jacob.

"I just couldn't help but notice you and Mindy tonight," Emily said as innocently as she could.

"Yes," Jacob laughed. "She's a wonderful person that I am enjoying getting to know."

"So, it's still in the getting to know each other stage?" Emily grinned.

"Yes, and if it changes, you will be the first person we tell," Jacob laughed.

"Really?" Emily said with more surprise than she intended.

"Of course," Jacob laughed. "You're like a sister to me, and I know hiding anything from your sister equals trouble."

"Oh," Emily replied, feeling her face turn red. "I'd better let you get to work then, bro."

Jacob shook his head, laughing as he walked past them to begin his shift.

"Are you done?" Shawn asked, rolling his eyes.

"For now," Emily chimed as she walked forward with him.

Emily and Shawn made their way back around the wall and down the stairs. Emily waited once again while Shawn put away his weapon and returned. They walked back towards Emily's house slowly. Emily could see that Shawn was right. The music on the street was turned off, and several people were cleaning up the tables and chairs.

"Damn," Shawn said. "I hoped I was wrong."

"Let's give them a hand," Emily replied, pulling Shawn forward. "It could be just as fun as dancing."

"I doubt that," Shawn laughed as he moved forward.

Emily walked over and folded up the chairs, and stacked them on a flatbed dolly. Shawn helped with the tables, and the street was clear before long. Emily waited while Shawn helped push the dollies back to the store where they were stored. Emily looked up the stairs and got lost in their beauty.

"Do you see something up there?" Shawn asked as he walked up beside her and wrapped his arms around her waist.

"Just the stars," Emily replied as she leaned against him.

"Well, stargazer," Shawn replied as he hugged her tighter. "I think it's time to get you home."

"But it's such a long walk," Emily said, looking over at her front door.

"Come on," Shawn said as he grabbed her by the hand and led her up onto her porch.

"Tonight was amazing," Emily said as Shawn stopped outside the door.

"Every moment I spend with you is amazing," Shawn replied. Emily and Shawn couldn't help but smile at how cheesy the statement sounded.

"Why don't you come in and…." Emily began.

"We're taking it slow," Shawn said, looking at the door. "I can't promise I can do that if I come in tonight."

"I guess it is harder to do that without Hope in the house," Emily admitted.

"Good night," Shawn said as he pulled her closer and gave her a light kiss.

"Good night," Emily replied as Shawn released her waist and she opened the front door.

Emily watched Shawn walk down the porch's steps and slowly close the wooden door. Emily made her way into the living room and collapsed on the couch. She was beginning to hate the word slow every time it was brought up. While they had only been officially dating a few months, she had cared for Shawn well over a year and knew that he felt the same way.

Emily was resolved to redefine the meaning of slow the next time she saw him.

Emily was pulled out of her thoughts by a knock on the door. Emily glanced at the clock to see that it was well after midnight. Fearing that something had gone wrong with the speaker systems, she jumped up and ran to the door. Emily completely forgot that someone would have called her on the walkie and would not be knocking on her door if there was an emergency. Emily threw open the door and was shocked to find Shawn standing on her porch.

"I walked all the way home and couldn't stop thinking," Shawn said as he walked past her and into the house.

Emily slowly shut the door and followed Shawn into the living room. Shawn was pacing in front of the television, constantly moving his hands.

"You were thinking and had to come back here?" Emily asked after a few minutes of awkward pacing.

"Yes," Shawn answered, pointing at her. His tone implied that Emily's question had explained everything, but Emily was still confused.

"I don't understand," Emily said as she raised and dropped her hands in defeat.

"I know we said we would take it slow," Shawn explained.
"But there's slow, and then there's stopped."

"I agree," Emily said as she took a few steps closer to where he was still pacing.

"And earlier, you said we have to enjoy the moments we have," Shawn continued.

Suddenly, Shawn stopped pacing, walked over to Emily, and pulled her into his arms.

"I love you," Shawn said as he looked softly down at her. "I have for a while, and I'm tired of hiding it."

"I love you too," Emily replied as she reached up and placed her hand on his face.

"I think we've moved slowly enough," Shawn said.

Before Emily could reply, Shawn lifted her from the ground and kissed her with more passion than Emily ever knew was possible. Emily wrapped her legs around his waist and allowed Shawn to pull her even closer. Emily felt Shawn begin to move, and soon he was carrying her up the stairs. Emily pulled back from the kiss and looked at Shawn. He looked rough and hardened on the exterior, but his eyes gave him away. They were a dark blue, and the softness that showed through them melted her heart.

Emily leaned back into the kiss just as they reached the top of the stairs. Shawn carried Emily into the bedroom. Emily pushed the door shut as they went by. Emily and Shawn continued to kiss as Shawn lay her gently on the bed. Emily relaxed her legs around Shawn as he slowly pulled away. Emily watched, biting her lower lip, as Shawn pulled off his vest, dropping it on the floor, followed by his shirt. Emily reached up and pulled Shawn close to her once more. They continued to kiss for several minutes. The passion in each made Emily feel as if she could explode at any moment. Shawn slowly pulled away once more and looked at Emily.

"Are you sure?" he asked her as he brushed the hair out of her face.

Emily placed her hand on his chest and gently pushed him to where she could sit up. Emily grabbed the bottom of her t-shirt and pulled it overhead, throwing it on the floor by his. Emily then reached up and pulled Shawn towards her as she lay back down.

"Positive," Emily assured him as they began to kiss once more.

Chapter 7

Emily woke the following day and couldn't help but smile. Emily could hear Shawn's heart beating under her ear as she lay on his bare chest. Emily slowly lifted her face to see that Shawn was already awake and looking at her.

"Good morning," Shawn smiled as he kissed her once more.

"Good morning," Emily replied as she continued to smile.

"Last night was…." Shawn began.

"If you say a one-time thing, we are going to have an issue," Emily warned him.

"I was going to say perfect," Shawn laughed. "But good to know it wasn't a one-time thing."

"It was not," Emily smiled as she made herself comfortable on his chest once more.

"We should probably get up," Emily said, hating herself for admitting after several moments.

"Let's just stay like this all day," Shawn replied as he wrapped his arms around her.

"I'm fine with that," Emily grinned. "But you get to explain to Hope what we are doing."

"Right," Shawn said as he flipped back the covers and sat up, dropping Emily onto the bed. "We really shouldn't spend all day in bed."

"Coward," Emily teased as she looked back up at him.

"That little girl scares the shit out of me," Shawn laughed as he began to get dressed.

Emily grinned and forced herself to stand up out of bed.

Emily made her way to the closet to get a fresh change of clothes. As she pulled a shirt off the hanger, Emily felt Shawn's arms wrap around her, and his lips softly grazed her neck.

"Are you trying to torture me?" Shawn whispered into her ear.

"Maybe a little," Emily smiled as she turned to face him.

"What time is she supposed to be home?" Shawn asked as he pulled her close once more.

"Mommy!" Hope's voice echoed through the house.

"Shit!" Shawn laughed as he finished buttoning his jeans and threw his wrinkled shirt back on.

"I'm thinking now," Emily laughed as she quickly dressed. "I'm getting dressed!" Emily yelled back down to Hope to keep her from coming into the room.

Both Shawn and Emily were dressed and heading downstairs in less than a minute.

"Did you guys have a sleepover too?" Hope asked as she spotted Shawn.

"We did," Emily answered, smiling while looking at Shawn. It was rare to see Shawn blush, but Emily could see the red building in his cheeks. This situation wasn't anything unusual. Shawn did sleepovers from time to time, and Hope knew that. But those times, it had been just to sleep, unlike last night.

"Good," Hope smiled. "Mommy needs to find her prince." "Her prince?" Shawn asked, looking from Hope to Emily.

Emily motioned that she didn't know what Hope was talking about.

"My daddy wasn't my mommy's happily ever after," Hope explained. "So, he wasn't her prince. My mommy deserves a prince."

"She does," Shawn smiled as he kneeled to Hope. "I hope I can fill the part."

"I think you can," Hope nodded. "But fairy tales say a princess has to decide if the prince is charming or not."

"Well, I guess I will just have to prove that I am," Shawn said to Hope.

"Good answer," Hope grinned. "I'm going to go get dressed." "Okay," Emily replied as Hope ran past her with Marley.

"So," Shawn said as he stood back up and turned to Emily.
"Am I prince charming material?"

"You have potential," Emily replied.

"Just potential, huh?" Shawn said as he pulled Emily close and began to tickle her.

"Yes!" Emily managed to reply between the laughs.

"I guess I will have to prove myself," Shawn said as he stopped with the tickle torture.

"Are you staying for breakfast?" Emily asked as she wrapped her arms around him.

"I wish," Shawn replied, looking at the clock. "I need to go check and see how things were on the wall this morning. I can meet you for lunch later."

"It's a date," Emily replied as she and Shawn shared a quick kiss.

Emily made her way to the kitchen while Shawn headed out the front door. Emily was cooking the eggs as Hope came into the kitchen. Hope set to work filling Marley's food and then sat down at the table.

"Did you have fun last night?" Emily asked as she began to divide the eggs onto two plates with toast.

"Yeah," Hope smiled. "I stayed up until nine!"

"Great!" Emily said as she rolled her eyes. "You're already turning into a party animal."

"It was fun," Hope said. "It was nice to spend the night somewhere for fun instead of because you are working."

The phrase was innocent enough, but it still cut Emily deep.

"I'm sorry about that," Emily said as she sat down next to Hope. "I know my work takes me away from you sometimes, and…."

"It's important, right?" Hope asked, realizing that Emily was upset.

"Very," Emily nodded. "I'm making sure this place is around for you and your kids one day."

"I don't mind," Hope smiled as she began to eat. "Does that mean I'll be in charge one day?" Hope asked, looking back at Emily. "One day," Emily laughed. "In the very distant future, when
I am older than Margaret."

"Promise?" Hope asked with excitement.

"Promise," Emily agreed.

Emily and Hope continued to eat their breakfast while Marley loudly ate his behind them. Emily did the dishes while Hope took Marley out in the backyard when they finished.

"Do you have to work today?" Hope asked as she and Marley came back in.

"For a little while," Emily smiled at her.

"Can I come with you?" Hope asked next.

Emily took a moment to consider Hope's question. Typically, her work was not something a one-year-old should be involved with. However, Hope was not a one-year-old. Emily had already explained to her the dead and how the world works. She wanted Hope to continue to grow and to learn. Today, we're going to discuss whether their plan was working and discuss the plans for Monday.

"Sure," Emily finally nodded. "You need to learn if you are going to lead one day."

"Yes," Hope celebrated.

Emily couldn't help but laugh at the scene unfolding in her kitchen. Hope was jumping around in celebration, and Marley joined. Marley had no idea what Hope was celebrating. He just wanted to be part of it.

"We'd better get going," Emily said as she put the last dish in the strainer. "Service starts in ten minutes."

"And then work after?" Hope asked.

"Then work," Emily laughed. "Let's get going."

Emily led Hope and Marley out the front door and onto the street. The crowd was already walking down the street toward the church. Emily led her small family into the group and walked with them. Shawn joined them as they reached the church and walked inside with them. They all sat down in their regular spot. Once everyone was settled, Marley lay down in the aisle. As Father Nathan began to speak, Shawn took Emily by the hand and pulled her close. Father Nathan was in his usual form, hitting on topics he knew were weighing on everyone's minds. Emily couldn't help but feel like he was staring at her when he began to speak about opening your heart to love to find true happiness.

When the service was over, Emily walked with everyone back outside the church. Even though it was Sunday, chores still had to be done. Most people were rushing home to get their work done so they could relax for the rest of the day. For the council, it was straight to the town hall.

"So, where are you going while we work?" Shawn asked Hope once they were outside.

"I'm going to work too," Hope beamed up at him. "Mommy said I can learn for when I'm in charge."

"She did?" Shawn asked, looking at Emily.

"I did," Emily smiled back. "I figured we could use the smartest person in Sanctuary."

"That we could," Shawn smiled at Hope. "We'd better get going before we're late for your first day."

They walked together to the town hall. Once they were inside, Shawn went to Emily's office and added a chair to the table for Hope next to Emily. Hope sat down at the table, grinning ear to ear. It wasn't long before the rest of the council began to join them. "Breaking out the big guns?" Cole asked as he looked at Hope.

"Thought it was time," Emily smiled back at him. Cole smiled back and took his seat.

"What's the verdict?" Emily asked as soon as everyone sat down. "Did our plan work or not?"

"Better than we thought," Shawn spoke. "No dead spots around the wall since we turned on the speakers."

"We need to get confirmation that they are in the pits before we set them on fire," Sarah spoke next.

"We just need to check one," Sam spoke. "If they're in one, then they are in all of them."

"And we can start the fire from inside?" Julia asked.

"Sure thing," Cole smiled. "We will have to go to each one once the fire dies to refuel and clean out the pits. But the actual deed can be done from right here."

"It should be only a small group that goes out," Howard spoke. "If it's just a quick look-see, we don't want to risk drawing attention."

"So, we tricked the monsters into big holes, and now we are going to set them on fire?" Hope asked.

"That's the plan," Emily said, looking at her. "What do you think?"

"I think it will work," Hope nodded with a serious face. "Are you and Shawn going to check on the hole to make sure the zombies fell for the trick?"

"Is that what you think we should do?" Shawn asked.

"Yeah," Hope nodded again. "Ms. Julia, can I come over for a little while today while mommy goes outside?"

"Sure," Julia asked with shock in her voice.

"Hey," Emily smiled at Hope. "I said you would be in charge when I was older than Margaret."

"You're getting pretty close," Hope smiled back at her.

"Alright, if there's nothing else," Emily said, looking back at the adults. "I'd better let Julia take this child before she goes missing."

"Love you, mommy," Hope laughed as she ran over to Julia.

Everyone couldn't help but giggle as they stood up and left the building. Hope waved back at Emily as she walked out the door with Julia. Emily waved back and stuck her tongue out at Hope, who returned the gesture. Emily laughed as Shawn walked up beside her.

"Did she just give us orders and call you old?" Shawn asked, trying hard not to laugh.

"I think so," Emily replied. "Maybe we should ignore her and prove she's not in charge."

"Right," Shawn nodded. "I'll get the truck ready."

"Coward!" Emily yelled after him as he headed towards the door.

"I told you she scares the shit out of me!" Shawn yelled back.

"Does she scare you, too?" Emily asked Marley. Marley wagged his tail and ran after Shawn. "I'll take that as a yes," Emily laughed as she walked after him.

Emily made her way to the armory, grabbed her knife and rifle, along with Shawn's weapons. Emily walked through the inner gate to see Shawn putting more fuel in the truck. Emily opened the passenger door and slid the weapons inside. Emily had just finished putting her knife in her waist as Shawn finished fueling up the truck.

"That should be enough," Shawn said as he set the empty jar in the crate. Emily knew that Cole would be picking up the empty jars when he did his next batch of moonshine.

"I'll get the gate," Emily nodded as she shut the truck door.

Marley jumped into the truck's bed as Emily turned and headed back through the gate. Emily heard the truck door shut and the engine roar to life as she entered the code. Emily walked out towards the truck and hopped up on the tailgate just before Shawn began driving. Shawn stopped the truck, and Emily climbed down. Emily entered the code, and the gate began to close. Emily walked back to the truck and climbed into the cab with Shawn.

"I thought you were just going to ride back there," Shawn teased as the door shut.

"Well, if you don't want me up here…" Emily began as she reached for the door handle.

"No, you don't," Shawn laughed as he grabbed Emily's arm and pulled her towards him.

Emily laughed as she leaned against Shawn's arm. Shawn put the truck in drive and then wrapped his arm around Emily.

"One of these days, I'm going to find a way to take you on a proper date," Shawn said as they drove down the logging road.

"I enjoy these drives together," Emily replied as she lifted her head to look at him.

"I do too, but I would like to enjoy time with you without zombies," Shawn said as he glanced back at Emily.

"They've become such a part of our lives. I don't know how to live without them."

Emily couldn't help but feel sad at her statement. It was unfortunate that zombies had become a regular part of their lives and that she couldn't imagine a life without them.

"Well, they are not invited on date night," Shawn smiled.

"Date night?" Emily laughed. "Does that still exist?"

"If school and barbeques exist, date night can, too," Shawn replied. "Do I have to propose this to the council?"

"No," Emily replied. "I think I can approve that on my own." "Good," Shawn said as he pulled her closer.

Emily lay her head on his shoulder and couldn't stop smiling. It was strange yet heartwarming that she had finally found a healthy relationship. It only took the end of the world for things to start going well in her life.

Shawn stopped the truck on the paved road and shut off the engine. Emily moved back to the truck's passenger side and grabbed her rifle. Emily opened the truck door and slid out, shutting the door behind herself. Marley and Shawn joined her by the wood line, and they began the walk into the woods. All three of them stopped as soon as they heard it, the loud sound of groans and moans ahead.

"Be careful," Shawn whispered to her as he took the lead.

Emily nodded and pulled her knife from her waist.

The sounds grew louder as the pit came into view. Emily walked slowly with Shawn and Marley towards the pit. Emily couldn't help but gasp at the number of zombies in the pit. The speakers were off now, and the zombies were agitated that they were stuck.

"Holy shit," Shawn said, looking at the zombies.

"I didn't expect that many," Emily replied, looking at the zombies as well.

"Neither did I," Shawn said, taking a step closer to the pit. "I knew there were quite a few hiding out here, but this…."

Emily felt like everything around her was suddenly in slow motion. Under Shawn's feet, the ground began to give way, and Shawn began to slide into the pit.

"Shawn!" Emily yelled as she reached for him.

Shawn reacted quickly and, with Emily pulling on his arm, was back on solid ground. Emily and Shawn both fell back, the pit of zombies all trying to find a way to get to them.

"That was too close," Emily breathed as she wrapped her
arms around Shawn.

"I'm sorry," Shawn said as he wrapped his arms around her.
"I knew better than that."

Emily couldn't find any words and just continued to hold on to Shawn.

"Let's get back and get these things burned," Shawn said as he released his arms from around her.

Emily nodded and pulled herself up to her feet. Marley sat staring at the pit, growling at the zombies below. Emily patted her leg and walked out of the woods with Shawn. Shawn opened the passenger door and allowed Emily to climb inside as they reached the truck. Emily slid over to the center of the bench seat and waited for Shawn to join her. Once Shawn was in the truck, Emily pulled herself close to him.

"Let's have them light it while we're here," Shawn said as he wrapped his arm around her. "That way, we can make sure it works and not have to come back out."

Emily didn't move away from Shawn as she pulled the walkie from her waist.

"Sanctuary," Emily said as she pressed the button.

"Emily," Margaret's voice responded.

"The pit is full," Emily continued. "Let's go ahead and light them."

"With you still out there?" Margaret asked.

"Yes," Emily replied. "Once they light, we will head back."

"It will only take a moment," Cole's voice rang out. "Let us know when you see the flames."

Emily forced herself to sit up and look into the woods. It wasn't long before the glow of the fire was visible between the trees.

"It's burning," Emily said into the walkie. "We'll be home in ten."

"See you then," Margaret and Cole both replied.

"Let's go home," Shawn said as he pulled Emily close and began the drive back to Sanctuary.

"Do you think it will burn hot enough?" Emily asked as they went.

"They say it will be hot enough to damage the brain," Shawn said. "But it won't be hot enough to turn them completely to ash." "As long as they're actually dead," Emily replied.

"They will be," Shawn said as he kissed her on the head.

They were nearly back to the logging road when he appeared —a man, a living man, standing in the middle of the road. Shawn released Emily, grabbing the steering wheel with both hands while slamming on the brake. Emily reached out and captured the dash with both hands. Emily knew that he wasn't getting it stopped before they reached the man. Shawn turned the wheel sharply, and Emily watched as the truck skidded towards a tree instead of the man. Shawn reached his arm back and tried to brace Emily.

"Shawn!" Emily cried as the truck approached the tree.

If Shawn did reply, Emily didn't hear it. The sound of the metal crashing around the tree filled the air. Emily felt herself fly forward, and her forehead slammed against the dashboard. Immediately, the world went dark, and Emily was trapped in the darkness.

Chapter 8

"The idiot wasn't supposed to wreck the damn truck!" a man's voice rang out.

Emily could feel warm blood running down her face, and the pain was too much for her to open her eyes or even speak.

"What are we going to do now?" a little girl's voice asked.

"We'll take what they have and leave them," the man's voice spoke once more.

"What about the dog?" another little girl spoke.

Emily could hear Marley barking and growling in the back of the truck. Emily was relieved that he was alright, but still couldn't get her body to respond.

"Just shoot it!" the man said, more agitated.

"Shawn," Emily finally managed to say above a whisper as her eyes slowly opened.

Emily could see that Shawn was still knocked out. Shawn had blood flowing freely down his face, and his arm was covered in Emily's blood.

"I can't," the little girl was saying outside the truck.

Emily knew that she needed to move, no matter how much it hurt. Emily reached for her rifle, but it was no longer sitting on the seat beside her. It was flung somewhere in the truck during the collision. Emily could see Shawn's shotgun still pinned between him and the truck door. Emily pulled Shawn slightly toward her to get to the gun.

"I said shoot it!" the man yelled at the girl.

Emily winced in pain as she forced herself across the seat and forced the truck door open. No one spoke as Emily moved out of the truck and lifted the shotgun towards a figure that she knew must be the man who was speaking. Emily's vision was still blurred, and the blood in her eyes did not help. The man was too far away for her to take him out clearly. Emily could see that a few small figures were standing around, but Emily couldn't see them either.

"Get back!" Emily forced herself to yell.

"You're a fighter, aren't you?" the man said as his figure moved further away.

Emily felt her stomach churn at the phrase. It was the same way that Jeff used to speak to her. Emily leaned against the truck's bed to steady herself and tightened her grip on the gun.

"You did this on purpose!" Emily yelled at the man.

"The plan was to get you to stop, not crash," the man said as his figure took a few more steps back.

"We could have helped you!" Emily continued to yell.

"All we wanted was the truck," the man replied calmly. "It's the first one we've seen run in a long time."

The pain in Emily's head surged, and she feared that she would fall.

"Just get out of here!" Emily yelled at the man. "I don't want to see you around here again, or I will shoot you!"

"Whatever you say," the man said as he moved further away. "Let's go, girls."

Emily watched as all of the figures moved out of sight and allowed her grip on the gun to loosen. Emily turned back to the cab of the truck and crawled back inside.

"Shawn," Emily said as she crawled over to him and touched his face. Emily could feel that he was still breathing, but Shawn did not respond. Emily grabbed for the walkie and pressed the button.
"Sanctuary," Emily struggled to speak.
"Is everything alright?" Margaret's voice rang out thick with worry.
"There was a man in the road," Emily began. "Shawn tried to stop, but we hit a tree. Shawn won't wake up."
"Emily, is he breathing?" Doc's voice answered.
"Yes," Emily said, trying to remain calm. "But I can't get him to wake up. He hit his head."
"Where are you?" Sam asked.
"Almost to the station," Emily replied.
"Just hold on," Sam answered. "We are on our way."
Emily dropped the radio on the seat and leaned over to check on Shawn once more. Shawn was still breathing, but Emily could not get him to wake up. The world around Emily began to spin, and Emily fought hard to keep from passing out. It didn't take long before she heard the sound of a car engine driving towards her. Emily lifted the shotgun once more and pointed it out of the passenger door.
"Emily!" Sam called out. "It's us."
Emily lowered the gun and allowed herself to lean against the seat.
"Get her in the truck," Doc spoke. "I'll make sure Shawn can be moved."
Doc had not come outside the wall since they had arrived, and Emily could not help but feel shocked. Emily heard the driver's side door open and knew that it was Doc.

"Can you walk?" Sam asked as he reached in towards Emily.

"I don't think so," Emily replied. "Everything is too blurry."

"I've got you," Sam assured her as he helped her out of the truck. Sam pulled Emily's arm over his shoulder and helped her walk towards the box truck.

"Marley," Emily said as she tried to stop walking.

"He's right next to you," Sam assured her. "We'll get Shawn next, but we have to get you into the truck."

Emily forced herself to keep moving forward. Sam walked Emily to the back of the box truck, where the door was already open. Alec was waiting for her and lifted her off her feet.

"You got her?" Sam asked as he let go of Emily. "I'll get her laid down and be there to help with Shawn."

Emily felt Alec climb into the back of the truck with her in his arms. Alec slowly lowered Emily onto what felt like a pile of blankets.

"Make sure she doesn't move," Alec said to Marley as he left the truck. Emily closed her eyes and felt Marley lie down close beside her.

Everything was quiet for a long time. Emily felt her anxiety growing as time passed. Finally, Emily heard voices approaching the truck.

"Careful with his head," Doc was instructing.

"God, he's heavy," Cole's voice spoke. Emily had not even realized that Cole was with them.

"Did you expect a guy his size to be light?" Jacob replied.

"No, but I didn't expect to be carrying him either."

Emily listened as they carried Shawn into the truck and laid him down on the opposite side.

"Emily," Doc said as he leaned down beside her. "Emily, are you still awake?"

"Yes," Emily replied.

"You can't fall asleep," Doc said.

"It hurts to have my eyes open," Emily replied.

"You can have them closed," Doc answered. "But you have to stay awake. Just talk to me."

"How's Shawn?" Emily asked.

"He hit his head pretty hard," Doc answered her. Emily heard the truck door shut and felt the truck begin to move.

"Is he going to be okay?" Emily asked, noticing that Doc hadn't answered her question.

"We'll take care of him," Doc answered.

Emily felt tears begin to roll down her blood-covered face. Crying only made her head hurt more, but Emily couldn't help herself.

"It's going to be fine," Doc tried to comfort her.

"I can't lose him," Emily cried.

"Then you won't," Doc replied.

Emily felt the truck stop and heard the doors shut. Light burst into the back of the truck as the doors were opened.

"Mommy!" Hope's voice rang in the back of the truck.

"Hey monkey," Emily forced herself to open her eyes and smile.

"Are you okay?" Hope asked as she appeared by Emily's side.

"We had a little accident," Emily replied.

"Why is Shawn sleeping?" Hope asked, and Emily could hear that she was scared.

"He hit his head," Doc explained. "He'll wake up in a little while."

"Mommy?" Hope said, turning back to Emily.

"We'll be alright," Emily smiled at her.

"We need to get them inside," Doc said to Hope. "Can you take care of Marley for a little while?"

"Yes, sir," Hope replied. "Come on, Marley."

Emily heard Marley stand up and follow Hope out of the truck.

"We're going to take Shawn in first, and then Alec will help you inside," Doc explained.

Emily nodded as she allowed her eyes to close once more and the smile to fade from her face. Emily listened as they lifted Shawn once more and carried him inside. It wasn't long before she heard Alec climb back into the truck.

"That didn't take long," Emily said as she felt Alec lift her.

"We drove up to the clinic," Alec explained. "Shawn woke up for a minute once we were inside."

Emily couldn't help but feel relieved as he spoke.

"He asked about you, and when Doc told him you were going to be fine, he passed back out."

"That has to be a good sign," Emily breathed as Alec stepped down from the back of the truck.

"Doc says it is," Alec replied as they walked into the clinic. "Where is she?!" Shawn's voice echoed through the clinic.

"Alec is bringing her in," Sam explained. "You have to lie still."

"I have to make sure she's okay!" Shawn yelled, and Emily could tell that Shawn was fighting to get up and look for her.

"Take me to him," Emily said to Alec.

"I'm not supposed to…." Alec began to say.

"He won't stop until he sees me," Emily replied. "Unless you think Sam can hold him down?"

"Right," Alec replied as he continued to walk.

Emily forced her eyes open once more and saw that Alec had taken her into the surgical room. Shawn was pushing everyone away from him and trying to get up. Shawn was having as much trouble with his balance and vision as she was, as he kept grabbing his head and bobbling around.

"Shawn!" Emily yelled over all of the noise in the room.
"Lay down and let Doc help you!"

"Emily?" Shawn said as he looked at Alec's arms.

"I'm fine," Emily said, as comforting as she could.

"You're bleeding," Shawn said with concern.

"Doc will clean it up if you let him finish helping you," Emily assured him.

"Help her first," Shawn said to Doc.

"Shawn," Emily said sternly. "Let Doc do his job."

"You're not going to win," Jacob said as he placed his hand on Shawn's shoulder and pulled him down on the table.

"I'll be right next door," Emily assured him as Alec carried her out of the room. Again, Emily felt the smile drain off her face, and her eyes closed again.

"You truly are an amazing woman," Alec said as he set her down on the bed.

"Everyone says that," Emily replied. "But an amazing woman wouldn't get so many people hurt."

"You defend those you love no matter how banged up you are and comfort those around you despite how much pain you're in," Alec explained.

Emily's head hurt too much to come up with an argument. Alec took her silence as a victory and sat down in the chair. Emily tried to lie still and remain silent while she waited for Doc.

"Are you going to put up a fight, too?" Doc asked as he walked into the room.

"You would win," Emily conceded.

"Alright," Doc replied. "Let's get your face cleaned up and see what's going on."

Emily lay still while Doc cleaned the blood off her face with a cool cloth.

"Definitely going to need some stitches," Doc said as he examined her forehead. "You've also got a concussion and whiplash."

"You can tell that from my face?" Emily asked.

"I can tell that by your pain, blurred vision, and trouble walking," Doc corrected her. "You will need to stay here tonight, and then you can go home. You will need to rest over the next few weeks."

"I have too much to do," Emily replied.

"You don't have a choice," Doc answered as he began stitching the cut on Emily's forehead. "You and Shawn will just have to enjoy your vacation."

"How is he?" Emily asked, remaining still.

"Same as you, but with a broken nose," Doc answered. "He has to stay here tonight as well."

"Can I see him?" Emily asked.

"As soon as I have you fixed up, we are going to move another bed in here so you can stay together," Doc answered.

"Thank you," Emily answered. Doc finished her stitches and placed a bandage on her head.

"Take these," Doc said as he handed Emily two pills. "They will help with the headache."

Emily took the pills and the bottle of water that Doc offered her. Doc watched as Emily took the pills.

"Knock, knock," Julia said as she walked into the room. "How's she doing?"

"She'll be fine," Doc answered. "We just have to get the power couple to rest for the next few weeks."

"I'll help how I can," Julia nodded. "Is it all right if I talk to her for a minute?"

"Just try to keep it short," Doc answered as he walked out of the room with Alec.

"Thanks for opening the gate," Emily said as she looked at Julia.

"That's what I wanted to talk to you about," Julia said as she walked towards Emily. "I didn't."

"What do you mean?" Emily asked. "If you didn't, who did?"

"Hope," Julia replied. "She heard the call over the walkie and ran up to the control room. She opened the gate for the guys when they left and opened it again when they returned."

"How did she know the code?" Emily asked, dumbfounded at what Julia was telling her.

"I asked her that," Julia continued. "She said that she watched you."

"That girl is too smart sometimes," Emily sighed.

"I don't think it's a bad thing," Julia said. "This way, it doesn't have to be written down, and no one knows that Hope has the code."

"You think I should leave it?" Emily asked.

"I do," Julia nodded.

"I'll think about it," Emily said after a few minutes.

"You just rest," Julia smiled. "I'll bring Hope in a little while."

"Thank you, Julia," Emily replied as Julia left the room.

"Your roommate is ready!" Jacob announced as he guided in a bed that Shawn was resting on.

"You guys can't drive for shit," Shawn said to Jacob and Sam.

"We're better than you," Sam teased.

"You should have seen that coming," Jacob laughed.

"Do you see how they treat me?" Shawn asked as Jacob and Sam put Shawn's bed in place.

"Kicking a man while he's down," Emily smiled. "How dare they?"

"Let's leave these two alone," Sam said as he walked out of the room with Jacob and closed the door.

"How are you doing?" Shawn asked with a more serious tone.

"I'm going to be fine," Emily assured him. "I got off easier than you."

"I'm sorry," Shawn said as he reached over and took Emily's hand. "I should have...."

"Don't do that," Emily interrupted him. "There was no way you could know that man was going to be on the road."

"What happened to him?" Shawn asked, suddenly remembering the man who caused their accident. "I didn't hit him, did I?"

"No," Emily assured him. "He walked away just fine."

"We need to send someone out to get him," Shawn continued with concern in his voice.

"He didn't want to come in," Emily explained. "He was trying to force you to stop so he could steal the truck." "What?!" Shawn asked, visibly angry.

"After you wrecked, he was angry and told the girls he was with to just take what we had," Emily continued. "I could barely see two feet in front of me, but I pointed the shotgun at him and told him if I saw him again, I'd shoot."

"Why didn't you?" Shawn asked, still angry.

"I couldn't see," Emily explained. "I didn't want to risk shooting one of the kids."

"He had kids?" Shawn was trying to remember anything from after the crash. Emily knew he wasn't going to be able to. He was out cold.

"At least two girls," Emily continued.

"So rather than come back with us where they would be safe, he put both our lives at risk over a damn truck!?" Shawn yelled.

"He said he hadn't seen one that ran in a while," Emily replied. "All that matters is that we're both okay."

"I just don't understand why anyone would do that," Shawn said, his temper visibly dying down.

"We don't know what they've been through," Emily replied. "Maybe they ran into Jeff or someone worse out there. You have to admit that what we have is hard to believe."

"It's still no excuse," Shawn said. "We're still people."

"Let it go," Emily said as she reached over and took his hand.

Shawn wrapped his hand around hers and closed his eyes. Emily knew that he was still angry, but tried his best to relax. Emily closed her eyes as well and tried to ignore the throbbing pain. The rest of their evening was quiet, except for a short visit from Hope. Hope and Marley stayed with Julia for the night until Emily and Shawn were allowed to go home. Doc came in every few hours and woke them each up. He said it was standard to make sure that they were alright.

"Emily?" Shawn said barely above a whisper after one of Doc's visits.

"Yeah," Emily whispered back.

"I love you," Shawn whispered back to her.

"I love you too," Emily replied as she squeezed his hand.

Emily lay in the dark and listened as Shawn fell back asleep. Emily wasn't sure if he was ever fully awake. Emily lay staring at Shawn in the dimly lit room for a long time. The throbbing in her head had lessened but was still making its presence known. Emily felt herself slowly close her eyes and drift off to sleep.

Chapter 9

Doc released Emily and Shawn the following day. While they were both still extremely sore, they were thrilled to be out of the clinic. Doc had told them both and everyone in Sanctuary that they needed to take it easy over the next few weeks. Everyone was taking things seriously and doing everything they could to relax. Cole had gone out with a group and towed back the pickup. While the front end of smashed up pretty good, he insisted that he still may be able to fix it. Cole had also towed back the SUV. Emily had tried to tell him how badly damaged it was, but Cole insisted. He said if nothing else, there may be a few usable parts that could help keep the other vehicles running.

Emily stood on the wall and watched as he towed it inside. It was strange to see it moving again. She had lived for months in it with Marley driving all over the state looking for her family and then for a home. Cole had taken it straight to his garage along with the pickup. He spent most of his days inside with only the sounds of curse words and metal banging escaping the walls. Emily found herself making her way to the garage this morning, laughing at the words she heard Cole yelling inside. Emily carefully opened the door but stood outside as a wrench flew across the room. Marley jumped as the wrench hit the wall and fell to the floor.

"Did I come at a bad time?" Emily yelled over to Cole, who was under the hood of the SUV.

"Come on in," Cole waved at her. "I think she needs a timeout anyway."

"You still think you can get it running?" Emily asked as she walked towards him.

"Almost done," Cole nodded. "The belt pulley is just being a...."

Emily couldn't help but smile at Cole's inability to cuss in front of women. "What about the pickup?" Emily asked, looking over at it.

"The frame didn't bend," Cole replied. "I can get the dents out, and we have a spare radiator. It's just the windshield that will be a problem. For now, we'll call it air conditioning." "You are a miracle worker," Emily smiled at him.

"Uh, oh," Cole laughed as he sat down on a stool.

"What?" Emily smiled back at him.

"When a woman speaks to you like that, it means she needs a favor," Cole explained. "And, guessing that you're complimenting my work on cars, you need me to fix something."

"You caught me," Emily admitted as she walked back over to him. "I wanted to try to get something together for Shawn, but I don't know how to do it."

"Let's hear it," Cole replied.

"He used to ride motorcycles before the flash," Emily explained. "I was wanting to see if there may be any way to put one together for him."

"I don't have one of those here," Cole said, looking around the garage. "But I did see a few backs at the dealership. If we could get one of those back here, and if they have some parts, I can get one going."

"Really?!" Emily replied, not trying to hide her excitement.

"You would just have to find a way for us to get to the dealership," Cole continued. "And a way to hide from Shawn what
we're doing if you want it to be a surprise."

"I'll think of something," Emily smiled.

"If we can get it soon, I can probably have it ready by Christmas," Cole nodded. "If the beast over there doesn't kill me first."

"She won't kill you," Emily laughed. "She's just used to being babied. I took her from an old woman."

"Well, that explains why she's stubborn," Cole laughed as he stood back up.

Emily headed back out of the garage as Cole climbed back into the engine. Emily walked back outside with Marley, excited about the idea of giving Shawn a motorcycle. The hot August air was giving way to the cooler temperatures of September. While winter was still a few months off, the relief that the change brought was welcome.

"Security to COM building," Sarah's voice came over the walkie.

"Must have new people," Emily said to Marley as she slowly jogged towards the building. While it had been a few weeks since the accident, Emily's body was still sore, and running was not an option. "What do we got?" Emily asked as she made her way through the open door.

"New group," Sarah replied. "They are near the road."

"How many?" Shawn asked as he walked in behind her.

"Six," Sarah replied.

"Just keep going," Margaret said into the microphone. "The road is safe, and we have people watching it."

Emily turned and made her way up the wall to the control room. While she could open the gate from below, standing up here let her see the people as they approached and leave the gate open as little as possible. Emily watched over the wall as a group walked into view. Emily quickly made her way to the control room and entered the code. The gate below her began to move, and Emily went back downstairs where Marley and Shawn were waiting.

"Every time I think there's no one else left," Shawn smiled at her.

"There's always someone out there," Emily replied.

Shawn nodded and walked through the inner gate to welcome the new people. Emily waited until she heard Shawn begin to speak before entering the code to close the gate once more.

"Here we go," Emily said to Marley as she walked to join everyone.

"Puppy!" a little girl yelled as Emily walked into view. The girl was about three years old and had bright yellow hair.

"Charlotte!" a balding man yelled as he reached to stop the girl, who was now running towards Marley.

Marley took a few more steps forward and sat down. He was allowing Charlotte to pull on his ears and pet his soft fur. The man stood watching, a look of both fear and shock on his face.

"He's great with kids," Shawn explained.

The man didn't reply and instead continued to watch Charlotte as she played with Marley.

"His name's Marley," Emily spoke to Charlotte. "I think he likes you." Charlette laughed as Marley began to lick at her face. Emily turned back to the man and took a few steps closer. "I'm Emily," Emily greeted him as she offered her hand.

"Ethan," the man replied, shaking her hand but still watching Marley and Charlette.

"It's nice to meet you, Ethan," Emily smiled.

"What is this place?" a woman with bright yellow hair asked.

"We call it Sanctuary," Emily explained. "A man built it to protect people. I found it, and together we have all turned it into a home."

Charlette came walking back over with Marley as Emily spoke.

"So, you all just live here?" Ethan asked. "Like in houses and with dogs?"

"Marley is the only dog," Emily smiled. "But yes, we all have houses and jobs, just like before."

"Daddy," Charlotte said as she reached her father. "I'm hungry."

"I know," Ethan said as he picked up Charlotte. "We saw the sign and hoped we might be able to find some food."

"Of course," Emily smiled. "Do you like applesauce?" Emily asked Charlotte.

"Apples?!" Charlotte asked excitedly.

Emily walked over to the clinic, where Doc handed her a jar of apple sauce and a few water bottles. Emily gave them to Ethan and the blonde woman. Emily watched as Ethan stared at the jar and then back at Emily.

"No offense," Ethan finally spoke. "But how do I know it's...."

"Oh," Emily smiled and held her hand out to back out to take the jar. Emily opened the jar and took a spoonful. "You must have had it rough out there if you worried we'd poison applesauce." Emily took a bite and handed the jar back to Ethan.

"That's one word for it," Ethan said as he carefully began feeding the applesauce to Charlette.

Emily still struggled with this part, knowing when and how much to say to people when they arrived. Emily took a few steps back to stand by Shawn and give them some space.

"We have plenty of food for everyone inside," Emily said to the group.

"Can we go in?" the blonde woman asked, looking at the open gate.

"First, we have to have you all examined by Doc," Emily explained. "Just to make sure no one is at risk of infection and keep those inside safe."

"We just want to get some food," Ethan replied. "This place isn't safe."

"Of course, it is," Emily said, offended.

"Not if you let people with bites in," Ethan said as he nodded his head towards Emily's wrist.

Emily couldn't help but feel embarrassed as she covered the scar on her arm. Though the bite had long since healed, the scar was still plainly on her wrist. It wasn't as easy to hide as the other one.

"She's immune," Shawn said as he took her hand. "She's been bitten twice now, and each time, she recovers."

"No one recovers," Ethan said as he continued to feed Charlotte.

"It's rare," Doc spoke up. "It's a rare genetic marker. Even
Emily's daughter didn't inherit it."

"The bite is healed," the blonde woman said. "Maybe they are telling the truth."

"You know how it works, Ellie," Ethan said shortly. "We will get what we need and get Charlotte and the others out of here."

"You don't speak for me," a middle-aged man said as he stepped forward.

"Hank," Ethan said with frustration. "I have kept us all alive."

"We kept each other alive," Hank corrected him. "Plus, a checkup couldn't hurt."

Emily smiled at Hank as he walked towards Doc and disappeared into the clinic. Emily watched as the others whispered among themselves, all being careful not to let Ethan hear them. After a few minutes, Doc and Hank came out, Hank holding a cold bottle of water.

"He doesn't bite," Hank teased as he walked out.

A woman and a man Emily assumed was her husband, stepped forward and followed Doc into the clinic. Ethan's frustration continued to grow. Emily remained silent and waited until the couple came back.

"She's been bitten!" Ethan said as the couple joined them once more. "She will turn any time."

"The doctor says she's immune," Hank spoke up. "I've never seen anyone who has survived long enough for a bite to heal. Have you?"

"And you don't think it absurd that they claim she's been bitten twice?" Ethan replied with sarcasm.

Emily didn't say anything as she let go of Shawn's hand and stepped forward. Emily pulled the neck of her shirt to expose her first scar. While it had begun to fade, it was still very pronounced.

Ellie stepped forward and took a closer look at the scar.

"It happened the day after the flash," Emily explained.

"How old's your daughter?" Ellie asked as she turned her gaze to Emily's face.

"She turned one in March," Emily answered. "She was born inside the wall."

"So, you were pregnant when you were bitten?" Ellie asked. "I didn't know it at the time," Emily explained. "But yes." "And she's okay?" Ellie asked next.

"Perfectly healthy," Emily answered. "She's growing fast." "They do that," Ellie smiled at her.

Emily felt a little bad about not telling the whole truth. Hope was growing increasingly accelerated, but she wasn't quite ready to share that information yet.

"Charlotte," Ellie called as she held out her hand for Charlotte. Charlette wiggled until her father set her down and came running over.

"Ellie!" Ethan yelled after her as Ellie led Charlotte towards Doc.

"There's no harm in making sure we're okay," Ellie replied.

Emily watched as Doc followed Ellie and Charlotte inside.

Emily could see that Ethan's face was turning red with anger.

"If you turn," Ethan said as he stepped towards Emily. Emily didn't have to look to know that Shawn and Marley

stepped forward as well. "I will put you down myself."
"Understood," Emily nodded.

Emily stood firm as Ethan walked toward the small clinic to join his family.

"I don't like him," Shawn said next to her.

"Ethan doesn't even like Ethan most of the time," Hank replied. "He's been through a lot."

"We all have," Emily said, sympathizing with what Hank was saying.

"Our group used to be much larger," Hank continued. "Ethan lost his oldest daughter a few months back."

"I can't imagine losing a child," Emily said, looking back at the clinic. "Especially in this world."

"She's the reason the reason he doesn't want to stay," Hank told Emily. "He wants to keep looking for her."

"She's still alive out there?" Emily said, surprised.

"There was an attack," Hank explained. "We lost a lot of people to the dead. Ava escaped and was alive the last time we saw her."

"He doesn't have to stop looking," Emily replied. "I know I wouldn't. This could just be a safe place for Charlotte and Ellie while he looks."

"I'm sure there are plenty of people here who would be willing to help," Shawn said. "I know I will."

"He will still be on edge," Hank replied. "But he will calm down a little the longer he's here."

Emily turned as Ethan and Ellie came out of the clinic with Charlette. Emily could feel her heartbreak as she looked at them. She couldn't imagine losing Hope out in the world, especially not knowing if she was alive, dead, or, worse, a zombie. "They're all clear of infection," Doc reported.

"Great," Emily forced herself to smile. "If you want to follow me, I'll give you the tour. Then we'll get you some fresh clothes so you can get cleaned up and some warm food."

Everyone remained silent as they walked through the gate. Emily went through her usual routine of explaining things as they walked. Emily stopped in front of the store and waited outside while the group all went in to get a few changes of fresh clothes.

"Ethan," Emily said just as he walked through the door.

"My wife has asked me to try, but there are things I can't just let go of," Ethan said as he stopped but didn't turn to look at her.

"You shouldn't let go of Ava," Emily replied. Ethan turned and looked at Emily for the first time without fear or hate in his eyes. "Hank told us about what happened," Emily explained. "We will get some volunteers together and help you find her."

"Why would you do that?" Ethan asked. "Why would anyone risk going out there for a girl they don't know?"

"We're family," Emily smiled. "And the second you came through that gate, you became part of it. We protect our family and leave no one behind."

"You realize it's crazy in here, right?" Ethan smiled slightly.

"Of course," Emily laughed. "And I'm the lead crazy."

Emily took the group back to her house, where they all washed up and she served them a big meal. There had been a period of shock when Hope came home from school. Emily explained to all of them her accelerated growth rate as best she could. Everyone was in disbelief but seemed to believe what Emily was telling them. Emily answered their questions throughout the evening, all of them asking the same questions that everyone asked when they arrived. Once everyone was settled into bed, Emily stayed up late to talk with Ethan and Ellie. According to her parents, Emily learned that Ava was thirteen years old and a very resourceful young girl. Emily reassured them that they would look for Ava and bring them back together.

Emily went to bed that night, with the thought of Ava sleeping in an abandoned building weighing heavily on her mind. Emily woke the following day and went straight to work. After breakfast, Emily sat down with everyone to discuss any concerns and answer any questions they had thought of since their last talk. When they finished, Emily was not surprised the next day when they all agreed to join Sanctuary and signed their name in the ledger. Emily had ensured that Ava's name was added as well. This small act seemed to bring comfort to her family. It helped confirm for them that they were going to find their daughter. Emily assigned each person a home and a job.

"I have to go check on something," Shawn said as they walked out the door. "I'll meet up with you once they are all settled."

"Alright," Emily replied as Shawn quickly kissed her and headed up the road.

Emily led Ethan's family to their new house and everyone else to the apartments. Emily walked back out onto the street with Marley and saw Shawn standing with a large group near the gate.
Emily made her way over to him to see what was going on.

"Again," Shawn was saying. "This is volunteer only. We don't know where she'll be or how long it will take to find her." "We're in," Cole answered as everyone else nodded.

"What's going on?" Emily asked as she walked closer.

"I am putting together the group to look for Ava," Shawn explained. "I want to get started first thing in the morning."

"And all of you are willing to do this?" Emily said, looking around.

"We have plenty of people to keep this place running," Jacob answered. "We are ready to do this."

"Alright," Emily nodded. "We'll see you all in the morning."

Everyone began to spread back out along the main street, leaving Shawn and Emily.

"I didn't want it to wait any longer," Shawn said as he walked closer to her. "The girl has been out there, alone, for months."

"I agree," Emily nodded. "I think Ethan will insist on joining us, though."

"I talked to him about it last night," Shawn replied. "Since he's assigned to security, Sam will give him the okay to go out. He knows we are meeting here in the morning."

"You've just thought of everything," Emily smiled. "Do you even need me?"

"Always," Shawn said as he pulled her closer. "But I was wondering if there is any way you would consider…." "I'm going," Emily interrupted him. "I know," Shawn sighed. "I had to try." "And you did," Emily grinned.

"I need to adjust the wall schedule and make sure that everyone is prepared for tomorrow," Shawn said as he hugged her.

"Are you coming by for dinner?" Emily asked, looking at him.

"I'll see you then," Shawn replied as he kissed her.

Chapter 10

The next day, Emily met everyone at the gate to begin the first search for Ava. Ethan still had a picture of Ava that he carried in his wallet. Everyone took the photo one at a time and looked at it carefully. Once everyone was ready, Emily watched as they divided between the vehicles.

"I thought you might want to drive," Cole smiled as he tossed Emily a set of keys.

"Why would I ..." Emily began as she looked down at the keys. Emily quickly looked back up and saw the SUV sitting with the other vehicles. "You fixed it?" Emily breathed.

"Finished it last night," Cole grinned.

"I never thought it would run again," Emily smiled.

The SUV, being not only inside the wall but also running, made her happier than she could explain. It reminded her of Ms. Tilly before the fence attack. It helped her to remember that her life before Sanctuary was real. The SUV also served as a reminder of everything that she and Marley went through on the road. But most importantly, climbing back into the SUV felt like going home. Emily opened the driver-side door and waited while Marley jumped in. Marley settled into the passenger seat while Emily climbed in.

"The rear hatch was broken," Cole said as he walked over.
"I'm not sure how that happened, but I managed to get it fixed."

"Marley wanted out," Emily grinned as she reached over and petted the pup.

"That dog is an army tank with legs," Cole laughed as he walked away.

"I'll drive it out the gate if you want," Shawn smiled. "But he is going to have to move to the back seat," Shawn nodded at Marley.

"I'll let you two figure that out," Emily laughed as she jumped down and made her way to the control panel.

Emily entered the code and walked through the gates. Once everyone was through,

Emily entered the code to close them once more. Emily walked back over to the SUV just as Shawn got out and walked around to the passenger door.

"I called shotgun," Shawn said to Marley while Emily climbed inside. "It's not my fault you forgot."

Marley huffed, jumped into the back seat, and allowed Shawn to climb in. Emily smiled as she put the SUV in drive and drove to the front of the line. Emily led the caravan back up the logging road and turned onto the pavement.

"Watch out for people in the road," Shawn said as she pressed down on the accelerator.

"I'm not stopping or swerving," Emily replied.

Emily led the group to town and drove straight through. The last place that Ava was seen was south of Springfield. Emily carefully led the group down back roads for about half an hour and pulled over. Emily put the SUV in park and climbed out. They were on a country road in farm country.

"We are going to split up from here," Shawn said to everyone. "Cover the sections on your map, radio if you find anything, and then meet back here."

Everyone nodded and returned to their vehicles.

"It's just the three of us?" Emily asked as they climbed back into the SUV.

"I think we can handle it," Shawn smiled. "Our area is ahead a little way."

Emily started the SUV and put it back in drive. Emily made her way through the country roads. Shawn watched the map and directed her when and where to turn. Marley stretched out across the back seat, obviously more comfortable than he was in the back of the pickup.

"This is it," Shawn said as he refolded the map.

Emily looked around to see that they were in a gated subdivision. The houses here were much more than she could ever afford before the flash, and some even more prominent than where she lived now.

"Geez," Emily said as she pulled over and put the truck in park.

"I never saw the point in these places," Shawn remarked.
"Who wants a golf course in their back yard?"

"Not me," Emily laughed. Emily was trying to hide the fact that being here made her uneasy.

While she had gotten used to going through abandoned stores, the idea of going through people's houses made her uncomfortable. She felt like she was disturbing something that should be left alone, almost as if the people would be back at any moment.

"Let's make it quick," Shawn said, almost as if he knew what she was thinking.

"It will be faster if we split up," Emily replied. "You can take Marley."

"You think I need a babysitter!" Shawn replied.

"Well..." Emily grinned.

"Thanks," Shawn pouted.

"I thought he might help if you find her," Emily continued.

"Little kids tend to have a better first impression of him than you."

"You know..." Shawn began. "You got a point there."

"I'll go into the house next door, so I won't be far," Emily assured him.

"Alright," Shawn said as he opened the door.

"Really?!" Emily had expected more of an argument about her going by herself.

"I've given up trying to argue with you," Shawn replied. "Plus, I don't have a better plan."

Emily opened the door to the SUV and climbed out. Marley climbed through to the front seats and out of Emily's door. Emily shut the door behind him and turned to look at the first house. "You take the keys," Emily said as she tossed them to Shawn. "Your pockets are deeper than mine, and the last thing we need is for me to drop them."

Shawn laughed as he stuffed the keys into his jeans pocket.

Emily walked towards the first house with both Shawn and Marley.

"You take this one," Shawn nodded. "We'll be right next door if you need anything."

"Keep an eye out for anything we can use," Emily reminded him.

"On it, boss," Shawn replied as he walked away and patted his leg to call Marley. Marley stood still, looking confused between Shawn and Emily.

"Go," Emily encouraged him, and Marley ran after Shawn.

Emily made her way up the front steps to the house. Emily reached for the door handle and turned it slowly. The heavy door opened without a sound, and Emily found herself standing in a large entryway.

"Oh my," Emily said as she looked around.

Everything in the house was covered in a thick layer of dust. The floor showed no signs of anyone walking in here for a very long time. Emily took her crowbar and banged it on the wall three times. Emily waited for anything to break the heavy silence in the house.

After a few minutes, Emily carefully began to make her way through the house. Emily couldn't help but look at everything as she went. Every room seemed to be grander than the next. She was sure the owner would have been appalled to see it all covered in dust. Everything was still in place, waiting for the owners to come back. There were no signs of packing and no car in the garage.

"They must not have been home when it happened," Emily said to herself as she walked back to the front door.

Emily opened the door and carried the few prescriptions she had found outside. Emily made her way down the porch just as Shawn and Marley came out of the second house. Emily made her way over to them, and they joined her on the street.

"Nothing except a few pill bottles," Shawn said as he walked up towards her.

"Same here," Emily replied as she looked out over the other houses. "This is going to take a while."

"We'd better not waste any time then," Shawn said as he walked towards the next house.

Shawn walked Emily to the next house and then continued with Marley next door. Emily headed up the front steps and stepped inside once more. Emily repeated her process to ensure that the house was empty and then searched the room. The owners of this house were home when everything happened and had packed in a hurry.

"Emily," Cole's voice rang out over the radio as she was heading back downstairs.

"Yeah, Cole," Emily replied after pulling the walkie from her waist.

"Just wanted to let you know I found your special request," Cole replied.

"You did?" Emily replied with excitement.

"It was just sitting in a barn," Cole answered.

"That's great. Thank you, Cole," Emily smiled.

"I didn't know we could make special requests," Jacob's voice rang out.

"You can't," Cole quickly answered in a playful tone.

"Then how come she can?" Jacob asked.

"Because we like her better than you," Cole laughed.

"None of that," Emily laughed. "Everyone, back to work."

"Fine," Jacob answered. "But my feelings are hurt, just so everyone knows."

"Noted," Emily laughed and then returned the walkie to her waist.

Emily finished searching the house and headed outside to Shawn, and Marley was waiting for her. Emily was still bouncy with excitement that Cole had found a motorcycle as she made her way off the front porch. Shawn, however, stood looking stern with his arms crossed.

"What's wrong with you?" Emily asked as she walked towards him.

"What's with this special request?" Shawn asked as they made their way to the next set of houses.

"That's between Cole and me," Emily smiled.

"And Sam," Shawn quickly replied.

Emily had forgotten that Sam was teamed up with Cole for the search. She felt confident, though, that Sam would keep her secret.

"Yup," Emily chimed.

"You know, secrets are never a good thing in a relationship," Shawn said as they reached the next front porch.

"Are you going to look me in the eye and tell me you have never kept a secret from me?" Emily asked as she stepped up on the porch and looked at him.

"That's different," Shawn replied. Emily could tell by the look on his face that he was trying to think of how quickly.

"No, it's not," Emily laughed. "I'm going inside now. I'll meet you in a few minutes."

"Come on, Marley," Shawn pouted as he walked away.

Emily continued to smile as she made her way into the house. Emily banged on the wall and waited again. Emily started to make her way through the house, which appeared just as empty as the other two. Emily barely saw her sitting in the armchair as she made her way into the living room. The woman looked like she had just fallen asleep in the chair and passed away. Emily knew better, though; this zombie was in hibernation. She quickly pulled the knife from her waist and stabbed it, then head.

Emily pulled back the knife and walked around the chair to look at the woman. She was very well dressed, and Emily noticed the wedding ring on her finger. Making a mental note that there may be more in the house, Emily moved on. Emily picked up a few more pill bottles and found the rest of the house empty. She looked back at the chair and couldn't help but feel sorry for the woman. She had been alone when everything happened, never knowing what had happened or having anyone to comfort her. Emily made her way back outside and waited for Shawn and Marley. It was only a few minutes before they joined her on the street.

"Trouble?" Emily asked as they walked out.

"Some still ones," Shawn replied.

"I found one in the other house as well," Emily added. "Not a good sign that Ava's around here."

"I was thinking the same thing," Shawn nodded. "Still, we'll keep searching, and we'll leave a message on the sign by the gate, just in case she finds her way here."

Emily, Shawn, and Marley continued to work through the remaining houses. They continued to find hibernating zombies in each and were sure to put each one to rest. The morning hours quickly turned to afternoon, and there were still no signs of Ava. With only a few houses left, Emily was beginning to think they would not find her that day. Most of the other teams reported no signs and headed back to the meeting place.

Emily's heart felt heavy as she walked into the last house. Emily went through the motion of knocking her crowbar on the wall and waiting. She was about to step forward when she noticed it, footprints in the dust. Emily bent down and took a closer look. They were fresh; no dust had yet fallen over the tracks, and they looked to be those of a child. Emily couldn't help but notice the other set of tracks in the dust. Based on the slide in each step, a zombie.

"Ava!" Emily called out before she could stop herself. "Ava, if you're in here, your daddy sent me to help find you!"

Emily followed the tracks as she called up the stairs. Emily could see a zombie standing in front of a closed door at the end of the hall. Emily quickly made her way down the hall and stabbed the zombie in the head. Someone had to have been here recently; he was the first one they had seen awake.

"Ava?" Emily said as she slowly opened the bedroom door.

A cool breeze greeted Emily, which was a nice change from the rest of the stuffy house. Emily slowly walked into the bedroom and saw that a window on the opposite side was open. Emily quickly made her way across the room, which belonged to a child based on the toys, and leaned out the window. Sitting on the edge of the overhang was a girl with tangled, dirty blonde hair. Emily recognized her instantly from her picture.

"Ava!" Emily called. "Your dad is looking for you."

"My dad is dead," Ava replied as she looked to be preparing to jump.

"No," Emily insisted as she pulled the walkie from her waist.

"Ethan!" Emily quickly spoke into the walkie.

"You find something?" Ethan's voice answered quickly. Emily held out the walkie as Ethan spoke so that Ava could hear it. Even from a distance, Emily could see the tears in Ava's eyes when Ethan spoke.

"Ethan, Ava's right here," Emily continued. "She can hear you."

"Ava?!" Ethan said, overjoyed. "Ava, are you alright?"

Ava looked at the walkie but did not move any closer. Emily no longer saw fear in Ava's eyes, but could see that Ava was still preparing to jump.

"Ethan, she said you were dead, and I can't get her to come off the roof," Emily said as she pressed the button.

"Ava, we're fine," Ethan replied. "Emily and her friends were helping us find you. Please, baby, trust her, and she will bring you home."

Emily looked at Ava and could now see the tears running down Ava's face.

"I can't," Ava finally choked out.

"Yes, you can," Emily replied as she crawled out the window to join Ava.

Emily heard the door downstairs open and close. She knew Shawn had overheard the conversation and was coming to join them.

"Please, Ava, Charlette needs her big sister."

"I'll find them when I can," Ava said as she moved closer to the ledge. "Tell Charlotte I had to help the other girls, but I'll find her."

"Ava!" Emily yelled as Ava jumped from the roof.

"Emily!" Shawn yelled as he ran up the stairs.

Emily didn't think as she moved towards the ledge and braced herself to follow Ava. Emily was not as nimble as the young girl and landed on her side. Emily felt her radio crunch under her body weight, and she heard the pieces fall to the ground as she stood.

"Ava!" Emily called as she pulled herself to her feet.

Emily could see the girl, already a reasonable distance ahead of her, running further south than they had planned to go today.

Emily forced her body to begin to run after the girl.

"Emily!" Shawn's voice bellowed from the upstairs window.

"She's right there!" Emily yelled back as she ran.

Emily forced her legs to run faster than they had in a long time, attempting to catch the girl half her age. Ava seemed to know her path well as she dodged in and out of buildings and around where groups of zombies had gathered. As the number of zombies around them grew, Emily was forced to stop calling after the girl.

Emily glanced behind her, half expecting to see Shawn or Marley.

The only followers she had, though, were a few zombies.

Emily continued to follow Ava for what seemed like forever. Every time Ava would take a breath and Emily would begin to catch up, she would take off once more. Emily had not run this much in her entire life, but was determined not to lose the girl. Ava led Emily into the small town downtown area. Emily was forced to stop following when Ava ran into a group of zombies. Emily braced herself on a cool brick building and watched, half expecting to see the young girl die.

Ava slipped through the crowd quickly, over a wooden gazebo, and into a large brick building in the center of the square. Emily couldn't help but celebrate as Ava closed the door behind her'.02

34, safe and sound.

"Way to go, kid," Emily whispered to herself.

Emily's presence did not go unnoticed for long, and soon the zombies were beginning to make their way towards her. Emily glanced back once more for Shawn and Marley. Emily found only more dead eager to make a meal out of her. Emily ran to the front of the building and through the first unlocked door. The wave of the dead crashed against the wooden door, eager to follow her.

Emily locked the door and turned to look at her haven. A long staircase greeted Emily with a closed wooden door at the top. Emily slowly made her way up the stairs, careful not to make noise. Any more noise would cause the zombies to stay longer outside the outer door. Emily reached the top of the staircase and slowly opened the wooden door. Inside appeared to be an office of some kind. There was a long wooden table set up in the front and two desks in the back. A large window let the last of the light from the setting sun flood the room. To her right, Emily found a small kitchen area. Emily quickly made her way through and grabbed a water bottle out of the flat on the counter. Emily drank it much faster than she should, but she was exhausted from her long run. A window in the kitchen gave Emily a view of the square, including Ava's door. Emily watched as more zombies found their way onto the square, drawn by both her and Ava's presence there.

"Dammit!" Emily said after reaching for her radio.

She had forgotten that she had broken it when she jumped to follow Ava. Everyone would be worried if she didn't contact them or come back tonight. Emily knew it would be morning before the zombies calmed down and began to spread out. Emily quickly made sure the office door upstairs was locked and began to look through everything. At the desk, Emily was happy to find a protein bar that would have to serve as her dinner. While the backpack was full of medication, there was nothing in it to eat. Emily sat down at the desk and looked through the papers as she ate. Emily figured out that this was some law office, not needed in this new world, based on what she saw.

Emily leaned back in the chair as the sun set. The dark ensured that there was nothing else she could do tonight. Emily closed her eyes and tried her best to rest. While her body was exhausted, Emily would find no sleep here. The sounds of the zombies outside kept her on edge, and the thought of Ava trapped across the street kept her mind racing.

Chapter 11

Emily was still awake as the sun began to rise the following day. She made her way to the small kitchen, grabbed another bottle of water, and looked out over the square. Some of the zombies had wandered off, and all of the attention seemed to be away from the door she was hiding behind. However, the dead all seemed to be focused on the stone building where Ava was hiding.

Suddenly, just as Emily took a sip of water, she saw what they were all attracted to. Emily set the bottle down on the counter hard and climbed into the window for a better look. Running across the gazebo was a young girl with chestnut brown hair. She could not have been more than five or six years old. Much like Ava, the girl weaved between the zombies with ease, avoiding the grab of each one. Emily couldn't just stand and watch while this child ran for her life.

Emily ran for the door, threw the lock open, and ran down the stairs. Emily tried to open the second door and cursed herself for forgetting the lock. Emily opened the lock just as the little girl ran in front of the door. The girl stopped in shock and stared at Emily.

"Get in here," Emily breathed as she reached out and pulled the girl in.

The girl remained silent and stood still while Emily closed the door and locked it once more. Emily took the girl by the hand and led her upstairs, where she locked the door once more.

"Are you alright?" Emily asked as she checked the girl's arms for bite marks.

The girl continued to remain silent and did not move.

"What were you thinking running through them like that?!" Emily scolded the girl once she was sure she was safe.

"It's my turn," the girl shyly replied.

"Your turn?!" Emily could feel her heart rate slowing, but still couldn't understand what the girl meant.

"Every day, we have to look for food," the little girl explained. "Daddy is too big, so we all take turns."

Emily couldn't help but be shocked at how normal this situation seemed to the little girl.

"So, it's just you guys and your daddy in there?" Emily asked, finally calming down.

"Yes," the girl replied.

"What's your name?" Emily asked the girl.

"Willow," the girl replied.

"Hi Willow, I'm Emily." Emily smiled at the child. "I'm looking for my friend Ava. I think I saw her run in there." "Ava's in there," the girl smiled.

"Her daddy is worried," Emily continued. "I'm here to take her home."

"You're here to take Ava away," Willow said as she backed up. "Daddy won't like that."

"I'm sure your daddy will be happy that Ava found her family," Emily said patiently. "We have a town not far from here. I would be happy to take you all there. There's plenty of food, and you wouldn't have to run through the zombies anymore."

"We are Ava's family," Willow said firmly. Emily couldn't help but notice that she sounded more afraid than angry.

"I'm sure you are," Emily smiled. "I have a family like that, too. But Ava's little sister is worried about her."

"Ava's first family?" Willow asked as she looked at Emily.

"Before the bright light?"

"Yes," Emily nodded, knowing that Willow referred to the flash.

"Those aren't our families anymore," Willow said, strong once more. "Daddy found us; daddy saved us. He is our only family.

Emily didn't know who *Daddy* was, but she hated the man. Something just seemed wrong with the entire situation. He remained inside and sent the children out for food because it was too dangerous. The girls weren't allowed to have any family besides him because he saved them. Emily knew that voicing these concerns to Willow would do no good.

"I understand," Emily nodded. "I would just like to offer your family a home where you all can be together and safe."

The words tasted like ash in her mouth as she said them. Emily didn't understand, and she didn't want to keep them all together. She wanted to get Ava back to her family and see if she could find the other girls' families. She didn't know who the man was in that building, but she didn't trust him. Emily hated to lie to Willow, but knew it was her only chance to gain her trust.

"Daddy said we need a new home," Willow said as she thought. "You have to promise to be good and not try to take any of us away."

"I promise," Emily smiled.

"Pinky promise?" Willow asked as she held up her little finger.

"Pinky promise," Emily nodded as she wrapped her finger around the little girl's finger. She knew that she wasn't lying. She was trying to be good. And she wouldn't take any of them away.

She would take them all away from here.

"Okay," Willow grinned as she released Emily's pinky. "You'll have to be quick, or you will get caught."

"I can be quick," Emily said as she stood back up. Her aching and exhausted body disagreed with her statement. Emily hoped that pure determination would be enough to get the job done.

"Follow me," Willow said as she motioned for Emily.

Emily unlocked the doors and followed Willow out onto the street. As soon as they were outside, Willow began to run. Emily took off at a run to keep up with her. There were too many dead to fight, so Emily acted just as the girls did. She was quick to spin and move throughout the crowd, over the gazebo, and into the building.

"Wait here," Willow instructed her once they were inside.

Small offices lined the hall on either side of the building.

The door to her left read

"Personal Property," and " Cashier " to her right. Emily concluded that this must be the town hall for this city. Ahead, there was an elevator that Emily felt confident did not work.

"What are you doing here?" A voice spoke beside Emily.

Emily looked down to see a ten-year-old girl standing beside her with a shotgun.

"Willow said your daddy was looking for a new home," Emily explained as she raised her hand to chest level. "I thought I would invite you all to stay in a city not far from here, where it's safe."

"Daddy won't like that," the girl replied. "I'm supposed to shoot anyone who comes in."

"Willow went to get your daddy," Emily sputtered. "Maybe we should wait for him to decide."

"Lower the gun, Zoey," a man's voice came down the hall.

Emily watched as Zoey lowered the gun before looking for the voice source. In the middle of the hall was a well-dressed, middle-aged man. The hair around his temples and ears was gray, while the rest of it was jet black.

"I do apologize for that," the man said smoothly. "We have to be on high alert these days."

"No apologies needed," Emily said as she lowered her hands and took a step forward.

"You must be Willow's father."

"That I am," the man nodded. "I'm Wesley."

"Nice to meet you, Wesley," Emily smiled. "My name is

Emily."

"Willow tells me you have a town nearby that is safe," Wesley replied.

Emily had never heard anyone, but politicians, speak the way Wesley was. It was like his voice was as smooth as silk, and he could make anything sound like a good thing.

"I do," Emily nodded. "I wanted to invite you and your daughters to join us."

"Is it an all-girl community?" Wesley asked as Willow walked up next to him.

"No," Emily replied, caught off guard by the question. "We are a collection of people trying to find a way to not only survive but live in this world."

Emily had just finished speaking when Ava walked into view. Ava's eyes grew wide, and Emily could see them pleading with her. Ava glanced at Wesley and then back at Emily. Ava slowly shook her head no but remained silent. Emily knew that Ava did not want her to tell Wesley that she knew Ava or her family was looking for her.

"I'm not sure it would be a good fit for us then," Wesley replied, not noticing Emily and Ava's exchange. "My girls have been through a lot, and I don't want them around men for their safety."

"I'm sorry?" Emily asked, confused. "However, us not being an all-girl community means that we can invite you in to join them. We will be able to give you a home where you can keep your family together and safe."

"Do you have other children that live there?" the man asked.

"We do," Emily nodded.

She had already decided that she would not tell him anything about the kids if he asked. Something about this situation still made her stomach churn and her blood boil.

"May I ask what happened to your girls?" Emily asked.

"A few months back, a group found us, a group of men," the man sighed with a sorrowful look on his face. "They were too much for me to handle on my own, and I had not allowed the girls to handle the guns. The boys beat my girls and did unspeakable things. Sophie!"

Emily watched as a girl, no more than sixteen, walked into view. Emily recognized the look on the girl as she gently rubbed a small bump on her stomach. The girl looked a few months pregnant, and her eyes told that she was traumatized by the event. Emily couldn't help the gasp that escaped her lips as she put her hand over her mouth.

"I'm so sorry," Emily finally replied. "We have a doctor who can help you."

"A woman doctor?" Wesley asked.

"No," Emily admitted. "However, I can vouch that he is a great doctor. I know children that he has helped bring into this world."

"Is he married?" Wesley asked next.

"No," Emily replied. "Nor is he dating that I know of. If your daughters are uncomfortable with him, they are welcome to ask either you or me to join them during any exams."

"He can deliver the child, though?" Wesley asked as he put his arm around Sophie. Emily couldn't help but notice Sophie cringe at his touch. "And there's food?"

"Yes," Emily replied. "It's quite a walk from here, but we may be able to make it before dark if we leave now."

Emily knew that she would need to find Shawn or one of the others with a truck to make it back. For now, however, she decided to keep that information to herself.

"Get the others," Wesley grinned at the girls. "It's time for us to go."

"How many daughters do you have?" Emily asked as she watched the girls run off.

"Seven," Wesley smiled. "They keep me busy, but knowing they are safe makes it all worth it."

"You are a brave man to raise seven daughters," Emily smiled. "How many sons?"

"None," Wesley said out of confusion. "Boys can survive anything, but girls are delicate flowers that need to be protected from this world.

Emily fought the urge to vomit as his velvet words made her feel in desperate need of a shower. Wesley seemed not to notice and turned to the girls as they ran towards him.

"Yes, Daddy," the girls all said in almost perfect unison, adding to the creepy level of the situation.

"We are going to go with Emily to check a town," Wesley said. "Where can we stay together as a family and be safe?" "Yes, Daddy," the girls said once more.

"Follow me," Emily said slowly as she turned and opened the door.

The dead had lost interest in the door and were strung out in the streets. Emily held the door open while the girls and Wesley ran out. Emily watched as the girls ran, drawing the attention of any zombies that neared, while Wesley casually walked across the square.

"What a piece of shit!" Emily said under her breath. She worked her way through the crowd, killing any zombies near the girls and gathering them all behind one of the stone buildings.

"Forgive my pace," Wesley smiled casually. "I fear that I was injured, and I'm unable to run."

"How were you injured?" Emily asked.

"Running," Wesley simply replied. "I hope this doesn't ruin our arrival time.

"We may have to hold up in a farmhouse overnight, but we will still arrive by tomorrow," Emily replied.

She hoped to even make it back to the subdivision by dark at the pace he was moving. Emily couldn't see any signs of injury as Wesley walked. There was no limp or any signs of discomfort. He looked to be just taking a casual Sunday stroll, leaving his daughters to keep the dead away from him.

"Why did you follow me?!" Ava angrily whispered to Emily while they were out of earshot from Wesley.

"I promised your dad I would find you," Emily whispered back. "Why did you run?"

"To protect the little kids," Ava whispered back. "I can't let what happened to Sophie happen to them."

"You think the group will find you again?" Emily asked in a whisper.

"You don't get it," Ava whispered in disbelief.

"Ava!" Wesley called out for her.

"You have to tell me what's going on," Emily whispered after Ava as she ran back to Wesley.

Emily knew something was wrong, but without the girls telling her, she couldn't be sure what it was. Emily led them towards the subdivision and finally reached it as the sun began to set.

"This is a place where I belong," Wesley said as he strolled through the streets towards the most prominent house.

"Wouldn't you agree, my loves?"

"Yes, daddy," the girls all replied in unison.

"It should be safe," Emily said as they walked towards the door. "My friends and I cleared these houses just yesterday."

"I hope there is food," Willow said as she followed Wesley up the stairs.

"If there's not young Willow, don't fret," Wesley called back at her. "You will still be beautiful to me."

Emily swallowed down the bile that rose in her throat once more as she shut the door and locked it. Emily looked around and realized that this was the house where she had found Ava. Emily glanced down at the footprints in the dirt. Shawn and Marley were visible. Emily suddenly feared that Wesley might run if he realized how large Shawn was. Emily dragged her feet as she walked, wiping their footprints away from the wooden floor.

"The cleaning staff must have the day off," Wesley mused as he sat down on the white couch. "Girls, see what you can find in the kitchen."

"Yes, Daddy," all of the girls replied at once.

Emily had not had a chance to check this house, so it stood the highest probability of having something to eat left in it. Emily made her way to the living room and sat down in a chair across from Wesley. Wesley looked as comfortable as a man on vacation. Emily was determined not to let him out of her sight until she knew more about what he was up to. She was sure to learn it all when they returned to Sanctuary, and Ava was reunited with her family.

"Do you have children?" Wesley asked as he looked at her.

"Yes," Emily replied shortly.

"How old?" Wesley casually asked next.

"One," Emily replied, vowing not to tell him that Hope was a girl or her name.

"Brilliant age," Wesley replied. "When they learn what's right and wrong before people have a chance to corrupt their minds."

"I do my best," Emily smiled. "Just as I'm sure you do with your daughters.

"Yes, but most of them remember at least something that their birth parents believe," Wesley replied. "It makes things harder but not impossible."

"Like what?" Emily asked, hoping to learn more about his relationship with the girls.

"Canned soups," Willow smiled as she walked back into the room.

"What kind?" Wesley smiled down at the girl.

"Tomato," Willow replied as she held up an open can with what looked to be a spoon in it.

"Not the most dignified way to eat," Wesley sneered as he took the can from Willow.

"I'm sorry, dadDaddyWillow said with tears in her eyes and fear spreading across her face.

"Don't whine!" Wesley suddenly snapped at Willow. "Get out of my sight and eat your food."

Willow ran from the room, trying not to cry, but Emily found herself frozen, staring at Wesley. There was something about his voice now that seemed extremely familiar. Emily was determined to place it and wouldn't let him out of her sight until she did.

"That was harsh," Emily said as she watched Wesley sip on his soup.

"There was no place for whining before, and there is even less of a place for it now," Wesley replied smoothly. "I am teaching the girls to be as strong as the noble ladies of old."

Emily had hoped to get him to speak in his rough voice once more, but he had already recovered.

"The ladies of old?" Emily asked, studying his face and trying to place it.

"Princesses and queens of olden days," Wesley explained. "You would never see one of them crying when they displeased someone. They were strong and kept their chin up."

"And you think women have become weak?" Emily asked, trying not to sound insulted.

"Yes," Wesley replied without hesitation. "They would rather cry than be strong. Women should face their challenges with both silence and grace."

"Why must they face them in silence?" Emily asked.

"It's their place," Wesley said, rolling his eyes. "One that you haven't learned."

Emily felt her fists clench around the arms of the chair. She would have put this man on his ass by now in any normal circumstance. But she couldn't risk him taking off in the night and taking the girls with him. Emily knew how to play the role of the dutiful woman; she had done it when she was married. Emily felt her hands relax and forced herself to give her best performance yet.

"I'm sorry if I offended," Emily replied as she looked at her feet.

"Maybe you do know," Wesley said as he stood up and thrust the half-empty can of soup at her. "I'll be going to bed now." Emily kept her eyes on her feet and nodded.

"Girls!" Wesley called in a rough voice once more.

Emily felt like the memory was just out of her grasp as the girls came running into the room and followed Wesley upstairs. Emily looked at Wesley as he climbed the stairs and finally knew where she knew him from. His face wasn't the clue she needed; she had never seen his face. Emily suddenly saw Wesley walking up the road, Shawn slamming the brakes on the truck, and plowing into the tree. It was Wesley they had come across that day in the truck.

Chapter 12

Emily had sat on the staircase all night, not allowing herself to fall asleep. Her body was beyond exhausted, but she didn't trust Wesley enough to close her eyes. She had even gone upstairs and opened the bedroom door, where he lay on the king-size bed and the girls slept around him on the floor. Emily had told them it was best to hear each other in case of an emergency. Wesley was not happy about it, but Emily did not care.

"Did you sleep?" Willow asked as she appeared on the stairs next to Emily.

"A little," Emily replied. "It's hard for me to sleep when I'm not home."

"I don't sleep much either," Willow replied. "I'm scared the monsters will get me in my sleep when I can't run."

"When we get to my home, you won't have to worry about that anymore," Emily said as she pulled the girl into a hug. "The monsters can't get in, and everyone can sleep."

"Sophie doesn't sleep either," Willow continued. "She cries all night long."

"Why?" Emily asked. "Is she hurt?"

"I don't think so," Willow said as she shook her head no. "Maybe she will be better when you all are safe."

"Maybe," Willow agreed.

"Why don't you go wake the others?" Emily smiled at her. "We need to get moving."

"Okay," Willow smiled as she stood and ran up the stairs.

Emily looked through the window at the dim light cast outside. Dawn was upon them, and there would be barely enough light for them to see. However, as slow as Wesley moved, they needed to get going as soon as possible.

"It is unbefitting to wake a gentleman before his breakfast is ready," Wesley said from the top of the stairs.

"We will have to look for something as we go," Emily said as she stood up. "There's nothing left in the kitchen."

"Did you eat the rest of my soup?" Wesley asked angrily.

"Yes," Emily replied. While she hated to eat after the man, it was the only food left in the house, and she wasn't about to take it away from the children.

"This is just the most…." Wesley was too angry with her to finish his sentence.

Emily had planned to continue her "good woman" act, but was just too tired for it this morning.

"The houses here have all been cleaned out," Emily said.

"The sooner we get to town, the sooner we can all eat."

"You searched already?" Wesley asked in confusion.

"I didn't want to disappoint you when you woke," Emily thought quickly. "The people who cleaned it out must have been chased away before they reached this house."

"Girls!" Wesley called out as he walked down the stairs. "It's time to go!"

Emily waited as the girls walked down the stairs. Emily looked at Sophie and could tell thethatllow had been telling the truth. The girl's eyes were red and swollen. An all-night crying look that Emily knew all too well. When she caught Emily looking at her, Sophie shifted her gaze to the floor.

Emily led them all outside and back through the subdivision. It took them an hour to reach the gate at the pace Wesley walked.

Emily looked again for any sign of injury but again found nothing. Emily couldn't wait for Doc to examine him and tell her nothing was wrong. She just may break his ankle for putting the girls at risk because he didn't want to walk fast.

Emily made her way slowly through the streets that she had driven through the day before with Shawn. The drive hadn't seemed that long, but at this walking pace, it would take them weeks to reach Sanctuary.

"I need a rest!" Wesley called up to her as she was killing a zombie.

"It's not safe!" Emily called back to him. "There are some houses up the road away we can stop in."

"I can't wait!" Wesley insisted. "You all will keep me safe while I gather myself."

"Yes, daddy," the girls all replied in unison.

Emily looked at each of the girls and could see the exhaustion on their faces. They hadn't slept well the night before and were now running in circles to protect Wesley. Wesley walked over to the side of the road and relaxed in the soft grass. He looked more like someone sitting beside the pool than someone stuck in the open with zombies all around.

Emily felt her anger boiling over as she turned and killed another zombie. He was going to get them all killed with this behavior. Emily had just made up her mind to give him a piece of it when she felt a sharp pain in her leg. Emily looked down to see that a zombie had decided her calf looked like its next meal. Emily pulled her leg out of the zombie's mouth and stomped on it hard several times until it went still.

Emily began to stomp towards Wesley. While she knew she would be fine, the girls would not be so lucky. She was going to get him up and moving, or he could stay here to die alone. Emily was only a few steps away from him when Willow suddenly looked up and pointed.

"Truck!" Willow yelled as she pointed up the road.

Emily turned to see a black SUV driving towards them. Even from a distance, she knew it was her SUV. Behind the SUV was a line of vehicles just as there had been the day before. Emily felt her heart swell in her chest as she waved to make sure they saw her.

"Get off the road!" Wesley yelled at the girls. Emily turned to see that he was suddenly on his feet and quickly ran towards the wood line.

"I knew it," Emily mumbled under her breath.

"No!" Emily called out to them. "It's my friends. They will give us a ride, so we don't have to walk."

The girls all seemed to freeze where they were. Emily could tell that they were all struggling not to do as Wesley told them, but they were also trying to trust Emily.

"I promise," Emily assured them. "None of them will hurt you."

"They're not like the bad boys?" Willow asked as she walked forward and took Emily's hand.

"No," Emily smiled. "I don't let the bad ones in."

"That will change," Sophie said low enough that she didn't think Emily could hear it.

Emily looked back at her just as Shawn brought the SUV to a stop in front of her.

"Emily!" he called as he jumped out of the SUV and ran towards her.

"I'm fine," Emily said as he wrapped her in a hug and lifted her off the ground.

Emily felt her anger take the back seat as she found comfort in Shawn's arms.

"What the hell happened?" Shawn asked as he sat her back down. "You jumped off the damn roof!"

"I had to," Emily assured him as she looked over her shoulder and smiled at Ava.

"Holy shit!" Shawn whispered as he looked at her.

"Don't even think about it!" Wesley yelled as he walked back onto the street. "She's mine!"

"She's what…." Shawn began.

"Ava!" Ethan yelled as he came around the SUV and spotted his daughter.

"Dad!" Ava yelled back as she ran to her father.

"I thought I lost you," Ethan breathed into Ava's long hair.

"I'm fine, Dad," Ava cried as she clung to Ethan.

"Why did you run?" Ethan asked as he pulled Ava back to look at her face.

"I had to," Ava replied sheepishly.

"But why?" Ethan asked her again. "You heard my voice; you knew it was me."

"Ava?" Wesley asked, confused.

"Yes, daddy?" Ava instinctively replied and then regretted it as she looked at the hurt on Ehtan's face. "No, I'm sorry, Dad," Ava said as she clung to Ethan's neck once more.

"It's okay," Ethan replied as he picked her up.

"You came to the square following Ava?" Wesley said, looking back at Emily.

"I did," Emily nodded. "Her family was searching for her, and I wasn't going to let them lose her again."

"You're bitten!" Willow suddenly exclaimed, pointing at Emily's leg.

"Again!" Shawn sighed as he looked down.

"Unfortunately," Emily said as she pulled up her pants leg. "Doc is going to get tired of stitching me up."

"That's it," Cole laughed. "We're making her a suit of armor if she wants to keep going out."

"I'll be fine," Emily laughed.

"Just keep rubbing that in my face," Cole said as he looked at her sternly.

"You were, too," Emily said as she wrinkled her nose at him.

"Are you all not going to take care of this!?" Wesley asked in disbelief.

"We'll have it stitched up at home," Shawn said. "She'll be fine by morning."

"You must be in charge," Wesley said as he took a step forward.

"Actually…" Shawn began.

"He sure is," Emily interrupted him. Shawn looked at her, confused, but decided to play along.

"I'm Wesley, and these are my daughters," Wesley had turned his smooth voice on once more. "I found them all, including Ava there, and took care of them all as if they were my own."

"Thank you," Ethan said as he still clung to Ava.

"It was my pleasure," Wesley nodded. "While she wasn't with us long, she was quickly becoming one of my favorites."

Emily felt her stomach turn once more as he spoke. Shawn still looked confused as he turned his gaze back to Wesley.

"I'm sure Emily told you about our community," Shawn spoke. "You and your daughters are, of course, welcome to join us."

"She had promised us a house and that we could stay together," Wesley said. "I just want to be sure you'll honor the promise of a woman."

Shawn's grip tightened on Emily's hand. He now understood, at least in part, why Emily wanted him to pretend to be in charge.

"I will," Shawn nodded, trying to remain calm. "Except for young Ava, there will be living with her parents."

"Of course," Wesley smiled. "It's always best when there can be a happy ending."

"We can take some of the girls in the SUV, and the others can divide between…." Shawn said, pointing at the trucks.

"We stay together," Wesley interrupted him. "I believe we can all fit in that truck."

Shawn turned to look at the box truck that Wesley was pointing at.

"It will be quite hot in there for the girls. I think it would be best if they could get some airflow."

"We will be fine," Wesley insisted. "Girls!"

"Yes, the girls all said in unison as they followed Wesley towards the truck.

"What the fuck was that!" Shawn whispered to Emily.

"I don't know, but it's not right," Emily replied. "And look."

Shawn turned his gaze back to Wesley as he walked towards the truck. It took only a moment for Emily to see the recognition in his eyes. Wesley's careful stroll was easily recognizable.

"That's the son of bitch that damn near killed us!" Shawn tried hard to whisper.

"I know," Emily nodded.

"Why am I not beating him into the pavement?" Shawn asked, his face turning red with anger.

"The girls," Emily explained. "It's like he has them brainwashed. They wait for him and protect him. He said that he's training them to be like the ladies of old. To serve and suffer in silence."

"You think he would run if he found out that you're in charge and take them with him?" Shawn said, putting the pieces together.

"We just need to get them back to Sanctuary," Emily replied. "We can figure it out there."

Shawn nodded and continued to look at Wesley as if he could kill him right there.

"Where's Marley?" Emily asked, looking around, expecting him to be demanding her attention and an apology for disappearing.

"He stayed back with Hope," Shawn replied. "She was a little worried about you and was afraid she would lose us."

"I feel awful," Emily said as she looked in the direction of Sanctuary.

"Don't," Shawn insisted. "She will be proud and brag to everyone that her mommy saved seven kids."

"And Shawn only killed one man," Emily joked, trying to lighten the mood.

"Today," Shawn smiled back. "Let's get you in the truck."

Emily climbed up in the passenger seat as Shawn shut the door behind her. Shawn joined her in the truck and began to lead everyone home.

"How long do you want me to pretend to be in charge?" Shawn asked. "I don't want to end up in the dog house for taking it too far."

"Until I learn the truth," Emily replied.

"Is there going to be some kind of signal?" Shawn asked, looking over at her.

"Believe me," Emily said, looking at the side mirror to get a view of the box truck. "You'll know."

Shawn simply nodded and continued the drive back to Sanctuary. Emily was surprised that the pain from the bite remained reasonably mild. She still felt like she could put pressure on it and wasn't getting weak. Emily held Shawn's hand as they drove through the small town, one step closer to Sanctuary.

"Julia didn't have to open the gate," Shawn said as they neared the logging road.

"Hope opened it," Emily said, remembering she had not told Shawn that Hope knew the code.

"I didn't know you decided to teach it to her," Shawn continued. "It's a pretty big risk with her being so small."

"I didn't," Emily insisted. "She must have seen me put it in and just memorized how it worked."

"She has been watching you do it since she was born," Shawn said. "But didn't you change it after I was shot?"

"I did," Emily nodded. "But she still figured it out."

"She is going to get away with everything when she's a teenager," Shawn laughed. "She's already smarter than us."

"That she is," Emily agreed. "Does anyone else realize she knows?"

"No," Shawn shook his head. "I figured out the luck thing and asked Julia if she needed it. She told me she had Hope and headed up to the control room."

"I meant to tell you," Emily admitted, feeling sorry that she had forgotten. Shawn was Hope's only father figure, and Emily wanted him to know these kinds of things.

"It's alright," Shawn smiled. "Let's just deal with this mess that we are bringing back."

"I don't know how to begin with that," Emily sighed. "I hope maybe one of the girls will say something to Doc. The oldest,
Sophie, is pregnant."

"What?!" Shawn asked in disbelief.

"Wesley says a group of men broke in, overpowered him, and took liberties with her," Emily explained. "I just find it hard to believe."

"I would think you would be the person to believe it," Shawn said, glancing at her. "Especially after Jeff."

"But that doesn't explain why Ava ran, even after hearing her father's voice or the creepy way they all behave around him."

"It is creepy the way they all answer him at the same time,"
Shawn agreed. "We'll figure it out."

"I hope so," Emily smiled as they approached the gate.

"Speaking of Hope," Shawn smiled as the gate opened.

Emily looked up at the wall and could imagine Hope sitting up in the control panel, watching the screens. Emily leaned out the truck window slightly and blew a kiss to where she knew the camera was located. Emily leaned back inside as Shawn parked the SUV.

"How's the leg?" Shawn asked as he shut off the SUV.

"Fine," Emily replied, looking down at her leg. Her jeans were covered in blood, but she still felt surprisingly strong.

"Can you walk on it?" Shawn asked.

"Definitely," Emily nodded as she opened the truck door.

Emily stepped out and glanced over at the gates that were closed once more. Emily shut the truck door and stood for a moment to take in how relieved she felt to be home.

"Mommy!" Hope yelled as she ran towards Emily with Marley barking and running beside her.

"Hope," Emily said as she bent down to hug Hope.

Hope ran into Emily's arms and wrapped Emily in a hug. Marley ran into both of them, knocking them onto the ground, and began to lick Emily on the face. Emily and Hope both laughed as they lay on the ground.

"That seems very improper," Wesley said as he walked onto the scene.

"It's best to let the women have a moment or two," Shawn said as he walked around the SUV. "It helps to ensure they do as they're told."

Emily could feel the confusion of everyone around them as Shawn spoke. They were not all in on their little hoax. Emily continued to smile as she stood up from the ground, holding Hope by the hand.

"With your permission, I will ask the doctor to fix my leg," Emily said as she turned to Shawn. "I'm sure it won't affect my ability to make your supper."

"Doc!" Shawn called out. "Please see to it that she gets some stitches."

"Alright," Doc replied out of confusion.

"You go with Ms. Julia, and I will find you soon," Emily smiled at Hope.

Hope nodded and took off towards where Julia stood with a confused look. Marley followed Emily towards the small clinic. Glancing back at Shawn, trying to figure out why they were speaking to each other as they were.

"What is going on?" Doc said as soon as the door was closed.

"Something is going on with that guy," Emily explained. "He thinks women are servants for men. We've decided to play along until we can find out what's going on, so he doesn't take the girls and run."

Doc had already rolled up her pants leg and prepared to clean the bite.

"You think it's more than him being an idiot," Doc asked as he cleaned the bite.

"The girls are like little drones," Emily continued. "It's not out of respect. You can see the fear in their eyes."

"You want me to see if I can get them to talk?" Doc offered as he began to stitch.

"If you don't mind," Emily winced. "I told them if they weren't comfortable being alone with you, either he or I could join them."

"I would much rather it be you," Doc replied.

"Me too," Emily replied.

Chapter 13

Emily walked back out of the clinic to hear Shawn doing her normal speech. It was no surprise that he knew it. He had been there every time she had done it. Emily walked towards Shawn, her leg freshly stitched and bandaged. Doc had told her that if she felt fine, he saw no reason to keep her in quarantine that night. As long as she didn't stay alone, she could go home. Marley was glued to her hip as she walked.

"I don't trust that man to be alone with my daughters," Wesley said to Shawn.

"We will give each of the girls a choice," Shawn nodded.
"They can have either you or Emily accompany them."

"Why the choice?" Wesley asked. "I'm their father. It should be me."

"Just to make sure they are comfortable," Shawn explained. "I don't need to deal with upset women with everything else I have to deal with."

"Understood," Wesley nodded. "I'm sure you have enough troubles without dealing with women's emotions."

"I'll go first and take young Willow here with me," Wesley said as he took Willow by the hand.

"As long as that's okay with Willow," Shawn answered, looking down at the girl.

"It's okay," Willow answered as she took Wesley's hand.

Emily watched as Wesley disappeared into the clinic with Willow. Emily felt herself shaking as each minute passed. She knew that with Doc in there, Willow was safe. But she couldn't shake the feeling of fear she felt. Emily breathed a sigh of relief as the door opened, and Willow came running out to rejoin the other girls. One by one, the girls went into the clinic, each wanting Wesley to go with them. Emily remained by the SUV, just in case a girl would say something different and want her to join them. Finally, Sophie was the only girl remaining. Sophie said nothing as she walked towards the clinic.

"Do you want him to accompany you or Emily?" Shawn said as they began to walk. "Emily has carried a child before and would be able to help talk you through the process."

Emily tried hard not to smile at how Shawn was playing the situation. Wesley turned and glared at Shawn for asking the question. He looked at Sophie with the same hate. Sophie looked at Emily, and Emily couldn't help but notice a change in Sophie's eyes.

"Well?!" Wesley asked impatiently.

"I would like Ms. Emily to come with me," Sophie finally answered.

Emily couldn't help the excitement she felt. She managed to contain it and simply followed Sophie into the small clinic. Once inside, Emily stood against the wall while Doc started his basic exam.

"How far along are you?" Doc asked once he finished checking her bite.

"Three months, sir," Sophie replied, looking at the floor.

"How have you been feeling?" Doc continued. "Any sickness?"

"No, sir," Sophie answered, still not looking up. "I don't eat enough to get sick."

"It must be hard to find food out there," Doc nodded.

"We found the food just fine," Sophie answered, looking up at him. "But *HE* has to eat first."

"That's not right," Doc replied. "Especially in your condition."

"He just hopes it's a girl," Sophie said, rubbing her stomach.
"If it is, I swear I'll make sure it dies before it calls him daddy."

"There's no need for that," Emily said as she walked over and sat down next to Sophie. "Children are so rare in this world."

"No child should have to call that monster daddy," Sophie said. "Is there something you can give me so that it looks like I just lost it?"

Doc looked at Emily, and she could still see the horror on his face. Emily knew that her face looked the same as his.

"We don't do that," Doc finally spoke. "We can find the baby another home after it's born if you want."

"If it's a girl, he won't allow it," Sophie said.

"Why?" Emily asked. "Why does he only want daughters?"

Emily knew that Sophie would be the one to tell her the truth about Wesley. It's why she wanted Emily to come in with her. Emily knew that outside, Wesley was probably afraid of precisely this happening.

"He doesn't want daughters," Sophie laughed out of disgust.
"He wants wives, young wives like they used to have in the old days."

Emily looked at Doc and could only imagine that her face was just as red as his. Emily tried to keep herself together while she turned back to Sophie.

"Is he the baby's father?" Emily finally managed to ask through clenched teeth.

Emily already knew the answer. She had feared it from the moment she saw Sophie. Sophie didn't speak but simply nodded her head yes.

"Does he touch the others?" Emily asked, swallowing hard.

"He didn't touch Ava or Willow yet," Sophie replied. "Ava was too new, and he used Willow to keep the rest of us quiet. If he finds out, I told you he'll…."

"We won't let anything happen to them," Emily assured her.

"You have to get them away from him," Sophie begged her.

"Stay with Doc," Emily said as she stood up.

"Game over?" Doc asked as he walked with her towards the door.

"Long over," Emily replied as she opened the door so hard, she was afraid she would rip it off the hinges.

Emily walked quickly and aggressively back outside towards where Wesley was standing. Marley ran over to join her, looking ready for whatever fight she was walking into.

"She is giving him trouble and wants her daddy?" Wesley smiled at her in a way that made her anger even worse.

"Emily?" Shawn asked as she didn't respond or slow her pace.

Emily began to reach for the knife on her waist when Willow looked at her, afraid. The other girls all knew what was going on, but Willow was oblivious to the worst of it. Emily released her grip on the blade handle and clenched her hand into a fist.

"What's going on with my…." Wesley said, agitated.

Emily hit him as hard as she could in the face before he finished his sentence. Wesley stumbled backward, clutching the spot where Emily had hit him. Emily didn't give him time to recover and hit him as hard as she could once more. Emily felt the blood on her hand as she pulled back. Wesley fell to the ground. Emily took a step to stand over him, intent on hitting him until he was dead.

"Emily!" Shawn said as he grabbed her around the waist and pulled her back. "What the hell is going on?"

"He's the father!" Emily yelled out. "That sick son of bitch is raping them!"

"They are like daughters to me!" Wesley yelled as he crawled away from Emily.

"You sick bastard!" Emily yelled as she kicked and felt her foot connect hard between Wesley's legs. "They are children!"

"Daddy loves us," Willow pleaded to get Emily to stop. "He is going to marry us, so no man can ever hurt us."

Emily watched as all of the girls looked at the ground. As if what had happened to them was their fault, and they were ashamed.
This did nothing but fuel the anger that Emily felt.

"Ava?" Ethan asked, looking at his daughter.

"He didn't touch me, dadDadAva insisted. "I had to go back, or he would take Willow as his next wife instead of me. I had to protect her."

"You did good, baby," Ethan said as he pulled his daughter close.

Shawn let go of Emily and turned his attention towards Wesley.

"Who would you rather your little girl be with?" Wesley asked Shawn. "A boy who will hurt her and leave her, or a man like me who will teach her a woman's place!"

Emily didn't even see Shawn make a fist or swing. However, the cracking sound that came when Shawn struck his face echoed all around her. Wesley went limp and didn't move.

"Is he dead?" Sam asked.

Shawn didn't answer as he stood back up straight. Emily looked down at Wesley and could see precisely where Shawn's fist had connected with his face. His face was bleeding and dented, but his chest continued to rise and fall.

"He's breathing," Emily replied to Sam. "Barely."

"Please don't!" Willow cried as she ran over to Wesley.

"Please don't hurt my daddy!"

Emily's heart broke for the little girl. She had no understanding that what Wesley was doing was wrong, if she even understood what he was doing at all.

"Willow," Emily said as she knelt. "Willow, he's a bad man."

"I know," Willow cried. "But he's the only parent I've ever had."

"Willow," Emily began thinking that maybe she was too young to remember her parents before the flash.

"No!" Willow yelled, still trying to protect Wesley. "I didn't have a mommy or daddy before. I live with people who were mean and changed houses all the time."

Emily finally understood what Willow was trying to tell her. Willow was an orphan before the flash, probably bouncing from foster home to foster home. It was a miracle that she had even survived the flash alone. Wesley promised her something she had always dreamed of, a family.

"He's not a good daddy," Ava said as she walked away from her father and towards Willow. "Daddies are supposed to love you, tell you stories, and make the monsters go away."

"Why can't I have a daddy?!" Willow cried, turning back to Emily. "What's wrong with me?!"

Emily didn't know what to say. There was nothing wrong with Willow, of course. She had just been a victim, and Wesley continued the trend. Emily searched for the words to convince Willow as the little girl looked at her with tears streaming down her face.

"There's nothing wrong with you," Doc spoke behind her. "You are an amazing little girl and deserve a great dad."

"Then why can't I find him?!" Willow cried, backing away from Wesley.

"Sometimes you have to go through a lot of bad before you find the good," Emily replied. "And I'm so sorry you had to go through so much bad."

"But we will help you find the good," Doc answered. "And we will all always be there for you, no matter what. We will take care of each other."

"Why?" Willow continued to cry as she wiped some of the tears from her face.

"Because we're a family," Doc smiled. "And that's what family does."

"Promise?!" Willow yelled at Doc. Suddenly, Willow jumped up off the ground and held out her little pinky to Doc. "Promise, you'll always be there."

Emily watched in silence as the scene unfolded. Doc looked at the little girl's finger as if it were the most important decision of his life. In truth, Emily knew that it was. Doc wasn't planning on just making a promise for the entire community, but for himself. He was going to be promising to take care of Willow, to be the father she never had.

"I promise," Doc said firmly as he wrapped his pinky around Willows. "I promise that until the day I leave this earth, I will always be there for you. I will love you. I will teach you. I will dry
your tears and work every day to make you smile."

Willow looked at Doc, surprised by how specific his promise was. Emily knew what had just happened. This was a postapocalyptic adoption, and she most definitely approved.

"Are you saying you'll be my daddy?" Willow asked, looking at Doc.

"Until the day I die," Doc promised. "And who knows if that will even stop me."

Emily felt a tear roll down her face as Willow threw her arms around Doc's neck. Doc hugged Willow and pulled her close. Everyone had momentarily forgotten about Wesley, who still lay bleeding on the ground.

"No!" Wesley yelled, ruining the perfect moment. "She's mine! They're all mine!"

"No!" Sophie yelled back at him. "We were never yours, and we never will be! I hope you burn in Hell!"

Emily watched as Wesley tried to pull himself back towards the closed gate. She knew that he had no way of escaping, but he seemed determined to do so.

"It's over, Wesley," Emily said as she walked towards him.
"You will never hurt another child again."

"Shawn!" Wesley yelled as he looked past Emily. "You need to get this woman in line!"

"I don't think so," Shawn replied through gritted teeth. "I'm not in the habit of telling any woman, let alone the boss, what to do."

Wesley seemed to panic as his eyes flashed back to Emily.
Emily simply nodded, confirming what Shawn had said.

"Get the kids out of here," Emily said to everyone. "Only the council is to remain."

Emily watched as Doc handed Willow to June, and the other girls followed June back into Sanctuary. It took a few minutes, but soon only the council stood with Wesley.

"What's your plan?" Wesley spat at Emily as they all gathered around him. "Stare at me until I'm a changed man?"

"Any arguments for life?" Emily asked, looking around her.
Everyone shook their head in response.

"We've never shed blood inside the walls," Doc spoke up. "I don't think we should change it for this piece of crap."

"I agree," Jacob added, his fists clenched hard at his side.

"I'll open the gate," Emily said as they turned to walk to the control panel.

"Mommy?" Hope said as she walked around the inner gate.

"What's going on?"

"The council is handling a problem," Emily replied as she entered the code. "I need you to stay with Ms. June while we take care of this."

"I'm part of the council," Hope insisted as she tried to follow Emily through the gate.

"No," Emily said as she turned to stop her. "Not this time." "But I have to learn," Hope pouted.

"Please," Emily softened her voice. "Not this time. I need you to help Ms. June take care of the new girls. You give them their tour and help get them fresh clothes."

"All by myself?" Hope asked, looking back at the girls.

"Yes." Emily breathed a sigh of relief that Hope was no longer insisting on coming with her.

"And I will learn about the council stuff you're doing later?" Hope asked, looking back at Emily.

"I pray you never have to," Emily smiled as she tucked Hope's hair behind her ear. "Can you please take care of them for me?"

"I got it," Hope nodded.

Emily watched as Hope walked over to June and the girls. Hope immediately began speaking, and June looked at Emily. Emily nodded to June, who understood and nodded back. Emily then went back through the gate, where Shawn was already dragging Wesley outside.

"You can't do this!" Wesley screamed. "This is murder!" "Shut up," Jacob spat at him as he kicked Wesley.

"You must have a daughter," Wesley said as Shawn let go of him outside the gate. "Is she pretty?"

Emily knew that while Terra was his niece, he loved her as a daughter. He was the only parent she had left now in this world, and he would protect that girl no matter what the cost. Emily closed the gate as Jacob punched Wesley hard in the face. Somehow, Wesley managed to laugh after the punch connected.

"I'll take that as a yes," Wesley smiled at Jacob.

"Two of you with such pretty daughters, and both of you probably stuck with old hags!" Wesley yelled. "I let you live here the way you want. Why not let me leave and live the way I want?
Jealous that I get the young ones?"

Howard was the one to step forward this time and slug Wesley.

"You're sick!" Howard spat as he stepped back.

"Sick implies I can help him," Doc said, shaking with anger.
"I don't know what the fuck he is."

Emily had never heard Doc talk this way before. She knew that his emotions were overtaking him. Their emotions were overtaking them all.

"Get him up," Emily said to no one in particular.

Shawn lifted Wesley to his knees and forced him to look at Emily.

"We've only had to do this one time before," Emily said, looking at him. "It was quick, and we ensured their souls were set free. But those girls are going to have to live every day for the rest of their lives with what you did to them."

"And I enjoyed every minute of it," Wesley smiled at her.

"You don't deserve to be free," Emily replied. "We'll remove your head and bury it in the woods. You will be stuck under the earth for all eternity, your soul unable to move on. Any objections?" Emily asked, looking around.

Everyone remained silent, and Emily had her answer. Emily stepped forward with her knife pulled from her waist. Wesley began to laugh as she walked towards him.

"You don't have the …."

Emily moved quickly as she slid the blade across his throat. Red blood quickly covered the front of his shirt and spilled onto the ground. Shawn let go of the body, and it collapsed into a heap on the ground. No one said anything but watched as the blood pooled around them.

"We'll burn the body and bury the head," Shawn said as he stepped around the body and towards Emily. "We'll be careful not to damage the brain."

Emily let go of her knife as Shawn pulled it from her hand.

"Emily," Jacob said, pulling her attention away from the corpse. "We need to get inside for a shovel."

"Of course," Emily said as she entered the code and opened the gate.

By the time Jacob returned, Shawn had removed Wesley's head, just as the eyes had opened, revealing their milky white color. Shawn carried the head by the hair into the woods, and Emily knew they were burying it. Jose and Doc dragged the rest of the body over to the woods, away from the gate.

"We'll add it to the pit tomorrow," Jose said. "It's nearly burning day anyway."

Emily nodded and watched as Shawn and Jacob returned from the woods.

"Did I…" Emily began to ask, thinking that perhaps she had gone too far.

"No," Shawn interrupted her.

"Even hell was too good for that bastard," Jacob said as he tossed the shovel over his shoulder.

Emily stood and watched as most of the council walked back through the gate. Ahead, she could see Hope pointing and talking to the girls, telling them all about Sanctuary.

"She's safe," Shawn said as he took her hand. "Nothing is going to hurt her here."

"If they do," Emily replied, not looking at him. "I know just where to plant their head."

Chapter 14

Time flew by in Sanctuary as the months went on. Each girl had found a new family inside Sanctuary, each seeming to have a perfect fit. Doc adopted Willow, and the little girl became his whole world. Doc confessed that he always wanted children but was too busy with medical school to make it a reality. Willow was thrilled with the arrangement and announced she wanted to be a doctor just like him.

Howard and June adopted Sophie. She was forced to grow up way too fast, so she seemed to relate to them easily. Howard and June had been unable to have children of their own and looked forward to helping Sophie grow up and her baby. Sophie had decided to keep the baby. She made it clear she never wanted the baby to know its father; she didn't want it to carry that burden.

Zoey found a home with Cole. She was younger than his daughter, but the two of them instantly had a connection. After school, Zoey could be found in the garage with Cole, helping to work on all of the cars.

The sisters, Becca and Riley, were adopted by Adam and Violet. While not big players in Sanctuary, they were awe-inspiring people. They had been teachers before the flash, and both currently worked at the school. Emily reassigned them from an apartment to a house to make room for the kids. The girls were thrilled to stick together, and Adam and Violet were finally excited to start their family.

The last girl, Brook, took longer to place, but eventually, the perfect home became apparent. Brook didn't speak much but seemed to open up when she was around animals. After one of her after-school trips to the barn, Jacob followed her home and insisted she stay with him. It was the first time Brook ever spoke a complete sentence since arriving when she told Emily the farm was her home and Jacob was her day.

Emily had considered adopting some of the girls herself. However, as the families stepped forward and saw what a perfect match they were, she knew it was not meant to be. Shawn had teased her that Hope was enough to handle, but Emily knew deep down that she wanted another child. She kept this to herself, though, unsure how Shawn would feel about having that talk. Even worse, she feared that he would tell her it was not something he wanted. For now, Emily wanted to enjoy the good times as they came.

The leaves shifted colors, and fall settled in on Sanctuary.

The town threw another Halloween party, with Hope dressed up as Dorothy. While Marley was way too big for the role of Toto, Hope insisted that's who he was this year. Emily dressed as Glenda, and Shawn modified his bear costume to go as the cowardly lion. Emily took every spare moment she could find to sneak away from Shawn and check on his Christmas present. The bike that Cole had found was in rough shape, but he slowly restored it as the months ticked by. The biggest challenge they were having was keeping it a secret. Sam had sworn not to talk about it, and both he and Cole had withstood many interrogations by Shawn regarding Emily's "special request." Fall quickly changed to winter, and the main street was once again decorated like a Christmas card. Emily knew that she would give Shawn the completed motorcycle tomorrow, and all of his conspiracy theories could be stopped.

"I want to make Shawn a present," Hope said as they walked towards the town hall.

"Did you have anything in mind?" Emily asked, looking down at her. "Christmas is tomorrow."

"I know," Hope sighed. "I'm not sure what to make."

"What do you know that he likes?" Emily asked.

"Hmmm," Hope said, obviously deep in thought. "I have an idea, but I don't want to make him mad."

"How could you ever make him mad?" Emily asked.

"I don't want to make you mad either," Hope admitted, looking away from Emily.

"Spit it out," Emily insisted as they walked inside. "I promise I won't be mad."

"Well, I know that Chad is my daddy," Hope began slowly.

"Uh-huh," Emily nodded.

"But all of those girls got new daddies because theirs weren't around. I was wondering if it would be okay if I asked Shawn to be my new daddy?"

Emily was caught off guard by the question and stopped to look down at Hope.

"It's not a good idea, huh?" Hope asked, looking ashamed.

"That depends," Emily said, clearing her mind once more.

"Do you want Shawn to be your daddy just because you don't have one?"

"No," Hope said, shaking her head. "He does everything for me that a daddy is supposed to do. He loves me, takes care of me, helps me get out of trouble, and I know he will always be there."

Emily felt pride as she looked down at her little girl. Her second birthday was only a few months away, but she already had such a great big heart and understanding of the world around her.

"Those are the perfect reasons to ask him," Emily smiled down at Hope.

"Do you think he'll say yes?" Hope asked with a touch of fear in her voice.

"I think he will for all of the reasons you just said," Emily grinned.

"Then I'll make him a card," Hope said definitively. "I drew us as a family and put his name down as dad this time."

"There's some paper in my office if you want to get started," Emily nodded. "We have to leave for the pageant soon, so don't take too long."

"I won't," Hope yelled back as she took off for the office with Marley.

Emily walked to the office and sat down at the desk while Hope made her card. She had come here tonight just to update her journal before the pageant. Emily felt herself writing more slowly, giving Hope more time to finish her card.

"Done!" Hope yelled from the floor as she ran over and showed Emily her masterpiece.

"What do you think?"

"I think he'll love it," Emily smiled as she reached into her drawer and pulled out an envelope.

There wasn't much use for them here, but it seemed perfect to wrap up Hope's gift. Emily helped Hope fold the card and slide it neatly into the envelope. Hope sealed the envelope and wrote
Shawn's name on the front, along with "Do Not Open Until

Christmas!!"

"We'd better get going," Emily said, glancing at the clock. "We don't want to be late."

Hope handed Emily her card for safekeeping and ran for the door. Emily followed her to the church. Emily watched as Hope made her way upstairs with Marley to get ready. Hope was much too big this year to play the role of a baby and had been determined to keep her part a surprise. Emily made her way to the front, where Shawn was waiting.

"What's that?" Shawn asked as he spotted the envelope in Emily's hand.

"A present," Emily grinned back.

"For me," Shawn said, trying to get a closer look.

"It clearly says on it not to open until Christmas," Emily pointed out. "You will just have to wait until morning."

"Fine," Shawn sighed. "So, did you ever get her to tell you what part she is playing?"

"No," Emily said, shaking her head. "She is getting way too good at secrets."

Just then, Father Nathan walked out on the stage and signaled for everyone to quiet down. Emily took Shawn's hand and held her breath as the play began. It didn't take long for Emily to discover Hope's role. She was the Christmas Angel. Emily and the others all gave the kids a standing ovation at the end, Emily wiping a few tears from her face.

"Were you proud, mommy?" Hope asked as she came running up to them.

"Very," Emily nodded as she hugged Hope.

"I don't think it was a good fit," Shawn said after a moment.

"You don't think I was a good angel?" Hope asked, sounding hurt.

"You are way too pretty to be an angel," Shawn smiled down at her.

Hope instantly smiled and hugged Shawn.

"We have to get home," Hope insisted as she dragged them both towards the door. "If I don't get to bed soon, Santa is going to skip me."

"We wouldn't want that," Emily laughed as Hope dragged them out the door, and Marley followed.

Once they were home, Hope quickly dressed for bed and hugged them both goodnight. Emily returned downstairs after tucking her in and tucked the card into the branches of the tree.

"I'm not even going to get a hint about what's in there, am I?" Shawn asked, looking at the envelope.

"Nope," Emily smiled as she looked back at him.

"Fine," Shawn laughed. "But grown-ups still get theirs on Christmas Eve," Shawn said as he handed a box to Emily.

"What's this?" Emily asked as she took the box and lightly shook it.

"Just open it," Shawn said, rolling his eyes.

Emily slowly opened the box and looked inside. Emily couldn't help but gasp at what it contained. Inside the box was a diamond ring. It had never occurred to Emily that she was holding a ring box. Emily looked back at Shawn, who had moved to one knee. Shawn took the box from her hand and pulled the ring out.

"I knew that first day I saw you that I would give my life for yours," Shawn said as he held up the ring to her. "I know you had a bad go of marriage before, and it's the most cliché thing ever to propose on Christmas."

Emily couldn't help the little laugh that escaped her lips.

"But Christmas Eve is when your life started over, and it's the day I want to ask you to be my wife. I love you. Will you marry me?"

"Yes," Emily replied without hesitation.

Shawn slid the ring onto Emily's finger and stood up from the floor. Emily wrapped her arms around his neck as he stood and felt him lift her off the ground as they kissed.

"You know this means you'll have to give up the apartment," Emily laughed.

"I'm here more anyway," Shawn smiled as he kissed her again.

"You just had to go and win Christmas," Emily said, looking down at the ring. "And I thought for sure my gift was a lock this year."

"I get a gift," Shawn said, sounding like a bit of a kid. "All I wanted was for you to say yes, but I'll take another present."

"Follow me," Emily said as she led Shawn to the dining room.

Cole had moved the motorcycle here earlier and covered it with a blanket. As they never used this room unless they had company, Emily didn't find it hard to hide from Shawn. Emily flipped on the light, walked over, and pulled the blanket off.

"Are you serious!" Shawn exclaimed as he ran over to the bike.

"This was the special request," Emily smiled at him. "Cole converted it and fixed it up for me. Do you like it?"

"I officially have the coolest wife ever," Shawn said as he looked over the motorcycle. "We're going for a ride."

"It's late, and Cole said this thing would be loud," Emily objected.

"Yeah, but I know he warned everyone because I wouldn't be able to resist," Shawn said as he began to push the bike out the door.

"Shawn, wait!" Emily called after him as she chased him out onto the porch. Shawn had already found the board Cole had used for a ramp and moved the motorcycle onto the street.

"Just one quick ride," Shawn said as he sat down and looked over at Emily.

"Quick," Emily repeated as she climbed onto the bike with him.

Shawn started the motorcycle, and even though Emily couldn't see it, she knew he was smiling. A wave of joy washed over him as the motorcycle began to move forward. Emily wrapped her arms around his waist and buried her face into his back to block it from the harsh, cold air. Shawn seemed unfazed by it as he drove through the streets. Emily knew he was driving the empty streets first and repeating. However, she remained silent and enjoyed the ride. Emily felt the motorcycle slow and come to a stop. She lifted her head to see that they were back at the house. Emily carefully climbed off and waited for Shawn to follow her.

"I should probably keep it inside," Shawn said, looking at his present. "The cold weather's not good for them."

"You can set it up where the tree is in the morning," Emily laughed. "But for tonight, it can be back in the dining room."

Cole had warned her that there was no way Shawn would leave it outside. When she suggested that it would become part of her new living room look, Emily hadn't realized.

"You just have to promise it won't fall over and crush Hope," Emily laughed as he pushed it back up the ramp.

"I'll teach her safety first thing in the morning," Shawn said as he entered the house.

"After Santa?" Emily asked.

"After Santa," Shawn nodded as he put the bike back up on the stand.

"You like it?" Emily asked as he walked back towards her.

"I love it," Shawn answered as he wrapped his arms around her. "You want to marry me?"

"Hell yeah," Emily smiled back at him.

Emily jumped from the ground as Shawn lifted her and wrapped her legs around his waist.

"Ready for your next present?" Shawn teased as he took off running for the stairs.

Emily laughed as she wrapped her arms around his neck, and Shawn ran up the stairs. Emily closed the door gently behind them as Shawn lay her on the bed.

"I love you," Shawn said as he ran his hand over her hair.

"I love you too," Emily replied, looking deeply into his eyes.

"Mommy! Shawn!" Hope's voice called out from downstairs. "Hurry! Santa came! Santa came!"

Emily slowly opened her eyes and looked up at Shawn.

"Does she ever sleep in?" Shawn asked as he stretched.

"Nope," Emily laughed as she kissed him. "You'd better get moving, or she'll come looking for us."

"And with the lack of clothes, that would be…bad," Shawn teased.

"Very," Emily nodded as she tossed back the blankets and stood up.

Emily quickly got dressed and brushed her hair. Shawn had just finished making the bed when Hope burst through the door.

"No time!" Hope yelled, looking at Shawn. "We'll fix it later."

"We're coming," Shawn laughed as he headed for the door.

Emily grabbed his hand as they walked out of the room and down the stairs. Hope was sitting by the tree, clutching an envelope in her hand.

"I know you guys do your presents at night," Hope said, looking at them.

"She said yes," Shawn smiled down at Hope.

"You knew?!" Emily said in shock.

"Shawn said he wouldn't marry you unless I was okay with it," Hope nodded. "I had to say yes before you could."

"You little stinker," Emily said as she reached out to tickle Hope.

"Stop!" Hope laughed. "This is for you."

Emily stepped back and watched as Shawn carefully opened the envelope and pulled out the picture. Shawn carefully looked over it, as he always does when she gives him a drawing.

"This is great--" Shawn trailed off. Emily knew that he had noticed the label under the drawing of him. He looked over at Emily, who just smiled, and then back at Hope.

"You are everything a daddy is supposed to be," Hope said to him. "You love me, and I know you will always be there. I thought since grown-ups can ask each other to be together forever, maybe kids can too. Shawn, will you be my daddy?"

Shawn looked at Emily once more, who could do nothing but smile.

"I had to say yes before she asked you," Emily said to let Shawn know that it was okay with her.

"It would be my honor," Shawn said as he kneeled and hugged Hope.

"This has to be the best Christmas ever," Emily cried as she bent down to join them.

"Alright," Shawn said after a few minutes. "That's enough tears on Christmas. You ready to open these things, kid?"

"Yes, dadDaddyHope smiled as she reached for her first present.

Shawn stood and wiped a tear from his eye as he watched her. Emily stood up and wrapped her arms around him.

"You okay there, big guy?" Emily asked him softly.

"I didn't see that coming," Shawn smiled.

"You sure you're okay with it?" Emily asked.

"This picture says, 'Dad," Shawn said, holding up the drawing. "I will fight the person who tries to take it from me."

"Two life-long commitments in one day," Emily smiled. "You think you can handle it?"

"Definitely," Shawn said as he kissed her.

Emily and Shawn turned their attention back to Hope as she opened a new book. Hope flipped through pages excitedly and thanked Santa, wherever he was. The gift under the tree that Emily had marked from Mom was a small necklace. She had found it at one of the houses, and the green reminded her of Oz. Hope saw the same thing and insisted it be put on her right away. Shawn gave Hope a toy gun that shot darts.

"She had to start somewhere," Shawn laughed as she opened it. "She asked for shooting lessons. I thought this was a good compromise."

"Good call," Emily laughed.

"Will it stop a monster?" Hope said, looking at Shawn.

"It stops closet monsters and bed monsters," Shawn answered.

"What about the ones outside?" Hope asked as she looked at the gun.

"Those are my job right now," Shawn answered. "But if you get good with the closet and bed monsters, we'll talk about moving you up to the outside monsters."

"Did you guys have to start with closet and bed monsters?" Hope asked.

"Oh, yeah," Emily nodded. "And I had to wait until I was older than you even to try those."

"Look out, monsters," Hope said as she pointed the toy across the room.

"Remember, she may only be one, but she is mentally and physically almost six," Shawn whispered to Emily.

"I would be nervous if she were six," Emily smiled.

"I should have asked first," Shawn said with apologetic eyes.

"No," Emily insisted. "It was a good compromise. Good call, Dad."

"That's weird," Shawn laughed.

"You'll get used to it," Emily smiled at him.

"Mommy? Daddy?" Hope asked as she stood up. "Can we have breakfast now?"

Chapter 15

All of Sanctuary was buzzing over the engagement, and Hope kept turning heads every time she called Shawn Daddy. Everything was finally falling into place for Emily. Everyone kept asking Emily when the ceremony would be, especially Father Nathan. Emily and Shawn decided to take it like the rest of their relationship. They weren't going to force it and let it happen as it would.

Shawn planned on officially moving out of his apartment in the spring, though he stayed at Emily's house every night. Once the Christmas tree was down, Shawn quickly moved the motorcycle into the living room. One of his new favorite times had become carefully wiping down each part. Emily was just thankful that it didn't have an oil leak that would get on the floor.

The following months flew by, and before Emily realized it, it was February. Shawn had been sneaking around for weeks, determined to give his girls a perfect Valentine's Day. Emily had tried her best to snoop, but the constant arrival of new people kept her busy. Hope had become a fixture at what they began to call the orientations. Jose had converted one of the office buildings into a classroom. Emily took to telling everyone about Sanctuary, answering questions, and assigning them jobs from there. Hope liked the setup more than taking everyone to their house. The people were still asked to wait at least a night to make their final decision, but most were put up with host families. Emily still took some into her house on occasion, but not regularly.

The newest group was still settling in, and the mood in Sanctuary was hard for them to adjust to. It was officially Valentine's Day, and love was definitely in the air. Jacob was working with Jessica to put together wildflowers for everyone to get. Julia was making extra sweets for everyone to share with their sweeties. Everyone seemed to be even more caring than usual.

"Daddy says me and him are doing lunch, and then it's you and him for dinner," Hope said as she walked with Marley and Emily.

"That's what he told me," Emily smiled down at her. "Are you excited?"

"Yeah," Hope said, almost jumping up and down. "He says I got a present."

"What about me?" Emily asked.

"I don't know," Hope said, shrugging her shoulders.

Emily smiled because she knew Hope was keeping a secret, just like she did at Christmas. Emily already knew that Shawn was giving Hope a new journal. Hope talked about how she wanted to keep one, and Shawn would make a big deal out of it. Emily felt sure that whatever Shawn had planned for her tonight, Hope was his co-conspirator.

"Do we have to get a baby monitor?" Hope asked as Emily opened the door to the store.

"It's either that or I will need to get you a babysitter for the night," Emily said as she ushered Hope inside.

"But Marley will be with me," Hope said as she petted the dog on the head.

"You both need a babysitter," Emily laughed. "It's just so if you need us. You have to call out."

"And I don't always have to keep it in my room, right?"
Hope said, looking at Emily.

"Right," Emily nodded. "You only have to have it when
both
Daddy and I aren't home at night."

"No room for negotiation," Hope said, looking at
Emily.

This was Hope's new favorite thing. She had learned
about negotiations in school and tried to negotiate every
chance she got.

"Zero," Emily replied.

Emily walked over to the counter where Jessica was
waiting with the baby monitor.

"You two have big plans tonight?" Jessica asked as they
neared.

"Daddy is taking us each on a date," Hope smiled.

"That sounds like fun," Jessica smiled.

"What about you?" Emily asked. "Any big plans?"

"Still the single life for me," Jessica smiled. "My prince
hasn't found this place yet."

"He will," Hope smiled. "Or we will go out and find
him." Jessica laughed as she handed Emily the baby
monitor.

"Don't work all night," Emily said as she turned with
Hope to leave. "Spoil yourself and put your feet up."

"I think I will," Jessica nodded. "You two have fun."

Emily walked back outside with Hope to find Shawn
waiting for them.

"Is it time?!" Hope asked excitedly.

"It sure is," Shawn said as he handed Hope a flower.
"Are you ready?"

"Yes!" Hope yelled as she ran towards Shawn.

"Have fun!" Emily called after them as they began to walk away.

Emily turned and walked back home with Marley. Emily made her way inside the house and set up a few household chores. It was rare that she was home alone these days, and she would take the opportunity to catch up on things. Emily had just finished the last of the laundry when the front door flew open.

"Honey, we're home!" Shawn yelled playfully into the house.

"Did you guys have fun?" Emily asked as she walked into the living room.

"Look what Daddy got me!" Hope said, holding up her journal. "Now I can write everything down, just like you!"

"That's pretty cool," Emily smiled as she pretended to look at the journal for the first time. "Why don't you go put that up in your room so you can write in it before bed?"

"Yes, mommy," Hope smiled as she took off for the staircase with Marley right behind her.

"What else did you guys do?" Emily asked Shawn as he sat down on the couch.

"We went to the farm and had a picnic and then went horseback riding," Shawn sounded exhausted. "Not as easy as I remember, and Hope didn't make it any easier." "What do you mean?" Emily asked.

"Jacob asked me if I had ridden before, and before I could answer, Hope told him I rode a hog," Shawn replied. "It took us twenty minutes to convince her I did not ride a pig!" "That's awesome!" Emily laughed.

"No, it's not," Shawn said, shaking his head.

"At one point, Jacob suggested I just ride the pig to make her happy."

"He better have called if you did," Emily continued to laugh.

"Keep making fun," Shawn warned her.

"And no surprise for you."

"I'm sorry," Emily pleaded as she crawled into his lap. "Please forgive me."

"That's better," Shawn said, trying to sound firm.

"So, when do we need to be ready to go?" Emily asked, looking down at her cleaning clothes.

"Hope ate a ton at lunch, so I'm not sure she'll want dinner," Shawn replied.

"Probably in the next hour or so."

"I'd better go get ready then," Emily said as she stood up.

"I have a few things to set up, but I'll be back in time to lay her down," Shawn said as he stood up as well.

"I love this," Emily said as she wrapped her arms around him.

"Domesticating me?" Shawn said as he looked down at her.

"You're still wild," Emily laughed. "I love having our little family."

"Me too," Shawn smiled and then kissed her.

"I love you!" Emily called after him as he made his way towards the door.

"I love you too!" Shawn called back.

Emily quickly made her way upstairs and took a quick shower. Emily looked through her closet, deciding what to wear, when Hope slowly opened the door.

"What are you doing?" Hope asked, looking at her.

Emily usually just reached in and threw on whatever. Hope had never seen her take so long to pick out what she was wearing. It had been years since Emily was on a date, and she realized she didn't remember how to do this.

"Trying to figure out what to wear," Emily replied as she looked through the clothes once more.

"You always know what to wear," Hope said as she climbed onto the bed with Marley.

"I always know where I'm going," Emily replied. "It's hard to pick something out when you don't know what you're doing."

"Daddy hung something new in there yesterday," Hope smiled. "Jessica helped him pick it out for tonight.

Emily moved quickly through the hangers and spotted something she hadn't seen before.

"This?" Emily asked as she pulled the hanger from the closet.

"That's it," Hope smiled, looking at the red dress.

It was pretty short with no sleeves. Emily couldn't help but think it would show all of her bite scars. While Shawn said they didn't bother him, she was still self-conscious about it. Emily stood staring at the dress, debating running down to the store and finding something else.

"Just put it on!" Hope laughed.

"I'll try it," Emily said as she stepped back into the bathroom.

Emily slipped into the dress and quickly fixed her hair. Emily stood and looked at herself in the mirror. The dress fit perfectly and, if it wasn't for the scars, she looked terrific in it.

"I don't know," Emily said as she opened the bathroom door.

"You look beautiful!" Hope said as her eyes widened.

"You think so?" Emily asked, tugging at the dress, trying to hide her scars.

"I know so," Hope nodded as she jumped down from the bed. "The shoes are down there, too."

Emily reached into the bottom of the closet and pulled out a pair of red flats as Hope left the room. Their date was dress-worthy, but heels were out of the question. Emily slipped into the shoes and looked at herself once more. She watched as she began to tug on the dress once more.

"Stop it!" Emily yelled at herself. "You got this."

Emily grabbed the baby monitor from the bed and headed to Hope's room.

"You hungry?" Emily asked as she walked in. Hope was lying on her bed with Marley, writing away in her book.

"No," Hope said, shaking her head. "I'm still way full."

"Alright," Emily laughed. "Let's get you changed into your pajamas before daddy gets home."

"It's still okay if I read a little while before I go to sleep, right?" Hope asked as she began to change her clothes.

"As long as you are in bed by the time the sun goes down," Emily smiled.

"Are we all ready in here?" Shawn asked as he walked through the door.

Emily turned and couldn't help but blush. Shawn had stopped mid-step and was staring at Emily.

"Wow," Shawn finally spoke.

"Good wow or bad wow?" Emily asked, placing her hand on her hip.

"Good," Shawn replied as he walked across the room.

Emily watched as Shawn scooped up Hope and her book and set them on the bed.

"You know the rules," Shawn said to Hope.

"You can read until the sun goes down, you don't leave the house, and you just speak into the monitor if you need anything."

"I got it," Hope nodded. "Doesn't she look pretty?" Hope whispered to Shawn.

"Very," Shawn whispered back. "You be good."

Emily walked over as Shawn stood up and kissed Hope on top of the head.

"Love you," Hope said as she leaned against her pillow and opened her book.

"Love you too," Emily and Shawn replied as they walked out of the room.

Shawn took Emily by the hand with a smile and started to walk towards the staircase. Emily felt her feet plant as they reached the bedroom door.

"What's wrong?" Shawn asked as he turned back to her.

"Maybe I should get a jacket or something," Emily said as she began to pull at the dress once more.

"You earned every one of those scars," Shawn said as he took both of her hands.

"Each one signifies at least one life you saved." Shawn moved his hand along her shoulder. "Hope," he said as he touched the scar. "Cole," he continued as he felt her wrist. "And seven little girls," Shawn said, looking down at her thigh. "If anyone can't see how sexy that makes you, send them to me."

Emily was blushing as she walked past the door and down the stairs with Shawn. Emily couldn't help but notice that the motorcycle was no longer in the living room when they reached the bottom. Shawn continued walking like nothing out of the ordinary was happening.

"I promise to go slow," Shawn said as he opened the door and pointed at the motorcycle.

"Not exactly dress-friendly," Emily laughed.

"I disagree," Shawn winked at her.

Shawn walked Emily down the stairs and helped her up onto the seat. Emily knew they could walk anywhere in Sanctuary without a problem, but Shawn was going to take every opportunity to drive the motorcycle. Emily held on to Shawn as he drove through the streets. Emily couldn't help but laugh as he returned to the main street and stopped by the stairs.

"We've arrived," Shawn said as he climbed off and then
helped Emily.

"I'm glad traffic wasn't horrible," Emily teased back.

Shawn took Emily by the hand and led her up the stairs. Emily smiled at Margaret, who was in the control room for her shift.

"Are you working?" Emily asked as Shawn began to lead her to the control room.

"No," Shawn laughed as they walked past Margaret as she left. Emily smiled as she looked at the meal set up on the small dining table.

"This is the first place I saw you."

"I didn't get to see you until the clinic, though," Emily looked back at him.

"I thought about that," Shawn nodded. "I think this location is better."

"Agreed," Emily smiled as she walked towards the table with Shawn.

Shawn pulled out her chair and helped her sit down at the table.

"This is just the first stop," Shawn told her as he sat down.

"So, don't overeat."

Emily set the baby monitor on the table and began to eat the plate of food that Shawn had set in front of her. They talked for what seemed like hours, and the sun started to set.

"Good night," Hope said to Marley. Emily and Shawn listened as Hope crawled under the blankets and, within minutes, was snoring.

"Before all of this," Shawn said, motioning all around. "People would have had our heads for leaving a one-year-old home alone."

"She's almost two," Emily corrected him.

"And it is the size of a six-year-old. I guess that doesn't change things."

"It just shows what you've created," Shawn said. "We know that if she sneaks out, there are over a hundred people here who will take her home and put her back to bed."

"It is amazing," Emily said as she took her last bite of food.

"Let's get you walking before you fall into a food coma," Shawn teased as he grabbed the baby monitor and stood up.

"Sounds good," Emily said as she stood up to join him.

Shawn wrapped his arm around her waist, and they walked
around the wall together. It had been a while since Emily
looked at their progress, but the trees were cleared a
reasonable distance back. Shawn stopped about halfway and
led Emily towards the ledge. Emily was glad not to be in heels
for this part of the date. She was never the best at walking in
them and probably would have fallen by now.

"Ready for your first present?" Shawn smiled at her as
he reached into his vest pocket.

"First?" Emily smiled at him.

Shawn handed Emily a box and then leaned back.
Emily carefully opened the box while Shawn leaned against
the wall and watched. Inside was a small locket which Emily
quickly opened. There was a picture of Shawn and Hope, and
on the other was a photo of her family.

"Jessica helped me get them the right size," Shawn
said.

"It's beautiful," Emily smiled as she closed the locket
and moved to put it on.

"Let me help," Shawn said as he took the chain, and
Emily turned around. "There," Shawn said as he connected the
clasp.

"It's perfect," Emily said, looking down at the locket.

"I have just one more surprise for you if you're up to
it," Shawn said as he took her hand.

"I think I can manage," Emily smiled.

Emily walked with Shawn around the rest of the wall
and back to the control room. Shawn led Emily over the ledge
where two glasses were sitting. Emily thought she was
dreaming when she looked inside.

"It took us a while to get the machine running," Shawn
    said.
"I hope you like vanilla."
Emily carefully picked up the class and lifted the spoon.
Emily slid the spoon into her mouth and felt the cold sensation
run over her tongue.
"Ice cream," Emily whispered as she swallowed the
first bite. "Oh, how I've missed you."
Shawn laughed as he picked up his glass and took a
bite. Emily smiled at him as she slowly worked her way
through the entire glass and set it back on the ledge.
"That decides it," Emily smiled at Shawn.
"Decides what?" Shawn asked as he set his glass down
as well.
"You are my Prince Charming," Emily replied.
"All it took was ice cream?" Shawn laughed as he
wrapped his arms around her.
"I thought it would take more, too, but here we are,"
Emily teased.
Shawn didn't say anything and instead lightly kissed
Emily. Emily felt like she was floating and was blissful for a
moment. Then the world began to spin around her, and she
attempted to cling to Shawn to keep from falling.
"Emily?" Shawn asked as he looked down at her.
"What's going on?"
Emily tried to find the words, but like her mind was
falling into a dark pit, the world was too far out of her reach.
"Emily!" Shawn yelled as he gently laid her on the cool
metal floor. Emily could hear everything around her but
couldn't get her body to respond.

"Doc, something's wrong with Emily!" Shawn yelled into the walkie. "Get to the wall now!"

Emily heard a muffled voice answer him, but couldn't make out the words.

"Hold on, babe," Shawn said as he ran his hand over her hair.

"Love you," Emily heard herself barely whisper. She couldn't even be sure if Shawn heard her. Immediately after, the dark came crashing down, and Emily was sealed away from everyone and everything.

Chapter 16

Emily was back at home and sitting on her couch. Hope had just come through the door from school and was upstairs playing. Shawn came in and walked past her without a word as Marley followed him. Emily tried to speak to each of them as they passed, but no words came out. None of them looked at or talked to her as they continually passed her. Emily tried to get up off the couch, but her body would not move. Emily's mind began to race as she tried to find a way to get her family to notice something was wrong.

Darkness began to creep closer from all corners of the room. Emily watched as it swallowed everything until she and the couch were all that remained. Silent tears streamed down her face as the darkness drew closer. Emily willed herself to scream, but no sound came out. All at once, the darkness swallowed her, and she was trapped once more.

"Was she allergic?" Shawn's voice spoke beside her.

"It wasn't the ice cream," Doc insisted.

"Then what was it!?" Shawn yelled out of frustration.

"I'm working as fast as I can!" Doc yelled back at him. "It could be a million different things!"

"You have to find it!" Shawn continued to yell.

"I'm trying!" Doc spat back at him.

"I can't lose her," Shawn's voice felt soft as he took Emily by the hand.

Emily could hear their voices, and she could feel Shawn's touch. The darkness had retreated, and she was her once more. However, Emily still couldn't will her body to speak or move in any way. Emily had been awake and unable to speak before, but she was always able to move in some way. She could feel Shawn watching her, looking for any signs of movement.

"Can she hear me?" Shawn asked as he adjusted her hand in his.

"I don't know," Doc admitted. "Everything I check says there's nothing wrong with her."

"What about the bites?" Shawn asked. "She didn't even get tired after the last one."

"Nothing obvious on the blood work," Doc said. "I'm trying to find something, anything, that looks out of place."

"Emily," Shawn said, choking back tears. "If you can hear me, hold on. Please, baby, just hold on."

Emily screamed inside her head that she was there. She willed her fingers to move, even a little, to show him that she could hear him.

"Mommy?" Hope's voice rang out heavy with tears.

"She's sleeping," Shawn said, quickly gathering himself.

"When will she wake up?" Hope asked as she moved closer.

'I don't know," Shawn replied, his voice breaking with pain once more.

"Mommy," Hope cried. "Mommy, please wake up."

Emily fought with everything she had. Her head began to ache from screaming so loudly in her mind. But her body remained still and her voice silent.

"I'm scared, Daddy," Hope said.

Emily felt like her voice was further away, almost down a long tunnel. Emily knew the darkness was trying to take her over once more. Emily clawed and fought to pull herself back up, but the darkness overtook her once more.

Emily continued this way for what seemed like years. She would have moments where she was in the clinic, listening to voices around her, and then being pulled back down. Other times, she was at home or even in the town hall, but no one noticed she was there. The darkness always crept back and always pulled her down.

"It's been almost a month," Shawn's voice was saying today.

Emily decided that the times she could hear and feel but not see were real.

"The toxin levels are dropping slowly," Doc replied. "I have no way of knowing how long it will take or if she'll wake up."

"She will," Shawn said firmly. "You hear me, Emily, you are going to wake up."

"We're waiting for my party," Hope said next. "It's not a birthday without you."

Emily felt her heartbreak as Hope spoke. For a moment, she thought she had imagined it as the warm tear ran down her cheek.

"Daddy, look!" Hope said as she came closer to Emily.

"Doc!" Shawn called out as he touched the top of Emily's head.

"What happened?" Doc asked as he began to check Emily's vitals.

"I told her I was waiting for my birthday," Hope said. "And she started crying."

"Still no response," Doc said as he took a step back.

"Does this mean she can hear us?" Shawn asked with hope in his voice.

"I can't know for sure," Doc admitted. "But I believe it does."

"She can," Hope said firmly. "She's been able to the whole time."

"How do you know?" Shawn asked Hope.

"I just do," Hope said. "You can't explain everything."

"She's right about that," Doc nodded. "Hold on, Emily," Doc said as he leaned down.

"You're through the worst of it."

As Doc finished speaking, the darkness came once more. Emily cursed it for pulling her away when they finally knew she was there. Emily stayed in the dark this time. No mental retreats to the light or hearing the voices surrounding her hospital bed. Just Emily's thoughts, all that she was, alone in the dark.

"Any change, Doc?" Shawn asked as he walked into the room.

"The toxin levels are gone, but she remains unconscious," Doc replied. "I do believe I found the source."

"What was it?" Shawn asked as he sat down beside Emily.

"It's the bites," Doc replied. "While her body is immune to the infection that most of us get, her mind is not."

"So, her mind shuts her body down to recover from the toxins?" Shawn asked.

"I believe so," Doc replied. "However, if that is the case, she should have woken up when the toxin levels dropped to zero last week."

"She will," Shawn said as he took her hand.

"When she does," Doc said as he stepped closer. "We now know the levels at which her mind will shut everything down."

"She'll be lucky if I let her outside the wall again," Shawn said as he kissed her hand.

"Try and stop me," Emily spoke.

The room fell silent, and even Emily was confused. She had thought it, but did she just say that?

"Emily?!" Shawn said as he leaned closer.

Emily tried to open her eyes for the first time in weeks. The room's bright lights made everything appear white and even caused her some pain, but she welcomed it. Emily squinted and allowed her eyes to adjust. Emily watched as Shawn's face slowly came into focus above her.

"I said, try and stop me," Emily smiled at him.

Shawn let out a slight laugh and pulled Emily into his arms. Emily tried to lift her arms to hug him back, but only got them a few inches off the bed before she was forced to let them drop once more.

"You're awake," Shawn breathed into her hair.

"I just needed a little nap," Emily replied.

"Two months is not a little nap," Shawn said as he pulled away.

"What's going on with your arms?" Doc asked as he walked back over.

"They just feel weak," Emily answered. "It's exhausting to try to pick them up."

"Just rest them for now," Doc said after checking all of her reflexes. "You can try to move them again in a few hours."

Emily watched as Doc walked out of the room and left her and Shawn alone.

"You scared the shit out of me," Shawn said, clinging to her hand.

"Sorry, I ruined our date," Emily smiled. "Is there any ice cream left?"

"All you want," Shawn smiled.

"How's Hope?" Emily asked.

"Officially two, but looking and sounding seven. She insists that everyone keeps saying she's one," Shawn explained.

"Because she couldn't have her birthday without me," Emily smiled. "I need to get up and get a party planned."

"You lie still," Shawn insisted. "You could hear us?"

"Sometimes," Emily replied. "I was only able to be here for so long, and then it was like I was pulled down into a pit. Sometimes I could hear you guys and get pulled away, and others I was in my mind and got pulled away."

"Shit," Shawn said as he ran his hand over her hair.

"What happened?" Emily asked. "Something about a toxin from the bites?"

"It took Doc a while to see, and he had to compare it to your other blood samples," Shawn explained. "Every time you are bitten, your body fights the infection before it can spread."

"That's supposed to be a good thing," Emily said, looking at him.

"It is," Shawn continued. "But every bit of the infection your body kills is turned into a toxin. The more of it that's in your blood and the longer it's there, it begins to shut down your body."

"So, two bites in a year was not good," Emily sighed.

"Doc had to put you on dialysis to get it out faster," Shawn explained. "But because it was so bad, he couldn't be sure if you would wake up. We couldn't be sure you were hearing us."

"Hope told you I could," Emily smiled at him. "You know how smart she is."

"Yeah," Shawn said as he moved his hand to Emily's cheek.

"We have to be more careful."

"We will," Emily replied. Emily hadn't realized she had moved her head until she felt Shawn's hand under her face.

"Hope will be here in a few minutes for her visit," Shawn said as he looked down at her.

"She comes by every day."

"Can you help me sit up?" Emily said as she pushed her hands against the bed.

"Doc said to wait and try again in a few hours.

"Please," Emily begged him. "She's seen enough of me lying here."

Shawn nodded and leaned over Emily. Emily wrapped her arms around his neck while he pulled her up into a sitting position.

When she was steady, Emily kept her arms tightly around Shawn.

Shawn said nothing and hugged her back.

"Mommy?" Hope's voice pulled them out of the embrace as she entered the room. "Mommy!"

Hope ran towards the bed and climbed into Emily's lap, wrapping her arms around Emily. Marley jumped up and put his top half on the bed to join them.

"Hey there, Monkey," Emily smiled into Hope's hair.

"I told them you would wake up," Hope grinned as she looked at Emily.

"I know," Emily smiled. "You were right about it all."

"Really?!" Hope smiled as she looked at Shawn.

"We were just talking about your birthday party," Emily smiled. "Thanks for waiting for me."

"I love you, mommy," Hope said as she hugged Emily once more.

"I love you too," Emily smiled.

The three of them sat for a long time discussing the plans for Hope's birthday. Shawn would be taking care of most of it, as
Emily would be forced to continue to rest. By the time Shawn took Hope home to put her in bed, Emily could move almost entirely independently. Her muscles were still stiff from lying in bed for two months, but she could live with that. Shawn returned the following day, delivering Emily a bowl of ice cream for breakfast.

"You pass out again, and you are never eating another bite of that stuff," Shawn teased.

"I won't," Emily smiled as she took a bite. "I promise."

Emily ate her ice cream with a smile while Shawn sat laughing at her.

"So, what did I miss?" Emily asked as she took her last bite.

"We have time to catch up later," Shawn replied. "You just need to rest."

"I have been resting for months," Emily insisted. "I hate feeling like I'm not doing anything."

"You're not going to let me out of here without telling you, are you?" Shawn asked, already knowing the answer.

Shawn took a deep breath and straightened himself in the chair.

"We had four new groups," Shawn began. "Hope let them all in. I helped her with their orientation, and they have all agreed to stay. There are twenty-seven in total."

"Wow," Emily said as she took a moment to let the number sink in. There were people inside the walls she had not met for the first time.

"They all seem like good people," Shawn continued. "I used your notes and gave them each a job."

"Sounds like everything is taken care of," Emily replied, feeling unneeded.

"Not quite," Shawn replied. "Hope told them all that it was just temporary. That they had to wait for you to make it official and sign the ledger."

"There was no need for that," Emily said, swallowing her pride. "If you both think they're a good fit, you could have made it official."

"Not a chance," Shawn laughed. "You're in charge. We were just filling in. The final call is and always will be yours."

"I'm just saying, in this type of instance…." Emily began.

"Nope," Shawn interrupted. "Hope and I both agreed that you had to make the final call."

"I hate that they have all been waiting so long," Emily replied. "Waiting to see if I'll kick them out or if they get to stay."

"It has been a little nerve-racking for them," Shawn admitted. "But they all say they understand when I check in on them."

"Anything else?" Emily asked.

"Sophie is due to have her baby any day now," Shawn continued. "I think the kid is waiting for you to awake before it makes its grand entrance."

"How's Sophie doing?" Emily asked.

"Good," Shawn nodded. "Better than expected. She had her moments, but I think she's got this."

"She's a strong girl," Emily agreed. "But I get the feeling there's something bad that you just don't want to tell me." "I was trying not to," Shawn said, more seriously.

"What is it?" Emily pressed.

"There were actually five groups," Shawn replied with a heavy sigh. "One of them started freaking out. They started screaming and shooting. The dead came out of the woods faster than we could get out of the gate."

"The dead got them," Emily summed up.

"Yeah," Shawn replied. "We buried them in the cemetery. We didn't know their names, but it just seemed like something we should do."

"I agree," Emily said. "We can't save everyone. Isn't that what you told me?"

"Yeah, but it's harder when you have to make the call that we can't save them," Shawn admitted.

Emily knew what he was feeling. It was challenging to make the final decision of who they could save and who they couldn't. However, she agreed with his decision based on what he told her.

"You did the right thing," Emily assured him. "Now, let's get the information on all of those new people, shall we?" "Tomorrow," Shawn said, shaking his head.

"I'll bring everything in the morning and have them come by to meet you in the afternoon."

"What am I supposed to do until then?" Emily asked, raising her arms and allowing them to fall on the bed. "I am going stir crazy in here. First, I was locked inside my head for two months, and now I'm locked in here."

"I hadn't thought of it like that," Shawn laughed. "I'll ask Doc if you can go for a *short* walk today to help build up your strength."

"And maybe we can...." Emily smiled at him.

"Just a walk," Shawn interrupted her. "You have to promise me, or I'm not asking."

"Just a walk," Emily said as pouty as she could. "I promise."

"Hope learns this from you," Shawn laughed. "You know that, right?"

"I think she's been a bad influence on me," Emily replied.

"Right," Shawn laughed as he stood up and left the room.

Emily tried hard to listen to the hushed voices on the other side of the door, but couldn't understand what they were saying. Emily quickly straightened herself in the bed as the door opened.

"The movement would do you good," Doc said as he walked in and looked at her. "I've told Shawn as long as he helps you up the stairs, you can walk the wall one time."

"Why the wall?" Emily asked, confused.

"Because in town, there are people you can talk to and try to work," Shawn answered.

"Exactly," Doc replied.

"I'll take it," Emily smiled. "Anything to get out and move."

"Radio if she gets dizzy or anything happens," Doc instructed Shawn as he walked out.

"Let's go," Shawn said as he reached down to help Emily out of bed.

"Actually," Emily said as she pulled away from him. "I'm not sure my current outfit is appropriate for the wall."

Emily looked down at the hospital gown she was wearing. While she was desperate to get out, she had no desire to show her bum to the world while she walked.

"I'll run home and get you some pants," Shawn laughed. "I think you look amazing, though."

"Of course, you do," Emily said, rolling her eyes.

Shawn winked at her as he left the room. Emily waited patiently until he returned with fresh clothes, a hairbrush, and a tie.

"Do you need help?" Shawn asked as Emily sat up.

"I need to try at least," Emily replied as she removed the gown and slipped on her shirt.

Emily pulled her pants onto her legs, but discovered that she was not strong enough to bend over and pull them up quite yet. Shawn didn't say anything as he helped her. Emily sat back down on the bed, brushed through her tangled hair, and put it back. She already felt more like herself. Emily took Shawn by the arm and walked out of the room. Emily stopped just outside the clinic door and felt the sun hit her face. Emily stood and enjoyed the warmth for quite a while. When she looked back at Shawn, he was simply watching her, smiling.

"What?" Emily smiled.

"Let's get married," Shawn replied.

"I already said yes to that," Emily said as she held up her ring.

"No," Shawn replied. "Let's set the date as soon as you are free to come home. I don't want to wait anymore."

"Me either," Emily replied as she leaned up, and Shawn bent over to kiss her.

Chapter 17

It had been nearly a week since Emily had woken up, and Doc had finally agreed she could go home. Emily felt that part of him felt guilty for not catching the toxin sooner. She had been walking on her own for days, but he still insisted that she stay.

Emily wasn't going to stay there today, and Doc knew it. Sanctuary had pulled together and was having Hope's second birthday tonight. Shawn had helped Emily secure a gift, but refused to cook anything. Emily knew that Shawn was okay with basic cooking. However, the last time he tried to bake, everyone thought their house was burning down because of the smoke.

Emily walked under the strings of lights that hung in the street towards the house. The motorcycle was propped up on the porch, telling Emily that Shawn was inside. He rode it every chance he got and had even snuck Hope on a few rides while Emily was down. Emily opened the front door and walked in.

Before she could speak, the sound of nails dragging on the hardwood floor filled the air. Marley came bounding towards her and jumped up to greet her.

"Hey there," Emily said as she petted his head. "I just saw you yesterday."

Marley continued, as if they had not seen each other in years, as he licked her face.

"You are going to get us both killed if you don't stop scratching these floors!" Shawn yelled as he walked into the living room.

"I think his nails need to be cut," Emily smiled at Shawn as Marley jumped down.

"I thought Doc said this afternoon," Shawn said as he looked around the house.

"I talked him into letting me go a little early," Emily said as she looked around the house. "What happened?"

Emily had just cleaned the house the night she got sick, and now she barely recognized it. Clothes covered most of the furniture; she didn't dare ask if they were clean or dirty, and toys were scattered everywhere. The house looked like it had not been cleaned in a year, and a pack of wild children had taken over.

"It got away from me a little bit," Shawn admitted as he looked around.

"A little bit," Emily laughed.

"I was going to have it fixed before you came home," Shawn smiled at her, trying to keep from getting in trouble.

"How bad is Hope's room?" Emily asked, trying to assess the damage.

"Pristine," Shawn sighed. "Much like you, she has the routine down."

"And the kitchen?" Emily asked as she took a step forward.

"I insist you don't go in there for your safety," Shawn said as he blocked their path.

"I think the things in there have taken on a mind of their own."

"Oh my," Emily laughed, craning her neck to try to get a glimpse. "Why don't I work out here and let you handle whatever monster you've created in there?"

"I can handle it," Shawn said as he looked around. "Why don't you go upstairs and rest?"

"Or I could sit on the couch and sort through laundry," Emily said as she walked over to the couch. "Please tell me all of this is clean?"

"Yes," Shawn smiled. "Just didn't have time to do the whole, put-it-away thing."

"You go slay the kitchen monster, and I'll work on this," Emily laughed.

"I didn't want you to have to come home and clean," Shawn said with regret in his voice. "It was just with my job and your work and taking care of Hope, it all got away from me."

"I don't mind," Emily assured him. "We are partners, and we are supposed to help each other. You made sure this place kept running. I can help catch up with a little laundry in exchange."

"Alright," Shawn smiled as he turned back to the kitchen. "I'm going in."

"My hero!" Emily yelled after him as she began to fold the clothes.

By the time Emily had finished, she felt confident there was not a single clothing item left upstairs. It looked like Shawn and Hope had been coming down here in the morning, finding what they needed and moving on.

"Hope!" Emily called out once she had finished.

It was only a moment before Emily could hear Hope running down the stairs.

"Mommy!" Hope celebrated as she ran around the couch.

"Hey, Monkey," Emily smiled at her. "I need you to pick up all your stuff in here and then take your clothes up and put them away."

"I guess we did let it get a little messy," Hope said, looking around.

"Shawn is battling the kitchen monster right now," Emily laughed. "I just need you to do your part, alright?"

"Yes, mommy," Hope smiled as she grabbed her first stack of clothes and headed upstairs.

"Are you making her clean on her birthday?" Shawn asked as he walked back into the living room.

"Did you win the fight?" Emily laughed as she turned to face him.

The front of Shawn's t-shirt was drenched with water and clung to his chest and stomach.

"I did," Shawn laughed. "The kitchen monster is no more."

"My brave knight," Emily smiled as Shawn kissed her.

"I'll get this stuff upstairs and then come back to finish cleaning up," Shawn said as he grabbed a stack of clothes. "Unless you want to come upstairs with me?"

"I can show you where the clothes go," Hope replied innocently behind him.

"Uh, I got it," Shawn smiled awkwardly as he walked past Hope and upstairs.

Emily straightened up the coffee table and anything she could reach from the couch while the laundry was carried up one load at a time. She was just getting ready to get up and move on to another section when Hope appeared to clean up her toys, and Shawn set to work on everything else. It doesn't take them long to finish, and soon Shawn was sitting next to Emily on the couch.

"I've figured out your secret," Shawn smiled at her. "I now know how you keep this place so clean." "Secret?" Emily laughed.

"Yeah, you make Hope help," Shawn smiled. "I was trying to do everything."

"I make her take care of her stuff," Emily laughed. "And Marley in the morning."

"She took care of Marley and her room," Shawn replied. "But I didn't realize she put away her laundry or picked up her toys down here."

"If she can make the mess, she can clean it," Emily smiled. "No wonder you got so overwhelmed."

"I will never call you lazy again," Shawn said as he leaned back against the couch.

"Do you still need help upstairs?" Emily teased.

"That was the worst timing ever!" Shawn said as he rubbed his face. "I couldn't even look at her."

"She is getting very good at that," Emily laughed.

A knock on the door interrupted their laughter. Emily waited on the couch while Shawn went to answer it.

"Who knocks on this door?" Shawn said as he walked towards the door.

Emily sat silent, as she already knew who was on the other side. Bobby was the only person in town who knocked on her door, especially during the day.

"She's on the couch," Shawn said, and moments later, Bobby walked into the living room.

"Hello, Bobby," Emily said as she sat up.

"I just wanted to make sure you are okay," Bobby smiled. "Mom said you were, but I haven't seen you in a while."

"I'm all better," Emily smiled. "You ready for the party tonight?"

"I made the cookies for you," Bobby smiled as he looked back at Shawn. "She said it was safer that way."

"Not funny," Shawn said as he sat down on the couch beside Emily.

"Tell her thank you," Emily smiled back.

Shawn rolled his eyes and let out an audible sigh. He was not finding either her or Bobby amusing today.

"I'd better get back," Bobby said as he turned towards the door. "I'm glad you're feeling better."

"Thank you," Emily replied. "I'll see you in a while."

Emily relaxed against the couch as the front door closed, and she was once again alone with Shawn.

"I think he's got a crush on you," Shawn suddenly stated.

"What!?" Emily laughed.

"I'm surprised he didn't bring flowers and come to steal you away from me," Shawn teased.

"Keep it up," Emily said as she pushed her shoulder into his. "I have options now."

"Oh my!" Shawn laughed. "Now I have to scare a child away from you."

"I don't think he'll scare easily," Emily smiled. "He used to bring me dinner when Hope was still in diapers to make sure I ate." "Really?!" Shawn said with a look of shock. "I got showed up by that little twerp?" "He's a real gentleman," Emily smiled.

"Who is?" Hope asked as she walked around the couch to join them.

"Bobby is," Shawn said shortly.

"He is," Hope declared as she sat between them on the couch.

"You too?!" Shawn exclaimed as he began to tickle Hope.

Hope squirmed on the couch as she laughed, trying to escape the tickles.

"Mommy, help!" Hope called when she realized she was trapped.

"Alright," Emily laughed as she reached over Hope for Shawn.

"Hey," Shawn said as he slid to the opposite side of the couch. "No fair, two against one."

"Men can be such babies," Hope smiled at Emily.

"I know," Emily laughed. "You'd better go get ready for the party."

Hope slid off the couch just before Shawn could catch her and run upstairs with Marley.

"I am so outnumbered," Shawn sighed. "We'd better have a boy so I can have a partner too."

"A boy?" Emily asked, both happy and surprised. She knew that she wanted to have another child, but she and Shawn had never had a chance to talk about it. Part of her feared that he might not want to have any children.

"Or a girl," Shawn said as he looked at her.

"As long as it's healthy and on my side of these fights."

Emily leaned across the couch and kissed Shawn.

"What was that for?" Shawn asked.

"Being perfect," Emily said as she lay her head on his chest.

"You know what, I'm just going to go with it," Shawn said as he wrapped his arm around her.

"I've been thinking about the date," Emily said as she listened to Shawn's heartbeat.

"How about August twenty-eighth?"

"Oddly specific," Shawn said. "And close. Can we have everything ready in time?"

"As long as we are there, everything else will work out fine," Emily smiled.

"I don't think I have anything planned," Shawn smiled. "Count me in."

"We'll tell everyone tomorrow," Emily said.

"We'll let Hope have her party tonight."

"Agreed," Shawn said. "Now you rest, or I'm going to make you stay home."

Emily wanted to argue with an intelligent comment, but she suddenly felt relaxed and exhausted. Emily had been afraid to sleep since she woke up. She was worried that the darkness would come back and she would lose more time. Emily let a yawn escape and felt herself drift off to sleep to the rhythm of Shawn's heart.

"Should we wake her up?" Hope was whispering in front of Emily. "I think the party has started."

"You go on out, and we'll be out in a few minutes," Shawn whispered back.

"You promise she'll wake up?" Hope whispered with concern.

"I'm up," Emily whispered to Hope as she opened her eyes. "You head out, and we'll be right behind you."

Hope smiled and took off out the front door with Marley.

"You were out," Shawn said as he stretched once Emily sat up.

"I haven't been sleeping well since, well, since I woke up last week," Emily explained.

"Doc says you're good," Shawn smiled at her. "That means you have nothing to worry about."

"Then let's get up and get out to the party," Emily said as she stood up.

"We're still keeping the date to ourselves until tomorrow," Shawn said. "Right?"

"Yeah," Emily nodded. "Hope's birthday and two-year town celebration tonight."

"You might want to fix your hair before you go out. Unless you want to look like that for the picture," Shawn laughed.

Emily reached up and felt that her hair was standing about six inches above her head. Emily quickly made her way to the bathroom and fixed herself so that she did not look like a mad scientist. Shawn took her by the hand once she returned and led her outside. Emily had met everyone who arrived while she was sick and officially welcomed them all to Sanctuary. The crowd was quite a bit bigger than the year before, but Emily knew each of their faces.

"Everyone, report for pictures," Sarah's voice rang out over the speaker system.

Shawn led Emily down the porch to their traditional spot on the front. Everyone squeezed into the yard while Jessica put them all in perfect position. Emily knew that the picture would have to spread to the street if they grew much more. Emily placed her hand on Hope's shoulder as she stood between her and Shawn while Marley lay in front of them.

"Ready!" Jessica yelled as she ran over to join them.

Emily smiled and looked at the camera as the flash went off. After checking the photo, Jessica ran back around and signaled that they were good. Hope immediately took off with Marley to play with the other kids. Shawn led Emily through the party, allowing her to talk to people she had not been able to see since she got sick. Everyone seemed thrilled to see her, and Alec nearly broke her spine. He hugged her so tight. Soon it was time for cake and presents. Hope took her time opening each gift, making sure to thank each person. However, the civilized lady turned into a cake monster as soon as Julia set her slice in front of her.

"I think she may have a problem," Shawn laughed as Hope inhaled her piece of cake.

"Do they have special meetings for people like her?" Emily smiled.

"There's no one like her," Shawn grinned.

Emily hugged his arm as they watched Hope enjoy a second slice of cake. Once she was done, the music was turned up, and everyone began to dance and celebrate. Emily danced a few songs with Hope while burning off her sugar high.

"Can I dance with Daddy?" Hope asked as the song ended.

"Of course," Emily smiled. "I need to sit down for a minute." "Are you alright?" Shawn asked with a face full of concern.

"I'm just tired," Emily assured him. "Consequences of spending two months in bed."

Emily made her way over to a chair and sat down. She watched as Hope and Shawn danced their way around the dance floor. Emily laughed and clapped for them when they did a big finish.

"So," Julia said as she sat down next to Emily. "Anything you want to tell me?"

"The cake's amazing?" Emily smiled at her friend.

"Not that," Julia said as she slowly shook her head no.

"Ummm, thank you," Emily said, not sure what Julia could be talking about.

"I mean wedding news!" Julia finally blurted out. "Any hints about what season we are looking at?"

"Definitely summer," Emily replied with a smile.

"This summer?!" Julia asked with excitement.

"We haven't decided that yet," Emily lied, hoping that Julia wouldn't notice. "We're not rushing."

"But I will be if you tell me last minute," Julia laughed.

"I promise you at least three months' notice," Emily said after a few minutes. "Will that work?"

"It's better than three days," Julia sneered, looking at Emily. "I get the feeling you're hiding something from me."

"May I have this dance?" Ben asked as he walked up beside them.

"Yes," Emily replied as she took his hand and stood up.

Emily knew that if anyone could make her crack, it was Julia. Emily followed Ben out onto the dance floor as a slow song played.

"You looked like you were a little cornered there," Ben smiled as they began to dance.

"Thank you," Emily smiled. "People are going crazy over this engagement."

"It gives them something to look forward to," Ben smiled. "If you and Shawn can make it down that aisle, it means that anyone here can do anything."

"No pressure," Emily laughed.

"None at all," Ben assured her. "You have earned your happiness. We want to help any way we can."

"I appreciate it," Emily said as she twirled around the floor with Ben.

"You off chasing younger women again?" Margaret said as the dance ended.

"He'll have to keep looking," Shawn replied as he took Emily by the hand. "This one's mine."

"Thank you for the dance," Emily smiled at Ben as Shawn began to lead her toward the house. Emily looked at the yard to see Hope curled up in her party dress, her head resting on Marley, asleep.

"She passed out a few minutes ago," Shawn laughed as he picked up Hope from the ground. "I thought you would want to say good night before I took her in."

"Good night," Emily said as she lightly kissed Hope on the forehead.

"Good night, mommy," Hope replied, not opening her eyes.

Emily waited in the yard while Shawn carried Hope inside and tucked her in. Marley followed Shawn in and didn't return when Shawn came back out. With Shawn sharing Emily's bed, Marley had moved to sleeping in Hope's room full-time. While Emily sometimes missed him, she was happy to know that Hope would always have him close.

"You got one more dance in you?" Shawn asked as he wrapped his arms around her.

"For you," Emily said as she pretended to think. "Always."

Chapter 18

Emily and Shawn made their announcement the following day. Julia nearly jumped out of her skin with excitement. It was now May, and Emily felt like her head would explode from all the wedding planning. Everyone seemed to want to contribute, even those who had not been there very long. Between running Sanctuary and the wedding plans, Emily found it harder and harder to sneak away with Shawn for even a few minutes. Emily was sitting at her desk at town hall, finishing going over the supply reports. Emily had just finished putting everything away when Shawn walked in. Marley immediately jumped up from the floor and ran over to greet him.

"Shhh," Shawn said to Marley.

"Are you trying to be sneaky?" Emily laughed as she closed the filing cabinet drawer.

"It's like every time we get a moment, someone appears to drag one of us away," Shawn continued to whisper as he walked towards her.

"Very true," Emily nodded as she whispered back.

"Hi," Shawn whispered as he wrapped his arms around her.

"Hi," Emily whispered back as she leaned up to kiss Shawn.

"Emily, Shawn," Sarah's voice rang out of the walkie just as their lips met.

"Damn!" Shawn said as he lowered Emily back to the ground. "Does she have a camera in here?"

Emily laughed as he looked around the room while she grabbed her walkie.

"Go ahead," Emily said as she pressed the button.

"We've got some new ones," Sarah replied.

"How far out?" Emily asked.

Emily had welcomed so many groups that she no longer asked how many, names, or anything like that. That information never helped when it came time to help them inside. There would be time to learn that once they were all safe.

"Fifteen, maybe twenty minutes," Sarah replied. "They are on the logging road now."

"On our way," Emily replied as she put the walkie back on her waist.

"I heard we have ten, maybe fifteen minutes before we're needed," Shawn said as he pulled her closer.

"And the second we start something, they will be at that gate," Emily smiled at him.

"Let's get these new folks settled, and I'll see if Hope can spend the night with a babysitter. We'll go radio silent."

"Alright," Shawn pouted as he let her go and took her hand. "I never thought I'd miss the days we went outside and fought the zombies."

"You miss it," Emily laughed. "We still go out to clean the pits."

"Yeah," Shawn said. "But I miss the runs where I would get to be alone with you in the truck."

"Me too," Emily said as she lay her head on his shoulder. "Maybe we should just take the bike out one day and look for people."

"Get lost for a day or two," Shawn smiled down at her.

"Sounds like a honeymoon in an apocalypse to me," Emily laughed.

"I'll make the reservations," Shawn laughed as well.

"We've got a problem!" Sarah's voice rang out.

"Told you," Emily said as she let go of Shawn and took off running for the COM building.

"You're nearly there!" Margaret was yelling into the radio. "Stop making all that noise!"

Emily had never heard Margaret yell before, especially at newcomers.

"What's going on?" Emily asked as she, Shawn, and Marley walked closer.

"One of the women is tired of walking," Margaret said, still angry. "She decided to start making noise so we could find them and come pick them up."

"Are you kidding me?!" Shawn said with disbelief.

"Sam reported hearing shots a few moments ago," Margaret continued. "We turned on the speakers, but with the noise she's making, I'm not sure it will help."

"Where the fuck are you people!" a woman's voice rang out.

"You are nearly here," Margaret repeated. "Our people will meet you at the gate when you arrive."

"Do you know who I am?!" the woman screamed at Margaret. "I am too important to walk another step. Get out here and pick me up."

Emily reached over Margaret and pressed the radio button. "With the noise you have made, I can't risk any of my people," Emily said with authority. "You will need to get moving, or the dead will overrun you."

"You're going to get us all killed!" someone yelled in the background.

"Shut up, old man!" the woman yelled back at him. "My father will have these people's heads if they do not come to get me."

"Shots fired," Sam's voice rang out. "We can see the dead making their way through the trees. They have to get out of there!"

"The dead are coming!" Emily yelled into the radio. "If you can hear me, run now!"

"Listen here, you, stupid bitch!" the woman yelled. "You come to get me, or you will regret it."

"That woman is going to get them all killed," Margaret said, looking at the walkie.

"We don't risk our lives for those who aren't willing to save themselves," Emily replied.

"We don't know them. This could be a trap to draw us out."

"So, we just let them die?" Julia asked, shocked.

"We have done all we can," Emily replied. "If they get close enough, we will help any way we can, but they chose this fate."

"She did," Margaret corrected her. "The young man I talked to before was very nice and reasonable. I gathered that he didn't care for this woman much."

"I'll go to the on wall and watch," Emily said to both Julia and Margaret. "If they get within range, we'll provide cover fire to help them inside."

"Seems more than fair," Shawn nodded.

Emily walked out of the COM building and headed up the wall. Emily stood beside Sam and looked out.

"If they get within range, provide them cover fire," Emily told him. "They have to make it that far on their own with the mess they've stirred up."

"We got it," Sam nodded.

Emily reached down and placed her hand on the handle of her knife. She had decided to keep it with her at all times inside the wall. With her being the first to meet new people and spending so much time around them, it made sense to make sure she could always defend herself. Standing here, watching the dead move in the trees and looking for the people on the road, it brought her comfort to feel the handle in her hand.

"There," Sam pointed down at the road. "They've got children with them."

"Shit!" Emily said as she looked down at the scene.

The group was out of range, and the road behind them was filled with zombies.

"I don't think they're going to make it," Shawn said beside her.

"Have Sarah turn up the speakers to max," Emily replied. "We'll help them as best we can."

Emily pulled her walkie from her waist and changed the station to the same one that the outside ones were set to.

"You have to get closer," Emily said. "We are trying to draw them away, but the ones closest aren't going to fall for it."

"If I make it inside…!" the woman's voice rang out.

"Please," a man's voice came over the radio. "If we tell the kids to run ahead, can you at least let them in?"

Emily stood in shock, looking at the walkie. Emily reached over, took Sam's rifle from his hand, and pointed out where the people were. They were still out of range, but the scope gave her a clearer view. Emily felt her heart leap into her throat as she pulled her eye away from the scope and handed the rifle back to Sam.

"I'm going out," Emily said as she turned and ran for the stairs with Marley.

"Emily!" Shawn said as he grabbed her arm.

"We risk our lives for family only. Not for dumbasses who summon an entire city of zombies down on their heads."

"They are family," Emily said as she pulled her arm out of his grasp and ran down the stairs. Emily entered the outer gate code and drew her knife as she walked out.

"Watch the gate!" Shawn yelled behind her.

Emily didn't stop to close it as she ran up the logging road with Marley. She knew that Shawn was behind her, but she had quite a head start on him. Emily confirmed what she saw as she ran closer and tightened her grip on her knife. Emily reached one of the children just as a zombie was reaching for them. Emily quickly killed it and threw it away.

"Get to the gate!" Emily yelled at the boy, who ran without looking at her with two little girls.

Emily made her way towards the adults and helped kill several. Most adults began to run to follow the children without even glancing at Emily.

Only one man continued to fight, and Emily ran over to help him.

"We have to go," Emily yelled at him as they killed the last walker within striking distance.

"Not until they're safe," the man yelled back as he turned to look at her.

Joe's hair was quite long, and his face looked like it had not been washed in months. His clothes were covered in holes and dried blood. Even with his shaggy appearance, Emily recognized her brother when she saw him.

"We have to go, Joe," Emily said as she pulled his arm.

Joe finally moved from where he was planted and followed Emily as she ran back towards Sanctuary. Emily could hear the dead swarming behind her and pushed her legs as hard as she could. She never saw the rock that caught her toe, but felt the hard ground as her body crashed on top of it. At that moment, she realized how close the dead were as the all too familiar pain of a bite spread through her leg.

"Emily!" Joe yelled as he turned back.

Joe kicked the zombie away from her and helped her off the ground. Joe kept his arm around Emily as they ran the final distance to the gate.

"Hope!" Shawn yelled just as they ran through.

Emily leaned against the wall as the gates closed shut beside her. She glanced down at her leg and could see a fresh bit right next to her scar. She knew she was in for stitches and blood tests to ensure the toxin levels did not rise again. However, Emily couldn't care less about that right now. Emily slowly lifted her head and looked at all of the new people who had just arrived.

"Not again!" Christine cried, looking at Emily's leg.

"It's fine," Emily replied, still trying to catch her breath. "I don't get sick."

Shawn walked up beside her and wrapped his arm around her waist to take some of the pressure off her leg. Emily looked at each of their faces to ensure they were all there. Charlie, Margaret, Joe, Rachael, Dwayne, JR, Ann, and Caroline. Emily took her time looking at each of the kids, as they had all grown so much from when she last saw them.

"Aunt Emily?" JR said as he took a nervous step forward.

"You still getting into trouble?" Emily smiled at him.

JR looked up at Rachael for confirmation that he wasn't imagining things.

"Mommy?" Hope said as she walked through the inner gate slowly.

"I'm okay, monkey," Emily smiled at Hope.

"Do you need my help?" Hope asked as she looked at each of the people standing there.

Emily could see that Hope was trying to figure out why they seemed so familiar.

"Let me have Doc take a look at this leg and make sure they are okay," Emily smiled at her. "I'll call you when it's time for the tour."

"Okay," Hope replied as she slowly backed through the gate.

Emily looked down at Marley, who was watching Hope with concern.

"Go," Emily said to him as she nodded toward Hope. Marley didn't hesitate as he ran off to join her.

"Sit," Doc said as he set a chair down beside her. "You talk, I'll stitch."

"It was an accident," Emily said as she could tell Doc was frustrated with her.

"I heard talk about getting her a suit of armor," Doc said to Shawn. "I'll pitch in the credits to help fund this project."

"It was a special circumstance," Shawn said, looking down at Doc.

"It always is," Doc said as he washed the wound.

"Doc," Shawn said firmly. "It's her family."

"It's her..." Doc looked back at the faces that were all now staring at them. "Oh, my."

Doc smiled at Emily and quickly stitched up the bite and put on a bandage.

"Come by for blood work in the morning so we can keep an eye on your levels," Doc said as he stood up. "I'm sure you all need a moment."

Emily nodded as she stood up from the chair and walked towards her family. Her leg was tender and sore, but she wasn't going to let that stop her. Emily walked straight to Christine and stopped.

"Hi, Mom," Emily smiled at her.

Christine burst into tears as she hugged Emily and pulled

Emily into a hug. Emily hugged her mother and felt the rest of her family join in.

"How is this possible?" Charlie asked as they all pulled away. "We saw you get bitten. You just got bitten again."

"It's a rare genetic condition," Emily explained. "My body can kill the infection, and I don't turn."

"Not that there isn't a price," Shawn reminded her.

"My body turns the infection into a toxin that, in low doses, does nothing. It takes a while to burn out, and if I get bitten too many times, I go into a coma," Emily explained. "It's only happened once, and now Doc knows to keep an eye out for it."

"I don't care as long as you're alive," Christine said as she put both of her hands on Emily's face.

"I am," Emily smiled. "I tried to find you, but you weren't at the cabin when I got there."

"That's because bright boy decided to turn on the generator," Charlie said as he turned his head.

Emily followed his gaze and found herself looking at Chad. Emily waited to feel small or angry as he stared back at her. However, she felt nothing. Emily turned her gaze to the woman standing next to him, clutching his arm. She recognized her from the pictures on his cell phone, Veronica. Veronica was holding the hand of a little boy who appeared to be about two.

"It must have been her on the radio," Emily said as she turned her attention back to her family.

"Who was that girl?" Ann asked as she looked back through the gate.

"That's your cousin, Hope," Emily answered.

"You have a daughter?" Christine said as she covered her mouth, and tears welled up in her eyes.

"Do the math!" Chad yelled as he took a step forward. "That girl was five or six. Emily found a lost child and took her in because she couldn't do what a woman is supposed to."

Emily had to move fast to block Shawn's path. She knew that it wouldn't go well if Chad and Shawn ever met. But even she didn't expect it to go wrong with the first thing Chad said.

"Side effect of the bite," Doc said as he stepped forward.

Emily continued to block Shawn as he clenched his fist and teeth so hard that Emily thought he might explode.

"I delivered her myself two years ago," Doc continued. "Because Emily was pregnant when she was bitten, Hope grew fast in her first year of life. She has slowed down to a normal growth rate this past year."

"You were pregnant?" Rachael finally spoke. "Why didn't you tell us?"

"I didn't know," Emily smiled. "It was Hope and Marley that got me through. That gave me the strength and drive to find Sanctuary."

"While this is touching," Veronica spoke up. "Can we move on to speaking to the man in charge? I have some things that need to be addressed."

"Excuse me," Emily smiled at her family.

Emily looked up at Shawn, who still stood ready to attack. Emily knew he wouldn't relax and hoped that he would let her handle this.

"I told you we couldn't risk our people," Emily said as she walked towards Veronica.

"The only reason I came out was that I was willing to risk my life for my family."

"Nice," Veronica said, looking past Emily.

"If you don't want to talk, I guess we can move on," Emily said as she walked back over to stand by Shawn.

"I'm not talking to you!" Veronica yelled at her. "I want to talk to the person in charge!"

"I guess it's story time then," Emily smiled, ignoring Veronica. "I found this place Christmas Eve, the year of the flash. The gate was open, and I found the body of a man named Robert upstairs. Robert had been forced to contribute to the flash but managed to escape. He, in turn, built this place to help protect those who survived until a cure could be found."

"However, the flash happened ahead of schedule. Robert lost everyone inside and took his own life. He left behind his research, his plans, and this place. I lived here alone, vowing to never open the gate after the evil I had seen took root outside of it until I went into labor. I was prepared to deliver by myself, but the baby was breached. I knew that we were both going to die. A group found the gate that had a doctor with them. They were running from a group of rapists that I had escaped after learning that I was pregnant. Desperate and with no other options, I opened the gate. They each played a role in saving my baby and me. They decided that since I had found this place, taken care of it myself, and was the only one who knew the codes, I would be in charge."

Emily stood and watched as the smirk on Veronica's face turned to anger.

"I don't care who your father is," Emily said, looking Veronica in the eye. "You pull that crap again, and I will leave you."

Veronica gave Emily her best death glare, but Emily was unfazed. She looked over at Chad and recognized the look on his face. He was prepared to put Emily in her place, just like he had done the entire time they were married.

"Who do you think you are?" Chad said as he stepped in front of Veronica.

"Emily," Emily replied. "Who do you think you are?"

"First, you tell me that girl is my daughter," Chad said. "A daughter that you stole from me, and now you attack the mother of my son."

"First, she is my daughter, not yours," Emily replied. "She has a dad and didn't need you. Second of all, I'm addressing the bitch who nearly got my family killed because she didn't want to walk."

"So, she doesn't even know who I am?!" Chad began to yell. "You replaced me with my child!"

"She knows who you are," Emily corrected him. "Just a fairy tale glorified version so I wouldn't have to burden her with what a piece of shit you are."

"You can't…!" Chad said as he pointed his finger at her, shaking with anger.

"I don't have time for this," Emily replied. "Now, why don't you shut up and let me do my job!"

Chapter 19

As Emily turned her gaze away from Veronica and Chad, the tension was thick in the air. She couldn't help but notice that the rest of her family was smiling at what she had just said.

"This is Sanctuary," Emily said as she addressed them all once more. "The price of admission is an exam to make sure you are not at risk of infection. For a reason I've explained, if you are at risk, we will invite you to stay in our quarantine area for the night. We'll bring you a hot meal, and Doc will do everything he can to help you through it."

"What happens if we're not?" Chad asked forcefully.

"You will be invited inside," Emily continued. "We'll give you a tour, explain how things work, give you some fresh clothes, and a chance to wash up. Tomorrow, you will all be given a choice to stay or leave."

"I'm game," Charlie said as he walked forward. "Let's get this done, Doc."

"Right this way," Doc replied as he led Charlie into the small clinic.

It was only a few minutes before Charlie returned, and Christine went in. The process continued until only Chad, Veronica, and their son remained.

"We're going together," Chad said as he walked forward with Veronica and his son.

"That's fine," Doc smiled at them. "It may be just a bit tight."

Shawn finally moved as he turned to watch Chad walk into the clinic.

"I'm going to kill him," Shawn spoke through his clenched teeth.

"I'll help," Joe said as he walked over.

Shawn seemed to relax as he finally turned to face Joe. Emily watched as Shawn introduced himself to each member of her family.

"Mommy?" Hope's voice called from the gate once more.

"Come here, monkey," Emily smiled as she held her hand out to Hope.

Hope ran towards her with Marley. Marley ran straight to the kids to say hello to his lost playmates. Hope walked right past Emily and towards her family. Emily noticed that Hope was holding her fairy tale book in her arms. Hope had figured out where she knew their faces from.

"Grandma, Grandpa, Uncle Joe, Aunt Rachael, Uncle Dwayne, JR, Ann, and Caroline," Hope said as she pointed at each of them.

"That's right," Emily smiled. "They found us."

"Hi," Christine said as she kneeled.

"Grandma!" Hope yelled as she wrapped her arms around Christine.

Emily couldn't help the tear that escaped as she watched Hope hug each member of the family that she had only read about. The moment was everything she had dreamed of. That was until the door to the clinic opened. Emily watched as Hope turned and looked at Chad, who walked towards her. Hope clenched her storybook and walked to meet him. Emily had to fight the urge to grab Hope and run back through the gate.

"Are you Chad?" Hope asked Chad as she stood before him.

"Yeah," Chad said, looking down at her with disgust.

"You don't know me, but I'm Hope, your daughter," Hope smiled at him.

Emily's heart broke at how sweet Hope was being. She knew Hope was excited for this moment, and Chad would find a way to crush her.

"Is this your princess?" Hope said, looking at Veronica.

"This is Veronica," Chad answered her. "And our son, Steven."

"My brother!" Hope said excitedly.

"Half, apparently," Veronica sneered at Hope.

"I'm two. How old are you?" Hope asked Steven, not paying any mind to Veronica.

"He's two and a half," Veronica answered for Steven. "He's your older half-brother."

Hope took a step back and could see the hurt on her face. Emily had told Hope that her dad was not her prince charming, and they had agreed to look for their happily ever afters. However, she had not told her that Chad had started looking before Emily knew. "What's wrong with her?" Chad said, looking at Emily.

"I never told her about you meeting Veronica before we separated," Emily explained.

"Well, you just did!" Chad yelled at her. "Are you trying to make sure she hates me!"

"No," Shawn said, shaking his head. "Veronica did by saying Steven was two and a half. That's older than she is." "No child could put that together," Veronica replied. "Especially one her age."

"She's probably the smartest person standing here," Shawn answered. "She figured it out."

"Is it true?" Hope asked, looking at Chad with tears in her eyes.

"Yes," Chad said, rolling his eyes. "But it was her fault."

Emily stood still while Chad pointed at her. She knew that Chad would blame her, and she would not get sucked into this argument, not in front of Hope. Hope turned away from Chad and ran to Shawn. Shawn picked her up and held her.

"Hope," Emily said as she rubbed her daughter on the back. "Hope it's okay."

"Are they ready?" Hope asked as she looked at Emily, wiping her eyes.

"They are," Emily said softly. "But they can wait until you are."

"I'm ready," Hope said as she put on a brave face. "Can you walk with me, daddy?" Hope asked, looking at Shawn.

"Of course," Shawn said as he set her on the ground and took her by the hand.

"Everyone follow me," Hope said as she walked back through the gate with Shawn and Marley.

"Wait," Chad said as he reached out for Hope.

Marley quickly turned and bared his teeth at Chad. He had not forgotten him and all the pain he caused Emily.

"Enough!" Emily yelled.

Marley turned and walked back up beside Hope, but glanced back at Chad. Emily followed Hope through the gate, with everyone else behind her.

"That damn dog is insane," Chad said low enough he thought Emily couldn't hear him.

"What idiot tries to grab a little girl with a monster of a dog on one side and a grizzly bear on the other?" Dwayne laughed at Chad as he walked past.

Hope led the group up the main street, pointing at the buildings as she went and explaining each one. Emily remained silent and let Hope handle this part.

"And here, Jessica will help everyone get a fresh set of clothes. By the time you are done, we will have host households that will take you each for the night, where you can go to the shower. Yes, we have hot water," Hope smiled at all of them. "Once you're cleaned up, we'll meet back at the classroom so my mommy can tell you all about how jobs and the cards work."

"Very nice job," Charlie smiled down at Hope. "You get your public speaking from me."

Hope beamed with pride as she watched everyone walk inside. Hope stepped behind Shawn as Chad and Veronica passed by.

"You did great," Emily smiled at Hope to coax her out from behind Shawn.

"I don't like him," Hope said, looking back at the store. "Why didn't you tell me?"

"It's a hard thing to explain," Emily replied. "Just because your dad didn't love me doesn't mean he won't love you." "You still should have told me," Hope insisted.

"I'm sorry," Emily said as she kneeled. "I'll tell you the whole story if you want me to."

"Why doesn't Marley like him?" Hope asked as she petted Marley.

"Marley watched him break my heart," Emily answered. "You know how protective he is. He doesn't want Chad to hurt you."

"Can our family stay with us?" Hope asked. "Not Chad and Veronica but everyone else?"

"They can," Emily nodded. "I'm sure we can make room."

"We're not finding any volunteers for your ex," Alec said as he walked towards her.

"He can't stay with us," Hope said with panic in her voice.

"He won't," Alec assured Hope. "I'm going to take them."

"Are you sure?" Emily asked. Alec and his family were so sweet. She hated to put a poisonous snake like Chad in their house.

"We got this," Alec nodded. "I'm not scared of that toothpick."

Just as Alec finished, the door to the store opened, and everyone began to file back out onto the street.

"Chad, Veronica, and Steven," Alec called out. "You all will be staying with me."

"I don't think so," Veronica said as she curled her nose up at Alec.

"It's either that or the quarantine area," Emily replied. "There are no showers out there, so…."

"Fine," Veronica snorted. "Maybe I can teach them some style while I'm here."

"I'd be careful," Emily warned her. "His wife is a little bit of a spitfire."

Emily watched as Alec led them towards his house. She could tell from how his hands were moving that he told them the rules and warned them not to make his wife angry.

"What about us?" JR said, noticing that no one else was standing there.

"It will be tight," Emily smiled. "But we would like you all to stay with us. You are family, after all."

"I'm in," Joe smiled at her, and everyone else nodded.

"Right this way," Emily said as she turned and led everyone to the house. "We're here," Emily announced a few minutes later.

"You stepped up in the world, Em," Joe said, looking at the house.

"The first one here gets first dibs," Emily laughed as she led them to the porch.

"You suddenly become a thrill seeker?" Charlie asked, looking at the motorcycle.

"It's Shawn's," Emily laughed. "I never drive, only ride."

"Me too," Hope smiled.

Emily opened the front door and allowed Marley to run ahead of her. Emily walked into the living room and let her family gather around.

"There's a shower down here and two upstairs," Emily explained. "Mom and Dad can use the bedroom at the end of the hall. Rachael, you guys can use Hope's room. I'll get some extra cots to set up in there, and Joe, you get the couch."

"Step up from the last time I stayed at your place," Joe said, looking around.

"Where will Hope sleep then?" Rachael asked, not wanting to put Hope out.

"I always sleep in mommy's bed when new people come," Hope smiled. "You guys can play with my toys if you want."

"Toys?" Ann repeated, looking at Hope.

"I'll show you," Hope said as she took off for the stairs with her cousins and Marley behind her.

"Not until you're showered," Rachael yelled as she and Dwayne ran after them.

"You go ahead, Mom," Joe said as he motioned to the downstairs bathroom.

"How long does the hot water last?" Christine asked as she walked towards the bathroom.

"Until we run out of water," Emily smiled. "I expect you'll be in there a while."

"I need to go check on the wall," Shawn said as he turned to Emily. "With all the dead that got drawn in, we may need to burn the pits sooner than planned."

"Just radio if you need me," Emily smiled at him.

"Nice to meet you all," Shawn nodded to Joe and Charlie as he headed out the door.

"So, you got yourself a boyfriend?" Joe teased her as soon as Shawn was gone.

"What?" Emily laughed.

"Joe, I do believe they are engaged," Charlie corrected him.

"How did you guys know?" Emily asked as she played with her ring.

"First, that ring is way nicer than the one Chad gave you," Charlie pointed out.

"And a guy doesn't park his motorcycle at a friend's house. They keep them close, like in their living rooms, close," Joe added. "And I thought there was going to be nothing left of Chad but a greasy spot when he spoke to you."

"Hope was another big tell," Charlie spoke again. "I had already guessed he was the dad she chose."

"Well, you two have become regular detectives," Emily laughed. "And the motorcycle goes over there when it's inside."

Emily pointed to the spot where the motorcycle sat for the winter. Shawn still brought it in from time to time, especially if it was raining. Emily didn't know why she felt embarrassed that her family knew she was with Shawn so quickly. She had been thinking about how to tell them during Hope's entire tour.

"And speaking of a greasy spot," Emily looked at both of them. "How did you guys manage to keep from killing them out there?"

"It was your dying request that we find that woman and keep the baby safe," Joe answered. "If I had known you were alive, I would have voted to ditch them a long time ago."

"I hate to admit it, but Joe's right," Charlie said, looking at her. "You were so strong and brave. None of us wanted to dishonor your memory."

"I appreciate that," Emily smiled at them. "But I'm right here now. No memory needed."

"Uncle Joe!" Hope yelled as she came running down the stairs.

Emily turned to see her carrying the bandana from her room.

"Mommy gave this to me so I could borrow some of your luck," Hope said as she held it out to him. "I thought you may want it back."

"Is that the one from my car?" Joe asked as he took it.

"I was surprised to see you left that death trap behind," Emily laughed.

"Baby was not built for the apocalypse," Joe said, sounding extremely sad. "Why don't you hold on to it for me?" Joe said as he handed the bandana back to Hope.

"Really?" Hope smiled as she took it.

"Yeah," Joe nodded. "I owe you a birthday present anyway."

"Thank you, Uncle Joe," Hope smiled as she ran back up the stairs.

"That is an amazing little girl," Charlie said as Hope disappeared.

"Careful what you say around her," Emily warned. "She hears and understands everything."

"Does she know what happened to you before this place?" Charlie asked, looking at Emily. "I know we've had a hard go of it together. I can't imagine what you went through alone."

"I wasn't alone," Emily reminded him. "Marley had my back every step of the way."

"That's a story I want to hear," Charlie said as the shower shut off in the bathroom.

Emily had told her story to people in the past, but telling it to her family seemed different. So much happened over the past two years, not all of it good. She didn't know if she wanted to tell her about Wesley's zombie head buried in the woods, about Jeff and how he tried to turn her into the same thing Chad wanted, or about what she had done with the guilty people from Jeff's camp.

"It's probably hard to talk about," Joe said softly. "How about we share our story, and then you share yours?"

"How many rapists are in your story?" Emily asked, looking at the ground.

"None," Joe admitted. "But we do have cannibals."

"I've had to do things," Emily began. "Things that I wouldn't have done before to survive and keep this place safe. I don't want you all looking at me differently."

"We always knew you were strong," Charlie said as he stepped forward and put his hand on her shoulder. "And seeing what you've done here, you've finally learned that for yourself."

"You're still Emily," Joe smiled. "Just maybe a bit more of a badass."

"After dinner," Emily agreed. "I'll tell everyone after dinner."

"That was amazing!" Christine announced as she came out of the bathroom, drying her hair. "Just burn those clothes. There's no saving them."

"Is there any water left?" Charlie asked as he walked to the bathroom.

"I saved you a little," Christine smiled at him.

Emily watched as Charlie disappeared into the bathroom and shut the door.

"What were you guys talking about?" Christine asked.

"Emily's fiancé, why Chad's still alive and wanting to know her story," Joe casually listed off.

"He seems like a nice man," Christine smiled at him. "How long have you known him?"

"I met him the day Hope was born," Emily smiled. "We started dating last year, and he proposed on Christmas Eve."

"Your dad likes him," Christine smiled. "The way he turned off his anger to comfort Hope. I'm not sure your dad even had the strength to do that."

"She has him wrapped around her little finger," Emily laughed.

"Did you tell them your story about what happened to you?" Christine asked.

"No," Emily shook her head. "I'll tell you altogether after dinner, after the kids go to bed."

Christine nodded and turned to look at the pictures on the wall. Joe and Emily walked over to join her.

"Are these?" Christine asked, touching the pictures one at a time.

"Jessica found a camera and a printer," Emily explained. "She takes a picture of the town every year on Halloween and our one-year celebration, Hope's birthday."

"She grew so fast," Christine remarked, looking at the pictures.

"How did she know who we were?" Joe asked, turning back to face Emily.

"The book she was holding, I gave to her last year for her birthday," Emily explained. "I had my photo album from the house and the pictures on my cell phone. I put them together in a fairy tale to help her get to know her family."

"You never gave up on finding us, did you?" Christine asked as she hugged Emily.

Emily let go of her mother and grabbed the locket around her neck. She opened it and held it up for her mother to look at.

"Shawn made it for me," Emily explained. "So, I could keep my family close."

Chapter 20

Emily continued to talk to her parents while Joe washed up. Joe joined them just as Rachael and Dwayne came downstairs with the kids. Emily led them all outside and to the classroom, where Alec waited for them.

"Everything go okay?" Emily asked as she walked towards him.

"The little man is scared now," Alec laughed. "They're waiting for you inside."

"Promise to tell me what happened later?" Emily asked as she opened the door.

"Promise," Alec laughed once more.

Emily walked inside and could see Chad, Veronica, and Steven waiting. Chad said nothing and didn't even look up as they entered. Emily made her way to the front of the room with Hope and Marley and waited while everyone sat down.

"Lunch will be here soon," Emily smiled at them. "I was just wondering if there were any questions about what you've been told so far."

"So, is this a dictatorship, or is there some kind of order to the leadership?" Veronica asked, her eyes boiling over with anger.

"There is a council," Emily explained. "A group of people whose thoughts and opinions I value and trust. On major decisions, we gather and talk about the best course of action, but the final decision is still mine to make."

"Of course," Veronica said, tossing her head.

"Knock, knock," Julia announced as she walked into the room carrying bags. Bobby followed behind along with Jessica, Sam, and Sarah.

"Sorry, it's late. I wanted everyone to have fresh bread," Julia explained as she and the others handed everyone a bag, and Bobby handed out bottles of water.

"Because I know you'll forget to eat," Julia scolded Emily as she handed her a bag.

"One for you, too, Hope," Bobby said as he held one out to Hope.

"Thank you," Emily and Hope said together.

"Good luck," Julia smiled as she walked out.

Sam was the only one who remained, and he took a seat at the back of the room.

"Those people are all part of the council," Emily explained. "Sarah is our communications expert, Jessica handles most of our supplies in the store, Julia is our baker, and her husband, Sam, is the head of our local police force. Alec, whom you met earlier, also works with Sam."

"Are there others?" Dwayne asked as he took a bite of his sandwich.

"Shawn, our head of security, Jacob, who runs the farm, Cole, our lead mechanic, Doc, and Ben, one of our teachers," Emily listed.

"Interesting group of people," Charlie nodded. "Definitely a diverse set of options to help you make your decision."

Emily opened her bag, pulled out the sandwich Julia had sent for her, and took a bite. She knew that Sam would tell Julia if she forgot to eat the sandwich when it was delivered to her.

"It is," Emily nodded. "They don't always agree, but help me to see it from all sides."

"How long do we have to stay with our host family?" Veronica asked.

"Just one night," Emily replied. "It gives us a chance to get to know you better and be around to answer any questions you may have to help you make your decision."

"Maybe you should tell them the rules," Hope offered as she took a bite of her lunch.

"Everyone in Sanctuary works except for children. Children are all required to attend school," Emily began.

"I can't work," Veronica interrupted. "I have a condition."

"We can find a job for everyone," Emily smiled. "Margaret, our radio operator, is in her eighties and can't stand for more than a few minutes at a time. If she can work, anyone can." "I can't," Veronica insisted.

"It's non-optional," Emily continued. "Everyone has to take a job and work a wall shift. We all live here, so we all help maintain and protect it. If you don't contribute, then you are not allowed access to what everyone else works to provide."

"So, we just have to work, and we get a free run of the supplies?" Charlie asked with concern.

"No," Emily laughed. "Robert, who built this place, had a card system in place. Each person is paid in credits, a set amount received for each child. You can use those credits to purchase things from the store. We make sure you have your basic needs and a house, but after that, it's up to you."

"So, you must be the richest person here," Chad said, finally looking at her.

"Everyone is paid the same amount regardless of their job or position," Emily explained. "No job is more important than the other, and therefore none pays more than the others. If you need or want to earn extra credits, you can volunteer for an extra wall shift. We can't guarantee that one is always available, but sometimes people get sick or such."

"Once you all decide to stay," Emily continued. "You will be given a job based on your skills before and after the flash. You will then be assigned a house or apartment based on your family size."

"And we have to wait until tomorrow for that?" Rachael asked with a smile.

"Even though I know all of you, it is a rule I put in place. It helps to give you a chance to think about everything and give me a chance to be sure I can trust you."

"So, tomorrow, you will give those you trust the choice and those you don't like the boot," Joe laughed, looking at Chad.

"I have been known not to offer the invitation to people," Emily admitted. "However, the reason for those was the unspeakable crimes that those people committed outside these walls."

"Is crime the same as it was before the zombies?" Joe asked. Emily could tell that her statement made him nervous.

"No," Emily said. "Everyone I refused had done unspeakable things to children."

"Oh my god!" Christine exclaimed.

"That's the basics of how it works here". Emily said as she folded back up the bag her lunch came in.

"What happens if you don't report to work?" Veronica asked. "Or if you can't work because your child is too young."

"Our school includes a daycare for those who are too young to attend classes," Emily explained. "If you do not report to work for any reason other than an illness or injury, you will not receive your credits that week. If it continues to happen, it can lead to jail time, or you may be asked to leave."

"So, you won't make us leave?" Veronica asked.

"She was just being polite," Sam spoke as he looked at

Veronica. "We'll give you a week's worth of supplies and toss you out the front door."

"And if I don't want to send my son to your school?" Veronica asked, turning back to Emily.

"We want to give the kids their chance at their best possible future," Emily explained. "All of the rules I have explained are nonoptional and, if broken, will result in the same set of consequences."

Emily had never had to explain so much about what would happen if someone didn't follow the rules. She knew that Veronica would give her trouble and was ready for the backlash it might cause.

"Any other questions?" Emily asked, looking around the room.

"When can I talk to my daughter?" Chad asked, looking at Hope.

"I'm not going to force that," Emily replied calmly. "If you choose to stay, she will be free to speak with and visit you as she wishes."

Chad went back to staring at the desk in front of him, silent once more. Hope made it a point not to look at him while Emily continued to speak.

"Hope is going to be giving you each a paper," Emily nodded to Hope, who began to hand out the papers to everyone. "On it, you will let us know how many are in your household and information about your skills, both pre- and post-flash. This way, we can be prepared for tomorrow and, hopefully, get you all settled into your new homes. Once you are done with those, we can get you all back to your host families."

"Mommy treats everyone the same," Hope explained as she handed out the papers. "If she doesn't, people will say she is showing favoritism."

"We don't mind," Christine assured her as she took a paper.

Emily watched as Hope stopped by Sam and handed him two sheets of paper. Sam walked over to Chad and Veronica and gave them their papers.

"Sorry," Hope said as she walked back up to Emily. "I couldn't do it."

"It's okay," Emily smiled. "You do what you are comfortable with."

"Would it be okay if I went to the farm?" Hope asked. "I feel like this room is getting smaller."

"Why don't you ask if your cousins could go with you?" Emily suggested.

"Okay," Hope nodded.

Emily watched as Hope walked over to Rachael and the kids and asked if they could come with her to the farm. Rachael looked at Emily to make sure that it was okay and safe. Emily nodded, and moments later, the kids tore out of the building.

Emily sat at the front of the room and waited while everyone filled out their forms. When they finished, Emily quickly collected them and slid them into the folder she would take home that night.

"If there's nothing else," Emily smiled. "I will see you all after breakfast."

Chad and Veronica were the first ones up as they bolted out of the room.

"I wonder what they did to that guy's wife?" Joe laughed. "Chad looked terrified."

"Alec's wife works at the store," Emily smiled. "I've never even seen her raise her voice. But Alec did tell me that his brotherin-law insulted their daughter in the kitchen one time. He said she broke a rolling pin over his head, dragged him outside, and threw the pieces at him. She never said a word and walked back into the kitchen, smiling as if nothing had happened."

"Dibs on the rolling pin," Joe said as he raised his hand.

"Let's get out of here," Emily laughed.

"Are you sure the kids will be okay?" Rachael asked as they walked outside.

"Oh yeah," Emily smiled. "Hope is probably convincing Jacob to give them all riding lessons."

"You have horses?" Dwayne asked in shock.

"Horses, cows, sheep, goats, chickens, and a large bull," Emily answered. "It's a full house down there."

"Where in the world did you manage to find them?" Dwayne asked as they walked back into the house.

"In the barn," Emily smiled at him. "They were here when I arrived. I took care of them as best I could, but Jacob got them all into top shape."

"Is there anything you guys don't have here?" Joe laughed.

"Still working on the movie theater," Emily smiled. "But until then, you guys are welcome to borrow anything from the collection."

Emily opened the movie cabinets as she walked in front of the television.

"Just be sure to put it back when you're done," Emily laughed.

Emily watched as her mom pulled out the copy of "It's a Wonderful Life."

"We used to watch this every Christmas," Christine said as she looked down at the case.

"We still do," Emily smiled. "Every Christmas after dinner."

Christine smiled as she slid the movie back onto the shelf.

"You guys relax while I go get dinner started," Emily said as she headed for the kitchen.

"You're not getting away that easily," Rachael said as she ran to catch up with her.

"I wasn't running away," Emily laughed. "I just need to get dinner started."

"Then I'm coming to help," Rachael smiled. "I want to hear all about Mr. Biker Man, whose clothes are in your closet."

Emily and Rachael worked together in the kitchen like no time had passed. They talked about Shawn and Hope. Rachael told her about how the kids were handling things. Time flew by, and soon they were getting dinner on the table. The kids arrived home while they were cooking, and the girls could hear them talking about everything they had seen on the farm.

"Is he often late for dinner?" Rachael asked, noticing that Shawn had still not come in.

"Never," Emily said, looking at the clock.

"Which means something wrong, or he's hiding."

"He better not be hiding," Rachael warned her.

"Shawn," Emily said into the walkie.

"Security Channel," Shawn replied. Emily quickly changed her radio station before pressing the button once again.

"Is everything alright?" Emily asked.

"We'll have to play the speakers through the night and burn tomorrow, but I think we have it under control."

"Are you still on the wall?" Emily asked.

"I thought I would give you some time with your family," Shawn replied.

"Most of my time is spent answering questions about you," Emily laughed.

"You told them?" Shawn asked quickly.

"Apparently, they figured it out in about two seconds," Emily laughed. "Are you coming home?"

"I'll be in a minute," Shawn replied. Emily turned her radio back to the general channel and set it on the table.

"Big baby," Rachael teased.

Emily heard the front door open and close as Shawn came in. Rachael gathered everyone for dinner, and soon they were all gathered around the table. Shawn told Rachael he had brought in some cots for Hope's room to all have a place to sleep. Things were awkward for only a little while when they first sat down. Shawn soon laughed and talked with everyone, just as if he had known them for years.

After dinner, the kids all began to rub their eyes. Rachael informed Emily that they had not been sleeping more than a few hours a night. Hope walked upstairs with them, insisting that she was tired as well. Once all of the kids were tucked in and the dishes cleaned up, everyone gathered in the living room.

"Do you want to go first, or do you want us to?" Joe asked, looking at Emily.

"You first," Emily replied, still not sure how to tell her family everything she had done.

"We weren't at the cabin long before dumbass rang the dinner bell for the zombies," Joe began.

"After that, we stayed on the move for a while," Charlie said, taking over the story. "We met up with this one group about four months in who claimed they had a cure. We had to know if it was true, so we traveled to their camp and lived there for a few months. It was then that they showed us the cure." "What was it?" Emily asked.

"There was no cure," Dwayne explained. "When you were deemed worthy, they had a zombie tied up that you were supposed to let bite you so you could ascend to the next level."

"We got out of there as fast as we could," Rachael explained.

"After that, we traveled alone for quite some time, probably another six months or so," Charles said, taking back over the narrative. "We came across this camp just outside of St. Louis. The first place we had seen that served fresh meat."

"I told you there was something wrong with it," Christine interrupted.

"Turns out that they slaughtered and cooked anyone they found wandering. Luckily, we discovered it before we were on the menu," Charlie continued. "The camp got overrun with zombies, and we slipped out in the chaos. After that, we didn't trust anyone. We stuck to ourselves and ate whatever we could find. The gas stopped working in the cars last year, and we have been on foot ever since."

"JR spotted the Sanctuary sign while we were making our way south, and here we are," Joe smiled.

Emily hated how tame her family's story was. They hadn't had to kill people, but managed to slip away from them.

"Your turn, Em," Joe said as he encouraged her to speak.

Emily heard the words start to come out of her mouth. She explained what happened after the bite and the theft of Ms. Tilly's SUV, about the day she learned she was pregnant, and about Jeff and his gang. Emily talked slowly when she discussed finding Sanctuary and letting everyone inside. Part of her hoped they would get tired and not want to hear the rest of the story. However, none of them moved, and all seemed to be hanging on her every word.

Emily told them about her fights with Derick and how he was now a changed man. Emily told them about Jeff attacking, kidnapping Shawn, and how she killed him. Emily explained the willing participants she and the council put down and burned outside the walls. Emily even said about Wesley, whose zombie head was still buried in the woods because Hell was too good for him. Emily ended on happier notes, telling them about her engagement, how Hope asked Shawn to be her dad, and explaining just how bright Hope was. When she finished, she sat in silence and looked at her family.

"Well," Charlie said after a few minutes of silence. "I knew you were strong, but even I didn't know you had all of that in you."
"Are you disappointed?" Emily asked as she looked at Charlie.

"No," Charlie insisted. "I'm going to be walking around here like a damn peacock, going, 'That's my daughter." "You are a badass," Joe laughed.

"I thought you guys would be upset about some of the stuff I've done," Emily said, looking around.

"I wish I had the strength to do what you did," Rachael said, looking at Emily. "Some of the assholes we met could still be alive out there, hurting people. We just slipped away, but you had the strength to make sure those people didn't get another chance."

"Told you," Shawn said as he took Emily's hand. "You are way too hard on yourself."

"She gets that from her mother," Charlie replied, making everyone laugh.

"Just to be clear," Joe said once the laughter died down. "You know your story didn't scare us away, right? We are all staying."

"I never count on that until decision time," Emily admitted. "Even with you guys, I'm trying not to get too attached in case you decide to leave."

"You are going to have to throw me off that wall to get me to leave you again," Christine spoke up. "Not to mention the hot showers. You are stuck with me for life."

Emily laughed as her mom compared her love for her child to the love of a hot shower.

"I second that," Rachael said, raising her hand.

"So why don't you go do what you need to with that folder?" Charlie said, looking at the folder on the table. "And we'll all get some rest so we can make this official."

"Maybe we'll get lucky, and Chad will take Veronica and go," Joe said as everyone stood up.

"You gave away your luck, remember?" Emily smiled at him.

"Maybe I could sneak up there and borrow it for just tomorrow," Joe said, looking at the stairs.

"You wake up those kids, and you get to sit up with them all night," Rachael warned him.

Emily laughed as she grabbed her folder from the table while Joe lay down on the couch. Everyone headed to bed, and Emily and Shawn each climbed in on one side of Hope. Emily began looking through the papers, trying to make objective decisions as she decided what job she would place them all in.

"You already know where they need to go," Shawn said as he lay down. "Stop second-guessing yourself."

"I'm afraid Sarah will kill him," Emily said as she shut the folder and turned off the light.

"She won't kill him," Shawn assured her. "She will want him to suffer first."

Emily laughed but knew deep down that Shawn was right. Emily slid her arm over Hope and felt Shawn take her hand.

Chapter 21

The next day, Hope was the first one to wake up. Emily woke and found Hope sitting on the end of the bed, flipping through her storybook. Emily lay still and watched as Hope flipped through the pages. Emily watched out of the corner of her eye as Shawn woke and began watching Hope as well.

"She's not okay," Shawn mouthed to her.

"I know," Emily mouthed back.

Emily looked back at Hope and watched her for a few more minutes.

"Hope?" Emily finally spoke. "What are you doing?"

"I don't understand," Hope said as she turned with tears running down her face. "You said you both knew you had to look for your happily ever afters, but how could I be born after my brother?"

"Come here," Emily said as she patted the bed.

Hope crawled back up between Shawn and Emily and set her storybook on her lap.

"Your dad," Emily began. "Found him happily after while we were still together. I didn't find out until the flash." "Why would he do that?" Hope cried.

"He had his reasons," Emily explained. "But that's between your dad and me."

"What am I supposed to do?" Hope cried.

"Get to know him," Emily smiled. "Just because he and I didn't work doesn't mean he won't be a good dad to you." "I don't trust him," Hope continued to cry.

"Trust has to be earned," Emily smiled. "But he can't earn it if you don't give him a chance."

"And what if he doesn't want me, or I can never trust him?" Hope continued to cry.

"Then it's his loss," Shawn spoke up.

"But does that mean you can't be my daddy anymore if I try?" Hope asked, looking at Shawn.

"I will always be your daddy," Shawn smiled. "I agreed to it for life, and nothing is going to make me change my mind." "That lady is mean," Hope said, her tears finally slowing.

"Just try to start with your dad," Emily encouraged her. "And if you need help, Daddy and I will always be here." "Right," Hope said as she straightened herself. "Thank you." Hope hugged Emily and Shawn before climbing out of bed.

"Just," Emily said as Hope reached the door. "Let us know when you are going to see him, and you will take Marley with you."

"Yes, Mommy," Hope nodded. "I promise."

Hope opened the door and ran out into the hall. Emily could hear that her family was awake and already working on breakfast.

"I don't know how you do it," Shawn said as he took her hand. "I don't know if I would have the strength to encourage her to get to know that piece of shit."

"I don't want her growing up hating me," Emily sighed. "I have to let her get to know him and decide for herself."

"But just so we're clear," Shawn replied. "If he hurts her, I will kill him."

"And I'll burn the body," Emily added.

"As long as we understand each other," Shawn smiled as he hugged her. "We'd better get moving."

Emily crawled out of bed and set to get dressed for the day. By the time they made it downstairs, Hope was dressed and had taken care of Marley. Her mom was putting the last breakfast on the table, and everyone was sitting down.

"I would have cooked," Emily smiled as she and Shawn walked into the dining room.

"I wanted to make sure I still could," Christine smiled at her.

"It smells good," Shawn said as he walked over and sat down next to Joe.

Emily sat down, and everyone began to eat. Hope was busy telling the other kids about school and everything she wanted to show them in Sanctuary. As soon as breakfast was made, Hope ran upstairs to finish getting ready for school.

"Can we go to?" JR asked as they all gathered around the front door.

"If you guys are staying, you can start tomorrow," Emily smiled at him.

"We're staying," Racheal insisted.

"Right," Emily nodded as she opened the door. "If you guys want to head over to the classroom, I'll be there as soon as Hope is at school."

"We'll meet you there," Christine smiled at Emily.

Emily and Shawn walked Hope to school and then back to the classroom. Emily walked in with Shawn and saw that everyone had arrived. She walked to the front of the room with Shawn and set her folder down on her desk. Shawn sat in a chair while Marley sat next to the desk. Marley sat quietly, but he stared at Chad.

"Does anyone have any questions?" Emily asked. "I guess you all have made your decisions," Emily said after a few minutes of silence.

"We're staying," Charlie said quickly.

"Chad? Veronica?" Emily asked, looking over at them.

"We're staying," Chad replied.

"But there will have to be a few changes around here," Veronica sneered.

"I welcome your suggestions," Emily nodded. "But you need to understand that you are agreeing to stay and follow the rules as they are."

"Fine," Veronica said as she leaned back in her chair.

"If you're all decided, it's time to sign the ledger," Emily smiled as she handed the ledger to Joe.

Emily made her way back to her desk and waited while the ledger made its way through the room. Once everyone had signed, JR returned the ledger to Emily.

"Joe, you're going to be working with Cole in the garage. Dad and Dwayne, you will be working with Jose, our construction foreman, Mom, and Rachael; you will be working with June at the school. Chad, you will be working with Sarah, who heads our communications, and Veronica...."

"I don't work," Veronica interrupted. "That's one of the changes that will need to happen."

"You listed almost no usable skills," Emily nodded.

"So, there is no job for me," Veronica smiled.

"I said almost," Emily smiled back at her. "You will be working with Jessica in our stores."

"She has to raise our son!" Chad yelled at Emily.

"You will drop your tone, or I'm going to drop you," Shawn said firmly from his chair.

"You think I'm scared of you?!" Chad yelled at Shawn as he burst out of his chair.

"You don't have to be scared to get your ass whipped," Shawn replied as he stood and walked over to Chad.

Emily noticed how much bigger than Chad Shawn was. Chad's head barely reached Shawn's chest, and she was sure Shawn could crush Chad's head with one hand. Emily intended to watch what happened until she looked at Steven. Emily couldn't let this happen in front of him.

"Shawn, please!" Emily yelled. "If they don't like it, they can just go!"

"We're not going anywhere!" Veronica yelled.

"Then you will report to work," Emily said forcefully.

"And you will sit down and shut up," Shawn said as he pushed Chad back down into his chair.

Shawn walked back over and stood next to Emily with his arms crossed.

"That was exciting," Joe laughed.

"Let's get you all to your houses," Emily breathed. "I think we'll take Chad and Veronica home first."

"It would probably be safer that way," Rachael smiled.

"Let's go," Emily said as she took Shawn's hand and led everyone out onto the street.

"Every time he speaks, it's like he's asking me to kill him," Shawn said as they walked outside.

"He's still trying to control me," Emily replied.

"If I can't, he sure as hell isn't," Shawn replied. "I know," Emily smiled at him. "I love you." "I love you too," Shawn said as his face softened.

Emily led everyone to the house she had assigned to Chad and Veronica.

"All of the basics should be inside," Emily said as she pointed at the house. "If anything is missing, Jessica will be able to help you, and Shawn will let you know when your wall shifts will be."

"Where do we find you if there's a problem?" Chad asked.

"I am mostly around town or at the town hall," Emily replied.

"So, my daughter is homeless?" Chad asked, not looking at her.

"House at the end of Main Street," Emily replied. "You can't miss it."

"So, you get that large house while we get this shack!" Veronica said, looking at the house.

"Again, you don't have to stay," Emily replied. "But you are going to have to be civil if you stay."

Veronica took Steven by the hand and led him into the house.

"When can I see her?" Chad asked, watching Veronica.

"She's working through it," Emily replied. "I encouraged her to get to know you, and she agreed she'd try."

"Thanks," Chad said as he took a step forward.

"Don't think that means I trust you," Emily continued. "She will be bringing Marley if and when she decides to see you."

"That dog will bite me just because he can," Chad said as he stopped.

"He didn't bite you today," Emily replied. "As long as you don't hurt her, you have nothing to worry about."

Chad said nothing as he walked towards the house.

"You were married to him?" Shawn said in disbelief as they turned to show Rachael and Dwayne their house.

"He was different when I married him," Emily replied.

"For the record, I never liked him," Joe spoke up.

"I know," Emily said, rolling her eyes. "But if I hadn't made that mistake, I wouldn't have had Hope."

No one had a comeback for that as they walked to the house. Rachael smiled and followed the kids inside as they ran to pick out their rooms. Dwayne was just as excited as the kids and ran with them.

"Last house is mom and dad's," Emily said as she pointed to the house next door.

"We only need one bedroom," Christine said as she looked at the house. "This is much too big for us."

"The last thing I need is you guys falling down the stairs," Emily smiled.

"I don't want anyone thinking we are getting special treatment because we're your parents," Charles said, looking at the house.

"You're not," Emily insisted. "June and Howard have a house along with Margaret and Ben."

"She's telling the truth," Shawn smiled at them. "This one is for you guys."

"If you insist," Christine said as she walked into the house with Charlie.

"Just so we're clear, I'm not opposed to special treatment," Joe said as he walked up beside her.

"Why don't you go get the cards done, and I'll show Joe to his new apartment," Shawn offered.

"Feel free to trip or push him on the stairs," Emily smiled back.

"I said special treatment, not abuse!" Joe said as he turned to follow Shawn.

"I know!" Emily called after him.

Emily smiled as she walked with Marley to the town hall. Emily made her way inside and set to work on the cards. She went ahead and put the first credits for everyone, just as she did for all of the arrivals. Emily sat at her desk after she finished, looking for something else that had to be done.

Emily knew that once she left, she would have to tell everyone about their new workers. Emily was still afraid to tell

Sarah that Chad would be working with her. Chad's experience with electronics and programming made him a perfect fit. But Emily knew that his attitude was going to drive Sarah crazy.

Finally, Emily accepted that she couldn't put it off any longer. She walked out of the town hall and made her way to the store. She gave Jessica the cards and let her know that Veronica would be joining her the next day. Emily warned her that Veronica was entitled but not to hesitate to call if she gave her any trouble. Jessica took the news with a smile, as always, and said she wasn't worried. Emily made her way through town and saved Sarah for last.

Emily and Marley walked into the COM building and could see Sarah working on the radio. Margaret was sitting in the chair, stitching and smiling as Emily entered.

"Everything alright?" Emily asked as she walked in.

"Work is just piling up," Sarah said as she stood up. "With it being just me, I keep falling behind on the upkeep around here."

"Well, you won't be the only one as of tomorrow," Emily smiled.

"A member of your family is good with this stuff?" Sarah said excitedly.

"Not exactly," Emily admitted. "My ex-husband is."

"Nope," Sarah said as she shook her head.

"I'll strangle him with speaker wire, I swear."

"If that's what you have to do, I'm fine with it," Emily replied. "He is good with this stuff, and I have to assign him where he will be most helpful."

"Damn you and always doing the right thing," Sarah sighed. "He does know I'll be the boss, right?"

"I told him to report to you," Emily nodded. "If you have any problems, I'm sure Shawn would be glad to set him straight."

"How's that going, by the way?" Sarah asked as she leaned against the desk next to Margaret. "Are the fiancé and the ex-best friends yet?"

"Shawn almost killed him again today for raising his voice to me," Emily admitted. "I think my dad and brother are taking bets on how long until Shawn hits him."

"I want in on that action," Sarah laughed.

"Me too," Margaret spoke up.

"Margaret!" Emily yelled as she and Sarah laughed hysterically.

"Did I miss something?" Shawn asked as he walked in.

"Nothing," Emily replied. "Just girl talk."

"Did you tell Sarah about her new employee?" Shawn asked as he stood next to Emily.

"She did," Sarah nodded. "She said if I have any trouble to call you."

"Aww, it's not even my birthday," Shawn said as he placed his hand over his heart and looked down at Emily.

"How's Hope handling all of this?" Julia asked as she walked in.

"She's confused and upset," Emily replied. "I'm just trying to help her find her way through it."

"We told her this morning we would support her if she wanted to get to know him," Shawn added. "She's just not allowed to meet with him without one of the three of us there." "Three of you?" Julia asked, confused.

"We figured Marley could handle it if something went wrong," Emily smiled.

"Oh, yeah!" Julia laughed.

"Does anyone know what he did to Samara?" Margaret asked. "I saw her last night sharpening her knives on her front porch."

"I have no idea," Emily admitted. "Alec promised to tell me the story, though."

"You have to tell us when you find out," Sarah smiled. "I've never even heard that woman raise her voice, and he pushed her to want to stab him."

"I'm sure the whole town will know by Friday," Emily laughed.

"No secrets in Sanctuary," Margaret laughed. "I know I wouldn't want that woman angry with me."

"I wouldn't want her angry with me!" Shawn added.

Everyone shared a good laugh as Shawn looked terrified at the idea of Samara attacking him.

"I shut off the speakers this morning," Sarah said to Shawn. "I had to replace some wires on the system here."

"Based on what we saw yesterday, I'm sure the pits are overflowing," Shawn said. "We should probably do a burn."

"We're going through the kerosene fast," Emily replied. "How's the process of making more?"

"Kathy says she's nearly set up," Shawn said.

"How does that work?" Julia asked.

"Kathy says you soak the wood in acid and then add calcium hydroxide, heat it, and boom, flammable oil."

"I'm sure it's more complicated than that," Emily grinned.

"Yeah, I'm pretty sure she gave me the watered-down version," Shawn agreed.

"But she's confident it will work?" Julia asked.

"I think so," Shawn nodded. "In truth, I was afraid I would insult her if I asked."

"Where is everyone?" Sam's voice came through the walkie.

"Leaving the COM building," Shawn replied.

"I guess we'd better get back to work," Emily laughed.

"Party this Friday, right?" Sarah said as she began to dance.

"You know it," Emily laughed as she walked out the door.

"Did I miss something?" Sam said as they all walked outside.

"Gossip," Shawn nodded. "You know how the women get."

"Excuse me?" Emily said as she looked up at him. "You were in there too, remember?"

"I…shit," Shawn said as he hung his head. "They sucked me in, and I didn't even realize it."

"It happens to the best of us," Sam laughed as he tried to comfort Shawn.

"Did you need something?" Emily asked, trying to break up the bromance unfolding in front of her.

"No," Sam shook his head. "Just wanted to make sure you all didn't run away and leave me to deal with all the crazy."

"You know," Emily said slowly. "That is an idea."

"Don't even try it!" Sam said, pointing a finger at Emily. "If you guys are running away, I'm coming with you."

Chapter 22

Everyone was always so excited when a new group arrived. Party plans were already in full swing by the afternoon. Emily stopped by the store and picked up what she needed to make her cookies. Emily walked through the door with Marley and could see right away that Jessica was frustrated.

"What's going on?" Emily asked her.

"Veronica was here," Jessica replied. "She said that her house was not fit for basic living and had a list of things she needed."

"What was missing?" Emily asked.

Jessica checked each of the houses every two weeks. She made sure that everything except for food, clothes, and personal items was stocked in each one.

"Labels," Jessica answered.

"Label?" Emily repeated, confused.

"She said that the sheets were so scratchy they should be illegal. She wanted silk sheets. The furniture was ugly, and she had a list of designers whose furniture would be acceptable, and wanted the name of a contractor who could remodel the house for her."

"You have to be kidding," Emily said as she rubbed her head.

"Nope," Jessica replied. "When I told her what she was asking for wasn't possible, she kept looking at me, asking if I knew who her father was. Who is her father?"

"I have no idea!" Emily admitted. "Not that it would matter now. It's not going to get her anything."

"Right!" Jessica agreed. "I'll admit, before the flash, I was spoiled. But now, I feel spoiled just being able to sleep in a bed at night."

"That's because you're a good person," Emily smiled at her.

"You should have seen the look on her face when she went to look at the clothes. She asked to be taken to the name-brand section since she had signed up to stay."

"Um, we have what we have," Emily laughed.

"She said she was going to talk to you about making this place more livable," Jessica replied.

"Jesus!" Emily exclaimed. "Anything else?"

"Just that she can't be on her feet a lot or lift anything, basically she plans on just sitting around doing her nails all day," Jessica smiled.

"You seem happy about it," Emily remarked.

"I told Samara not to stock the flour or anything over four pounds today," Jessica smiled. "She is going to have a lot of work to do."

"I like it," Emily nodded.

"I survived, Derick," Jessica replied. "I'm not afraid of a spoiled rich girl."

"I'm here if you need me," Emily reminded her.

"I have your stuff by the counter," Jessica said as she led Emily over to the counter. "I gave you enough to make double the usual."

"I'll make sure to set you a few back this time," Emily smiled as she grabbed the bag.

"I haven't gotten one all year!" Jessica teased. "I don't want to have to tackle a child."

"I'll make sure you get some," Emily laughed as she headed for the door.

Joe walked in just as Emily reached it. Emily held open the door while Joe walked in.

"Here to get my card," Joe chimed as he walked in.

"Jessica has it," Emily said as she nodded towards Jessica.

"Also, I am missing a couple of things in my apartment," Joe said, looking at Jessica. "Is that something you can help me with?"

"Depends on what it is," Jessica replied cautiously.

"A pillow?" Joe asked slowly. "I can live without one if it's a problem."

"No," Jessica replied gently. "Just had some ridiculous requests today. Feel free to grab what you need. Just stop by here so I can update the inventory with what you take."

"Sounds like you met Veronica," Joe smiled. "I wish I could say she grows on you, but I'd be lying." "Good to know," Jessica smiled.

Joe headed into the store to find the missing things, and Emily headed outside. Emily quickly made her way home to put away the groceries. Emily had just put away the last of everything when she heard the front door open.

"In the kitchen!" Emily yelled as the door closed.

"Hey there, beautiful," Shawn smiled at her as he walked into the kitchen. "How are you holding up?"

"I'm thrilled to have them here finally," Emily smiled at him.

"I meant with Chad and Veronica," Shawn smiled at her.

"I'm happy that Hope can finally meet him," Emily tried to look at the positive side.

"Now she can make her own decision about him and not have to wonder about him the rest of her life."

"I asked how you were doing," Shawn said, looking at her knowingly.

"Honestly, I would have been happy never to see him again," Emily sighed. "I forgot how much of an ass he is."

"How did you stay married to him?" Shawn asked as he sat down.

"When we got married, he was almost sweet," Emily admitted. "He didn't change until I had a miscarriage. I felt like it was my fault, no matter what the doctors said. I knew he blamed me, and I felt like I owed him."

"Your spirit broke," Shawn said as he looked at her.

"Completely," Emily nodded. "It wasn't until right before the flash that I finally snapped and stood up for myself. We tried the therapy because you know how I felt about vows."

Shawn nodded slowly, showing that he understood.

"I found out the night of the flash that he had no plans of changing. He was trying to build a case to get as much as possible in the divorce. He had already met Veronica, and she was pregnant."

"He made you pay for the miscarriage?" Shawn said as he looked into her eyes.

"Yeah," Emily said with a choke.

Shawn took Emily by the hand and pulled her onto his lap.

"You deserved better than that," Shawn said softly. "You know I would never do anything like that, right?"

"I'd be lying if I said I wasn't afraid of it," Emily replied. "I love you more than I ever knew was possible. I don't know what I would do if...."

"Not going to happen," Shawn said as he lifted her face to look into her eyes. "Ever."

Emily wrapped her arms around Shawn's neck and hugged him tightly. Shawn pulled her close and held her for a long time.

"I know I haven't been helping," Shawn said when Emily finally loosened her grip on him.

"What are you talking about?" Emily asked him, confused.

"I've wanted to beat him to death twice now," Shawn answered. "Me losing my temper like that isn't going to help the stress you feel. I know you already have enough stress trying to help Hope through this."

"You're not adding to my stress," Emily assured him. "You are just trying to protect me."

"But I don't want to take away your fight," Shawn said. "I find it sexy as hell when you knock a guy on their ass." "I know you do," Emily laughed as she kissed him.

"What do you have to do now?" Shawn asked her.

"I could start on the cookies," Emily said, looking at the cabinets. "That way, I don't have to try to do them and dinner tonight."

"So, if I make dinner, you are free right now?" Shawn asked with a smile.

"Yeah," Emily smiled at him. "I have to pick up Hope soon."

"Right," Shawn smiled. "I'm going to help you relax."

"How are you…!" Emily's sentence was cut off as Shawn stood from the chair and began to run towards the stairs. "Shawn!" Emily squealed as she held onto his neck.

"No time to wait," Shawn said as he ran up the stairs and into the bedroom, closing the door behind him.

Emily rested her head on Shawn's chest as they lay on the bed. All of her stress and worries about Chad and Veronica were long gone. Shawn had his arm wrapped around her and rubbed up and down her upper arm.

"Are you relaxed?" Shawn asked softly.

"Totally," Emily smiled.

"Good," Shawn said as he exhaled.

"My family is probably looking for me," Emily laughed.

"Probably," Shawn laughed with her. "We should probably get up."

"Probably," Emily said as she continued to lie still.

"You're not moving," Shawn laughed.

"Nope," Emily smiled.

"Come on," Shawn said as he began to sit up.

"No," Emily whined as she slid off his chest.

Shawn began to get dressed while Emily continued to lie in the bed.

"Get up," Shawn teased as he threw a pillow at her.

"Fine," Emily smiled. "You big bully."

"Bully?!" Shawn said as he jumped back into the bed and tickled Emily.

"I'm sorry," Emily squealed as she tried to escape him.

"Shawn," Sam's voice came through the walkie.

"I'll let you off easy this time," Shawn said as he stood up and grabbed his walkie.

"Easy?!" Emily laughed.

"Go ahead," Shawn said into the walkie.

"I wanted to see if you had updated the wall schedule yet?" Sam asked.

"Not yet," Shawn replied. "Is there something you need me to change?"

"No," Sam quickly replied. "I just…"

"I'll be at the security building in ten," Shawn answered. "Why don't you meet me there?"

"Will do," Sam replied.

"I have to get to work," Shawn said as he leaned over and kissed Emily.

"Don't forget, you are cooking tonight," Emily reminded him.

"I'm on it," Shawn said as he walked out the bedroom door.

Emily got out of bed, quickly dressed, and made the bed. Emily made her way downstairs and found Marley asleep on the couch. Emily didn't bother him as she made her way to the kitchen and got to work on her cookies. Emily worked the next few hours, making sure to put a few cookies on a separate plate for Jessica.

"Emily?" Christine's voice rang out as the front door opened.

"In the kitchen, Mom!" Emily yelled back as she pulled the latest batch out of the oven.

"Is this where you have been all afternoon?" Christine smiled as she walked into the kitchen.

"Mostly," Emily nodded. "It's my contribution to the welcoming party."

"Are these your grandma's cookies?" Christine smiled as she picked up a cookie.

"As close as I can get them," Emily nodded. "Help yourself."

"I shouldn't," Christine said, putting the cookie down. "I can wait until the party."

"That's risky," Emily laughed. "The kids go nuts."

"In that case," Christine said as she picked the cookie back up and took a bite.

"You want some milk?" Emily asked as she opened the refrigerator and pulled out the glass milk container.

"Please," Christine said as she took another bite.

Emily poured Christine a glass and set it in front of her. Emily slid the last cookies into the oven while Christine helped herself to a second cookie.

"I'm sure you didn't come over just to sneak some cookies," Emily smiled as she sat down with her mom.

"I just wanted to see you," Christine smiled. "I keep thinking that I'm imagining that you are here."

"Mom," Emily smiled as she reached over and pulled her mom into a hug.

"I didn't want to believe that you were gone," Christine said as she hugged Emily back. "I even kept calling your cell phone for a while and leaving messages."

"I got a few of them," Emily smiled as she sat back. "I could never get a call to go through, though."

"You heard them?" Christine said with tears in her eyes.

"It's part of what kept me going," Emily nodded. "All of you called at least once, even Dad."

"Really?" Christine smiled. "He told us he didn't believe you were gone but acted like we were crazy when we called."

"You know how dad is," Emily replied. "He always has to be the strong one."

"True," Christine laughed. "I'm just glad we're all together now."

"Me too," Emily smiled.

"And you have a daughter!" Christine added. "I feel like I've missed so much."

"You were here the whole time," Emily assured her. "Hope has been hearing about all of you since she was born."

"And Shawn?" Christine eyed her as she spoke.

"What about him?" Emily laughed. "He is a great man."

"I like him," Christine insisted. "He's just the opposite of Chad."

"That's part of what I love about him," Emily laughed.

"What's his story?" Christine asked with a more serious tone. "Who was he before?"

"He was in the Marines," Emily replied.

"That's it?" Christine said with suspicion. "That's all you are going to tell me?"

Emily considered telling her mom the entire story Shawn had told her. Emily was afraid of telling parts of Shawn's story that he didn't want to share. However, she didn't want to start keeping secrets from her mom again.

"He's had a rough go of things," Emily began to explain. "When he came out of the military, he found it hard to adjust and find a job."

"A story heard too much about soldiers," Christine said, shaking her head.

"He did find a group that accepted him. They became like his brothers and helped him to find work," Emily explained.

"What group?" Christine asked.

Emily knew that her mother would not let her be vague about the details.

"A biker gang," Emily answered, and then waited for her mother to process what she said. "The vest he wears shows that he is part of it."

Christine sat quietly and looked at Emily. Christine had done this since Emily was a child. It was her way of making Emily talk.

"Everything his brothers did wasn't exactly legal," Emily continued. "He says that he did things to protect his brothers, but nothing different than he did to protect his fellow marines when he served."

"But he's a good man?" Christine asked softly.

"The best," Emily nodded. "He has protected Hope and me since the day he arrived."

"All I care about is that he's a good man," Christine smiled. "And that he makes you and my granddaughter happy." "I don't think I've ever been this happy," Emily replied.

"Just don't let Chad find a way to destroy that," Christine warned. "The last time you two saw each other was tense, to say the least."

"I don't want to waste any more of my life on Chad," Emily replied. "If he can build a relationship with Hope, great. But there's nothing left between us."

"I just know how he gets in your head," Christine continued. "I don't want him to ruin what you have here."

"I won't let him," Emily replied.

"I know you wouldn't do it on purpose," Christine said. "But Chad has always had a way of pushing you down the wrong path."

"I know," Emily nodded. "But it's not going to work this time."

"You do seem different," Christine smiled. "Stronger."

"I am," Emily nodded. "The world forced me to either fight or die. I had to find my strength."

"I'm proud of you," Christine smiled as she grabbed Emily's hand. "But I'm still going to try to protect you."

"Everyone does," Emily said, rolling her eyes.

"It's your fault for being so amazing," Christine teased.

Emily was pulled out of their conversation by the timer signaling that the cookies were done. Emily stood up, took the cookies out of the oven, and placed them on the cooling rack. Emily and her mom continued small talk while Emily packed up the cookies.

"I'd better get home and finish supper," Christine said as she stood up. "It should be ready about six."

"Something never changes," Emily smiled. Her mom had always had dinner at the table by six in Emily's entire life.

"Make sure you get there early," Christine said, walking towards the door. "I know your dad wants to talk to Shawn some more. Especially since you're marrying him soon."

"Actually," Emily said as she stopped Christine. "Shawn is cooking us dinner at home tonight."

"I talked to him earlier, and he said that you guys were free," Christine replied, confused. "Didn't he tell you?"

"Not exactly," Emily smiled. "We'll see you guys for dinner."

"Okay," Christine replied slowly as she left.

Emily finished cleaning up the kitchen after Christine left. Once she finished, Emily headed to the school with Marley to pick up Hope. Hope was in a much better mood than she was that morning. Hope was in an even better mood when Emily told her about their dinner plans. Emily walked with Hope to the Security building just as Shawn walked out.

"You ready to cook dinner as you promised?" Emily asked him as she walked up to him.

"Uh-oh," Hope smiled. "Daddy's in trouble."

"You talked to your mom," Shawn said, looking down and then back at her.

"She came by right after you left," Emily said, trying to look annoyed.

"I'm sorry," Shawn said, pouting at her.

"Don't you try to get out of this," Emily said as a smile began to spread across her face.

"I'm sorry," Shawn said, pouting at her.

"Not going to work," Emily said, turning away and walking towards her parents' house.

Chapter 23

Dinner at Emily's parents' house made it seem like the flash never happened. Charlie, Joe, Dwayne, and Shawn instantly bonded. There was no awkward silence, and it seemed like they had known each other for years. Hope spent the evening with her cousins, telling them all about school and the party happening the next day. Emily got caught up in conversations with her mom and sister, who wanted to talk about the upcoming wedding.

Emily walked home that night with Shawn, who was carrying Hope. All of the excitement of the night had led to her falling asleep before they left. Marley walked slowly beside them, full of all the table scraps that the kids had given him. Shawn took Hope up to bed as soon as they got home, and Emily went to take a quick shower. When Emily came back into the bedroom, Shawn was lying on the bed.

"You still mad at me?" Shawn asked as she crawled under the covers.

"I was never mad," Emily smiled.

"Good," Shawn said as he slid closer and hugged her.

"Are you not coming to bed?" Emily asked, noticing that he was still fully dressed.

"I have to take a shift in a few hours," Shawn replied. "Julia needs some rest, and I told Sam I would cover it."

"Is she alright?" Emily asked with concern.

"Sam insists she's fine," Shawn answered. "He said she was just feeling run down."

"I'll check on her in the morning," Emily replied. "I can't believe she didn't say anything."

"You've had a lot going on," Shawn answered. "She probably didn't want to bother you.

"No excuse," Emily replied.

"I know," Shawn said as he kissed her on top of her head. "Just try to get some rest tonight, and I'm sure everything will be fine tomorrow."

Emily felt a yawn escape as Shawn spoke. She was more tired than she realized, and her eyes felt like they were being pulled shut.

"I'll try," Emily said as she lay her head on her pillow.

Shawn wrapped his arm around Emily as she closed her eyes. Emily knew he would be leaving, but having him there when she fell asleep was comforting. It didn't take long before Emily was fast asleep.

Emily woke the following day and reached over to Shawn's side of the bed. She was surprised to find him asleep next to her. He had changed and was under the blanket. He must have come home after his shift and gone straight to bed. He couldn't have been home more than a few hours. Emily slid out of bed and quietly got dressed. Emily walked out into the hall, quietly closing the door behind herself as she went.

"Where's daddy?" Hope asked as she walked towards Emily.

"He worked last night," Emily explained. "He's catching up on some sleep."

"So, it's just you and me this morning?" Hope asked.

"Just like old times," Emily smiled as she led Hope and Marley down the stairs.

Hope ran with Marley to the kitchen and let him outside. Hope set to fill Marley's bowls while Emily made breakfast. As soon as everyone had eaten, they headed out the door. Hope took off running as soon as she saw Rachael and the kids.

"Does she ever slow down?" Rachael laughed as they neared each other.

"When she's asleep," Emily answered with a smile.

Rachael and Emily walked the kids to school. Hope insisted on walking everyone in by herself.

"I have to go in," Rachael laughed. "I work here."

"Oh, okay," Hope smiled. "But mommy doesn't need to come in."

"I feel loved," Emily laughed.

"I do love you," Hope said as she hugged Emily.

"I love you too," Emily smiled. "Now, get to class."

Hope smiled as she led Rachael and the kids inside. Emily waved to Christine as she headed into the school. Emily knew that she needed to check on the others to ensure that everyone reported working. The only ones she was really worried about were Veronica and Chad. Emily looked around and didn't see Veronica anywhere with Steven. Emily waited until all of the parents left for work and saw that June was still standing by the door. June shook her head at Emily, confirming that Steven had not arrived.

Emily didn't feel anger or even surprise. She had guessed from how Veronica acted the day before that this might happen. Emily turned and headed back towards the main street with Marley. Emily considered running straight to Chad's house to confront them, but stopped herself. She had to do this fair and make sure everyone else was at work first. She hoped that maybe they were running late and would report to work by when she was done. Emily knew that it wouldn't happen, but she hoped it would anyway.

Emily made her way to the construction area first. Charlie and Dwayne were there and already hard at work. Charlie was giving Jose tips that may help make things easier or more efficient.

Charlie kept telling Jose he knew Jose was in charge, but just couldn't help himself. Emily found Joe in the garage, helping Cole work on the pick-up that she and Shawn had wrecked. Emily went into the store and wasn't surprised that Jessica hadn't seen Veronica. Emily then made her way to the COM building. She felt confident that Chad wouldn't be there, but she had to check anyway.

"This setup is very primitive," Chad's voice spoke inside.

Emily stopped outside the door in shock and listened.

"In this world, it's the best we can do," Sarah replied.

"Still primitive," Chad sneered.

Emily walked into the building with Marley to confirm that her ears were not playing tricks on her. She saw Chad standing with Sarah by the radio.

"Good morning," Margaret smiled at her as she entered.

"Good morning," Emily replied. "I just wanted to check to make sure everyone was settling in."

"Did you check on everyone?" Chad asked. "Or just me?"

"This is my last stop," Emily replied calmly. "I checked on everyone else first."

Chad said nothing as he looked back at the radio.

"Actually," Emily said, making him turn back to her. "I wanted to talk to you for a minute if I could." "Go ahead," Sarah nodded to Chad.

Chad walked towards Emily and followed her outside. Marley was visibly tense as he stood next to Emily outside.

"Did I do something wrong?" Chad asked as he stood in front of her.

"No," Emily assured him. "I just noticed that Steven was not at school, and Veronica did not report to the store."

"She was getting ready when I left," Chad replied. "I'm sure she's just running late."

"Maybe you would like to go check on her," Emily suggested. "I don't think she will take it well if I do."

"Maybe you can give her a few more days to adjust," Chad replied. "She's never had to work before. Her dad gave her everything she wanted."

"That's not an option here," Emily answered. "Money and a title don't get you anything in this world. You have to work to survive. Please, I'm trying to be as gentle as I can about this."

"I expected you to drag her out kicking and screaming if she didn't do what you said," Chad admitted.

"What happened before doesn't matter," Emily replied. "There's no point in us attacking each other in here. Zombies are waiting to kill us. We shouldn't be trying to kill each other."

"You're different, Em," Chad said, looking at her softly.

"Not really," Emily said. "I'm just who I was meant to be."

"I'll go check on her and make sure Steven gets to the school," Chad nodded as he walked past her.

Emily let out a breath she didn't realize she was holding as soon as Chad was gone. Emily looked down at Marley, who was beginning to relax. Emily walked through the main street for a while, pretending to have something to do while watching Chad return.

Thankfully, she did not have to pretend for long. Emily watched as Chad walked with Steven towards the school. Veronica was upset and was giving him an earful as they walked. Chad didn't look happy as he carried Steven to the school, and they disappeared inside. After a few minutes, they both came back out. Emily watched out of the corner of her eye as Chad walked to the store and stopped.

"We have to do this," Chad said in a frustrated tone.

"My father will have her killed for this," Veronica spat, looking at Emily.

"If he's alive, we'll deal with that then," Chad replied.

"Of course he's alive," Veronica replied. "You have no idea what he is capable of."

"Then why did he let you and his grandson travel out there for so long?" Chad asked. "If he's alive, then why didn't he come to get you and take you home?"

"He will," Veronica replied. "He just expects you to make sure I'm taken care of until then."

"Just get in there and try not to cause any trouble," Chad sighed. "We don't have a wall shift today, but we both have to attend a weapons class on Monday."

"I don't fight," Veronica sneered. "You will do my shift."

"I will if they let me," Chad said in defeat.

"Don't give her a choice," Veronica said as she flung open the door to the store and stormed inside.

Chad said nothing as he walked past Emily and back into the COM building. Emily couldn't help but feel sorry for Chad. He was used to being the most important person in a relationship. However, Veronica made it clear she was the most important.

"Where are you going to let me sleep the day away?" Shawn asked behind her, making her jump. "Didn't mean to scare you," Shawn laughed.

"Sorry," Emily smiled at him. "I was just thinking."

"About what?" Shawn asked.

"It doesn't matter," Emily said as she waved it off. She didn't know how Shawn would react to her admitting she felt sorry for Chad. Christine had warned her not to let Chad ruin what she had. She couldn't see how her concern would do anything but hurt Shawn.

"How'd everything go this morning?" Shawn asked.

"Veronica tried to hide in her house with Steven," Emily replied, rolling her eyes.

"And Chad?" Shawn asked, looking at the COM building.

"He was on time," Emily replied. "He just got back from taking Steven to school and forcing Veronica to work." "That's surprising," Shawn said, shocked.

"Not really," Emily said, looking at Shawn.

"He's probably trying to get me to drop my guard so he can take over."

"Do I have anything to worry about?" Shawn asked, smiling at her.

"No," Emily laughed. "But just as a heads up, Princess plans on Chad working her wall shift."

"Not going to happen," Shawn responded.

"I know," Emily agreed. "I just wanted to warn you."

"I'll deal with that on Monday," Shawn sighed. "Today, I just want to focus on you."

"Any particular reason?" Emily smiled as Shawn pulled her into a hug.

"Do I need one?" Shawn asked.

"Not really," Emily replied as she leaned up and kissed Shawn.

"I need to go check on Julia," Emily said as she looked at the bakery. She knew Julia was working as the smell of bread flowed out.

"I'll meet up with you a bit," Shawn nodded. "Let me know if she needs anything."

"I will," Emily nodded as she walked with Marley towards the bakery.

Emily walked inside with Marley behind her. Julia pulled the bread out of the oven, and Emily felt her concern rise. Julia was as white as the flour that covered her apron. Her hair was messy, and she looked like a slight breeze could blow her over.

"Let me help you with that," Emily said as she rushed over to take the pan from Julia.

"I'm fine," Julia insisted as she wiped her forehead. "Just a little tired."

"I heard," Emily said as she placed the pan on the rack. "What's going on?"

"Nothing," Julia insisted. "I'll be fine."

"Maybe you should see Doc," Emily said with concern as she looked at Julia.

"I have," Julia sighed.

"What's going on?" Emily asked as she walked closer to Julia.

"It's nothing," Julia insisted.

Emily looked at Julia and could tell she was hiding something.

"What happened to no secrets?" Emily asked. "Maybe I can help."

"I wish you could," Julia said with tears in her eyes.

"Julia," Emily said as she pulled Julia into a hug. "What's going on?"

Julia said nothing as she broke into a heavy sob. Emily tried her best to comfort her but wasn't sure what to say. Julia was talking, but Emily couldn't understand her through the sobs.

"Doc says we can try again in a few months," Julia sobbed clearly. "But it's still hard to accept."

Emily understood what was going on. Julia had a miscarriage.

"I know," Emily replied. "But you can't let it consume you."

"I thought if I kept myself busy here, it would help," Julia said, looking around the bakery. "But putting buns in the oven wasn't as comforting as I thought."

Emily noticed a slight smile spreading across Julia's face, and Emily smiled with her.

"Why don't you take off the rest of the day?" Emily smiled. "I think we have enough here for the next few weeks."

"I need to help set up for the party and pick Bobby up from school and...." Julia began.

"We got the party, and I'll pick up Bobby," Emily interrupted her. "Anything else?"

"I have to take all of this to the store," Julia said as she began to walk towards the racks.

"I got it," Emily said as she stepped in front of her. "You go home and rest."

"Are you sure?" Julia asked.

"Positive," Emily replied as she led Julia to the door.

Julia gave up trying to argue and headed home. Emily set to work moving the baked goods to the store. Jessica confirmed what Emily had thought. Julia had overbaked today. They decided to use some of it for the party; otherwise, there was no way they could use it all before it went bad. By the time Emily finished, it was time to head to school. Emily waited by the fence and watched as Hope and Bobby came out. Bobby looked around for his mom for a moment, but came running over to Emily when she waved to him. "Is my mom okay?" Bobby asked as he ran over to Emily.

"She's fine," Emily assured him. "I told her I would walk you home today."

Emily couldn't help but admire the resilience of children. Bobby didn't question her any further and instead walked ahead with Hope and Marley. Though Hope was so much younger than him, no one would ever know it watching them together. They were talking about a new game they learned at school. Emily followed them, smiling at Julia's house. Emily followed Bobby inside.

"Mom!" Bobby yelled as soon as he opened the door.

"Living room!" Julia's voice yelled back.

They all walked into the living room and found Julia relaxing with her feet up on the couch.

"How was school?" Julia asked as Bobby ran in.

"It was good," Bobby asked, flopping down into a chair. "You feeling okay?"

"Yeah," Julia nodded. "I was just a little tired. Why don't you get your chores done so we can go to the party in a bit?"

"Yes, ma'am," Bobby said as he jumped up and ran upstairs.

"Let me know if you need anything," Emily smiled at Julia as she walked with Hope and Marley to the door.

"I will," Julia replied. "We'll see you tonight."

"See you tonight," Hope said as they walked back outside.

Emily, Hope, and Marley made their way back towards their house. People were already filling the street in front of her house. Emily could see that Shawn had been put on light duty, and Joe was helping him. Emily couldn't express how happy it made her that Joe and Shawn got along. She felt like it was a sign that she was with the right man this time.

"I'm going to go help Ms. June," Hope said as she ran off with Marley.

"Alright," Emily laughed as she walked towards the crowd to help.

"We don't have the best track record for these types of things," Racheal teased as she walked over to Emily.

"I spent the last two years getting it right," Emily laughed.

"Hopefully, the world won't break this time."

"It better not," Rachael laughed. "I don't want to know what would happen."

"Me either," Emily smiled.

Rachael and Emily finished setting up the tables together. Emily headed into the house to grab her cookies. She had just picked them up off the counter when Shawn walked into the kitchen.

"You need a hand?" Shawn asked as he walked over and grabbed one of the containers.

"We just have to make sure the plate goes to Jessica," Emily said as she nodded to the plate on the counter.

"I thought those were for me?" Shawn teased as he picked it up.

"You can fight the kids," Emily smiled as she began to walk towards the door.

"So, I don't get any?" Shawn concluded.

"I guess not," Emily laughed as they walked back outside.

Emily and Shawn set the cookies down on a table and then delivered the plate to Jessica. Jessica smiled and began to eat them as she walked away.

"You may want to take Julia off the wall schedule for the next week," Emily said as she turned to Shawn.

"Is she alright?" Shawn asked.

"She'll be fine," Emily nodded. "She just got some bad news and needs to rest."

"I didn't put her on the schedule tonight, but I will make sure she has the week off," Shawn nodded.

"Thanks," Emily smiled back at him.

Emily loved that Shawn didn't press her for details. He simply trusted what she was saying. It wasn't that she didn't want to tell Shawn what was going on with Julia, but she didn't feel that it was information that she was supposed to share. Julia didn't want everyone to know, and Emily wasn't going to break that trust now.

Chapter 24

The party went smoothly, and Emily couldn't help but have fun. Hope was in bed by eight-thirty, but the adults continued well past midnight. Joe had spent most of the night talking to Sarah. Emily recognized the look on his face and tried to steer him away from her. However, Joe just seemed more and more interested the more Emily tried. Emily finally gave up and decided that Sarah could handle Joe independently.

A couple of weeks went by, and almost everything was back to normal. Julia was back to being herself, and everyone was back to their routine. Veronica continued to resist working and had to be forced out of her house every morning. Emily had allowed Chad to do it until this point, but had finally lost her patience with the situation. Emily had just found out that Veronica had not reported working again and was going to Veronica's house. Emily walked with determination up the stairs and knocked on the door aggressively.

"Leave me alone!" Veronica's voice yelled from behind the closed door.

"You were supposed to be at the store an hour ago!" Emily yelled back.

"Fuck you!" Veronica yelled back.

"Stay," Emily said to Marley as the anger that filled her caused her entire body to shake.

Emily twisted the door handle and walked into the house. Emily knew that Steven was already at school and Chad was at work. This was going to be the first time she and Veronica were alone, and it wasn't going to be pleasant. Veronica stood with her arms crossed and glared at Emily as she entered.

"Get out of my house!" Veronica yelled at her. "Get out, or I'll call that rent-a-cop to drag you out!"

"You have to get to work!" Emily yelled back. "I've tried to be patient, but you just want everything handed to you!"

"My father would never…." Veronica began to yell.

"I don't give a shit!" Emily interrupted. "Get your ass to work or get out! It doesn't matter to me!"

"You're just trying to get back at me for Chad!" Veronica yelled.

Emily felt her anger drain away and heard herself begin to laugh. She knew that Veronica would probably use this excuse. However, hearing her say it sounded ridiculous.

"What's so funny?!" Veronica asked, and Emily couldn't tell if she was angry or embarrassed.

"He's all yours," Emily laughed.

Veronica scrunched her red face while Emily tried to compose herself.

"Here's the deal," Emily said after she finally gained her composure. "You didn't report on time once over the past two weeks. Half of your credits will be docked for that." "You can't do that!" Veronica yelled.

"I can, and I have," Emily replied. "And if you don't go to work again, you will be put in quarantine for three days. You can decide if you want to stay or go. If you stay and still don't go to work, you're out."

"You are going to throw me out because I won't stock shelves?" Veronica asked in a huff.

"I told you when you decided to stay, we all work and help this place run. There are no free rides," Emily explained. "The choice is yours."

"You will pay for this," Veronica sneered as she shoved past Emily.

"I know," Emily sighed as she followed her out of the house and closed the door.

Marley glared after Veronica as she left, but greeted Emily with excitement. Emily petted him and began to walk through town once more. Emily did all of her usual morning check-ins and then headed for the town hall. Emily had just sat at her desk when she heard someone walk in. Emily looked up with a smile, expecting Shawn, when Chad stepped into the doorway. Marley remained on the floor by her but began to growl.

"You need something?" Emily asked as she looked back down at the reports.

"Veronica said that you dragged her out of the house?" Chad asked as he continued to stand in the doorway. "She says that you are trying to get even with her for our affair."

"She walked out on her own," Emily replied. "And I don't even care about the affair anymore. She's the one looking for that drama."

"I figured," Chad said as he cautiously took a step forward. "She's been trying her best to make drama wherever she goes."

"I told her that next time she will be put into quarantine for three days, and her credits have been halved," Emily continued.

"That's fair," Chad nodded. "You've been more than fair since we arrived."

"I treat everyone the same," Emily replied, looking up at him.

"The last time I saw you, I know things went bad, and that's my fault," Chad said. "I didn't realize how much I loved you until I saw that thing biting you."

"Chad," Emily sighed. "Don't go there. There's no point. I think we both have realized we don't belong together and moved on."

"I just can't help but think about it," Chad answered, taking another step forward. "Maybe it's fate that we find each other. A husband and wife reunited after years apart in all of this."

"Ex," Emily corrected him. "Ex-husband and ex-wife."

"I don't see it that way," Chad said, shaking his head. "I love you, Em."

Emily looked at Chad in disbelief. Other than Hope, who was still not talking to him, they had nothing left between them. She got an all too familiar feeling in the pit of her stomach. Not love, but the feeling she would get when Chad tried to sweet-talk. His words oozed with deceit and manipulation.

"I love Shawn," Emily replied. "This is never going to happen," Emily said, pointing back and forth between them.

"Em," Chad said softly as he took another step forward.

"You need to leave," Emily replied as she felt herself grab onto the edge of her desk. "Now."

Marley seemed to recognize what was happening as he stood up from the floor. Marley slowly began to advance towards Chad, still growling.

"Just think about it," Chad said as he reached the door. "Please."

"Go!" Emily heard herself yell.

Chad nodded and left. Marley returned to Emily's side and lay his head in her lap.

"Good boy," Emily said as she patted him on the head. "I think he's gone truly crazy if he thinks we're getting back together."

Suddenly, Emily felt like the entire room was spinning around her. She frantically reached for the waste bin and lost what was left of her breakfast. Emily set the bin down and felt the room slowly stop spinning. Things were still shaky, but she felt well enough to walk.

"What the hell?" Emily said as she placed her hand on her forehead.

Emily didn't feel warm but knew there was only one way to be sure. Emily slowly stood and made the walk to the clinic. Everything around her seemed so unstable, like walking on a giant marshmallow. Emily opened the door to the clinic and stepped inside. Isabelle was sitting at the desk, but jumped up as soon as she saw Emily. Emily leaned against the wall as things began to spin around her once more.

"Doc!" Isabelle yelled as she ran over to Emily.

Doc came running, and soon each of them was standing beside Emily.

"What's going on?" Doc asked as he and Isabelle walked Emily to the exam room.

"Everything began to spin, and then I...."

Emily caught sight of the waste bin just in time to throw up. Doc and Isabelle stood with her and helped Emily to a chair as soon as she finished throwing up.

"Have you been feeling sick all day?" Doc asked as he began to take her vitals.

"No," Emily replied. "It just hit me out of nowhere."

"Nothing's jumping out at me as wrong," Doc said as he looked at her.

"But something is," Emily said as she closed her eyes, trying to get the spinning to stop.

Emily felt Doc prick her skin with a needle and knew that he was drawing blood. He was probably going to check her toxin levels.

"Just sit here," Doc replied. "This shouldn't take long."

"I'm not going anywhere," Emily replied as she rested her head against the cool wall.

"Stay with her," Doc whispered to Isabelle as he left.

By the time Doc returned, Emily was back to feeling pretty much normal. She was tired, but the world had stopped spinning, and she no longer felt like vomiting.

"Stress?" Emily asked as Doc walked back in, trying to explain her symptoms.

"Not exactly," Doc said as he sat down beside her. "Though this diagnosis is known to produce stress in the long term."

"What?" Emily asked, frustrated with whatever joke Doc was trying to make.

"Emily, when was your last period?" Doc looked at her with knowledge in his eyes.

"It was…" Emily suddenly realized that it had been a while. "It was two months ago," Emily finally answered. "Doc, am I pregnant?"

"You are," Doc smiled. "Did you not have morning sickness with Hope?"

"No," Emily said, shaking her head. "I did have a dizzy spell towards the end, but I thought it was because I wasn't drinking enough water."

"Well, apparently, this one is going to make you work for it," Doc laughed. "I would just keep some crackers close by, drink plenty of water, and know that it will eventually pass."

"I'm pregnant," Emily said again to herself, trying to ensure she understood it correctly.

"And no riding on that motorcycle," Doc smiled. "We don't want anything else jiggling up your stomach."

"Right," Emily replied as she felt herself begin to smile.

"Would you like us to get Shawn?" Isabelle asked. "I assume he is the father?"

"Yes, he is," Emily laughed. "But no, I want to tell him tonight."

Isabelle nodded and smiled.

"I would go home and rest for today," Doc suggested. "It's still too early for an ultrasound, but we should be able to do one in about four weeks."

"Okay," Emily grinned as she stood up and headed for the door.

Emily walked out of the clinic, still smiling, to see Shawn walking towards her with concern on his face.

"Everything alright?" Shawn asked as he took her hands. "People said you walked to the clinic and looked almost like you were drunk."

"I probably did," Emily laughed. "It was just a dizzy spell."

"Are you sure?" Shawn asked, still looking concerned.

"Doc checked everything," Emily assured. "He said I'm fine, but to go home and rest."

"Then let's get you home," Shawn said as he took her by the hand.

Emily continued to smile as she laced her fingers around his and walked home. Shawn led her and Marley inside and to the couch.

"Do you need anything?" Shawn asked as she sat down.

"Water and crackers," Emily smiled up at him.

"I'm on it," Shawn said as he took off for the kitchen.

Shawn reappeared a few minutes later and set what Emily had asked for on the table.

"I heard, right before you got sick, that Chad was in your office," Shawn said as casually as he could while he lifted Emily's legs and sat down.

"Yeah," Emily laughed. "I think he's lost his mind."

"How so?" Shawn asked.

"Oh, he tried to say it was fate that we found each other and that he loved me," Emily said dismissively.

"And what did you say?" Shawn asked, holding her hand.

"I told him I love you," Emily insisted. "And then Marley tried to eat him."

"I'm surprised he didn't try to use Hope against you," Shawn admitted.

"I'm sure he will," Emily sighed. "But it won't work." "I mean, he is the father of your child," Shawn admitted. "It's a pretty strong argument."

"And are you going to let him shove you out of your child's life without a fight?" Emily asked, grinning.

"You know that Hope is my daughter to me, but Chad is her biological father," Shawn replied.

Emily couldn't help but feel disappointed that he didn't catch on to what she said. She continued to smile, though, as she thought of another clever way to say she was pregnant.

"I just want the two of you to be happy," Shawn replied.

"It's the three of us," Emily grinned.

"I know," Shawn said, patting her hand. "But you know what I mean."

Emily couldn't help but think of this as a game now. How many times could she talk about being pregnant and Shawn not realize?

"I mean, maybe with everything as it is, you too could make it work," Shawn continued. "I mean, if a mother and father can make it work, they should be together."

"I agree," Emily grinned. "So, we still have so much left to decide on for the wedding."

"You're sure it's over with him?" Shawn asked.

"Positive," Emily nodded. "Now, can we talk about the wedding?"

"Sure," Shawn laughed. "I was thinking maybe we should push it off a month or two with everything that's happened."

"That won't work," Emily smiled, shaking her head. "I don't want to have to adjust the dress."

"Why would you have to adjust the dress?" Shawn asked.

"I'm going to put on weight," Emily said, if it was apparent. "I'm not going to have a big belly and walk down the aisle."

"You think you are going to stress eat that much?" Shawn laughed. "I promise to hide the food if you try to."

"You take food away from a pregnant woman, and we are going to have a funeral instead of a wedding," Emily replied.

"Pregnant woman?" Shawn asked, looking at her. "Emily, are you pregnant?"

"That's what Doc's diagnosis was," Emily smiled.

"Are you serious?" Shawn smiled as he came closer to Emily.

"Yeah," Emily laughed.

Shawn quickly scooped her up and pulled her onto his lap. Emily wrapped her arms around his neck while he placed a hand on her belly.

"You okay, Daddy?" Emily smiled at him.

"Perfect," Shawn smiled as he looked at her.

Shawn and Emily pulled each other close and shared a soft kiss.

"Did you talk to her?" Veronica asked as Chad walked into the bedroom

"Of course," Chad nodded. "But she didn't have it. She kept saying how much she loved Shawn."

Chad walked over and sat down on the bed beside Veronica.

"We can end that easily enough," Veronica sneered. "You just make her think you love her and learn that code."

"That could take years," Chad said, rubbing his neck. "Can't the General just hack the panel or break down the gate?"

"No way he can break it down, and you said you couldn't hack the panel," Veronica answered.

"How long until he arrives, another week?" Chad asked, trying to figure out his timeline.

"He couldn't say for sure," Veronica replied. "He said it could take longer."

"Great," Chad sighed as he turned off the light and lay down.

Author's Note

Thank you for joining Emily and Marley on their journey. I hope you enjoyed their story as much as I did. If you could please review it, it would be greatly appreciated.

Are you looking for more? Please check out my other books.

Scan the QR code below for links to my social media, mailing list, and other books.

J.D. Crist